Slow Ride

Kat Morrisey

CRIMSON ROMANCE

F+W Media, Inc.

This edition published by
Crimson Romance
an imprint of F+W Media, Inc.
10151 Carver Road, Suite 200
Blue Ash, Ohio 45242
www.crimsonromance.com

Copyright © 2014 by Kat Morrisey.

This is a work of fiction. Names, characters, corporations, institutions, organizations, events, or locales in this novel are either the product of the author's imagination or, if real, used fictitiously. The resemblance of any character to actual persons (living or dead) is entirely coincidental.

ISBN 10: 1-4405-7484-7
ISBN 13: 978-1-4405-7484-9
eISBN 10: 1-4405-7485-5
eISBN 13: 978-1-4405-7485-6

Cover art © 123rf.com

Acknowledgments

First and foremost, thanks to my editor, Julie. I think you are the most patient person I know. Thank you for teaching me that there is always more to learn when it comes to the writing process and not making me cry. Too much. I am also extremely grateful for the kindness you and Tara showed when things got crazy for me and working with me to adjust deadlines. The unexpected snuck on me but between the three of us, it all worked out.

To my friends, both online and off, who have supported me through the years with my dreams of wanting to be an author. I never thought the day would come when the hard work and constant re-writes would pay off, but it finally did. Lauren, Julie, Juliana, Fallon, Em, Lena and everyone else who cheers each other on during sprints, NaNo, and writing challenges, you all rock and without you and our writing adventures, I wouldn't be where I am today. And a huge hug to my CPs, Fallon and Elli especially, who helped me stay on track when my characters needed some discipline.

To my best friend, MB: You're my rock and no matter what is happening in my life you can make me laugh. You are the wisest person I know. Even when I'm staring death right in the face, I know I can count on you. And MA, there is nothing better than to find your book twin (among other things), and you're mine. How about we take another trip to Hawaii?

To my family, who put up with me: I love you and thank you for all your support throughout the years, no matter where my journey has taken me. I have to give a special thank you to my mom who all those years ago let me pour over the Scholastic book order forms and change my mind a zillion times as I tried to decide what I wanted; the endless trips to Waldenbooks; and for reading with me all the time. And to my sister, you're the best big sister a girl could have. Thank you for helping me through the toughest and scariest time in my life. To my niece and nephew, I love you guys with all my heart.

Lastly, to you the readers, who have decided to take a chance on me, a new author. I've dreamed of becoming an author since I was a little girl, and finally that dream is coming true. I hope you enjoy Kyla and Cooper's story as much as I enjoyed writing it. Have fun in Ashten Falls and happy reading!

Chapter 1

Kyla belted out the chorus of Tom Cochrane's *Life is a Highway* as it blared from the external speakers of her MP3 player. The song was perfect for her road trip, and when he screamed out the chorus she did, too. Where Kyla was going, she had no idea. She was just glad to have her latest troubles behind her and nothing but the future in front.

She was singing about riding the highway all night long when the car jolted underneath her, a horrible clanking noise that even she, someone who knew next to nothing about cars, recognized as a very bad thing. She gripped the wheel tightly and guided it to just off the shoulder, setting the car in park. Her shaking fingers turned off the ignition and waited a moment before she tried to turn it over. A choking, sputtering noise was the car's angry reply, with an added belch of smoke that drifted from the hood into the sky.

"Please, please no, no, not here, come on, please don't do this."

Kyla tried to turn the car over one more time, whispering to it, and whatever saint might be the guardian of American classic cars, all to no avail. He or she must have been on vacation. She sat still for a long moment, her eyes closed, taking in slow, steady breaths. Of all the things she'd considered that could happen on this trip, her car giving out on her hadn't been one of them. It was an American original, strong, loyal, and had yet to let to her down. Until today anyway.

"It looks like we have to rely on the auto club, Lola. And yes, I know how you feel about strangers getting near you." She rifled through her messenger bag, tossing out receipts and scraps of paper on the floor with the rest of the detritus already there. She found her card and dialed the number, requesting a tow. It would, in the words of the customer service representative, be there "shortly."

Slow Ride

Kyla twisted and pulled herself out of Lola, her '67 Mustang Coupe, lifting her arms up over her head to stretch. She'd been in the car for hours since leaving the truck stop at lunch. She needed a hotel and a soft, comfy bed she could crawl into and sleep for days, but she could see by the lack of civilization around her that was unlikely. There was thick brush about ten feet from the shoulder of the road, wildflowers and bushes mixing with tall trees of all shapes and sizes. Further into the woods, she could see rays of sunlight hitting the forest floor where it wasn't blocked by the towering pine trees climbing up to the sky.

Kyla listened to the soft sounds of nature, until the sound of a car cut through the air. She was unable to stop her initial reaction, her muscles contracting into a mass of tension, shoulders pushing back to straighten her spine. Despite the beauty around her, it was at that moment that she realized she was a woman traveling alone in an unknown area.

The driver stopped just off the road's center stripe, his window rolled down, and he called out to her. "You need some help there, girl?" His demeanor conveyed an easy friendliness, and her irrational fear of being vulnerable fled when he spoke those first soft words. But she stayed where she was. She wasn't totally stupid.

Her eyes focused on the driver, who looked to be somewhere in his fifties, and if appearances were any indication, he had lived a full life. He had a wide mouth, a slightly crooked nose, and soft, gray eyes covered by wire-rimmed glasses, silhouetting a face tanned from spending too much time in the sun without the use of sunscreen. His hair, a mass of shoulder-length gray with specks of black in it, was held back by a faded blue bandana around his forehead. When he smiled at her, she saw well-worn laugh lines around his mouth and eyes.

"No, thanks. Called a tow. They are on their way." She offered a bright smile. "He should be here in a few minutes." She had no idea if that was the case, but she hoped to hell they were. "Thank god for auto club, right?"

"Well all right then. Don't stand near the road; someone is going to come around that curve and smack into you. People drive this road like a bat out of hell." His head bobbed up and down once, and then she heard the strained whir of the electric window as it rose between them. She lifted her chin as he drove off and looked down at the map feature on her phone to try to determine where she was exactly.

She'd been wandering for a few weeks now, taking a meandering road trip through the northeastern part of the country. She had seen some beautiful sites and had a ton of pictures to show for it, but she'd always packed up and kept going after a few days. Now she was in Maine, but she couldn't remember the name of the last sign she'd passed. Somewhere north of Portland was her best guess. There had been so many small towns she'd passed on her journey, the names ran together after awhile.

She bounced on the balls of her feet and glanced around again. It was early in June, but the weather this far north still made the air cool. She shivered and took a deep breath, the corners of her mouth tipping up. Salty sea air. The scent was faint, but it was there. That was a good sign; she was still near the coast. The water in this part of the Atlantic might be cold compared to warmer climes, but Kyla didn't care much about that. The smell and sound of the waves, her toes curled into the sand—that was all she needed.

Kyla hummed a song under her breath, determined to not let her car's misfortune get the better of her. She'd called the auto club, and they would send someone to tow her somewhere close by. There was no sense in worrying about it or overthinking the situation. She did enough of that. The whole point of this trip was to let go of the worry and fear she'd been living under. Kyla was free. Free to sing, free to drive where she wanted, and free to let go of the past. It wouldn't be easy, but she'd damn well try. And her determination to do that, coupled with her stubbornness, would hopefully bode well for her success.

As the minutes ticked past, it was obvious her definition of "shortly" was much different than that of the auto club's. She grabbed the mp3 player from the front seat and unhooked the external speakers she used in her car. She connected her ear buds and climbed up on the trunk, lying back at a reclined angle against the back window. She stared up at the trees and sky above, and found herself swept up in the music of Lana del Ray's *Off To The Races* in that throwback voice that always made her shiver. The raw emotion the singer exuded struck her deep, and Kyla joined in at the chorus. She sang into the second verse, oblivious to anything going on around her, as was always the case when the music took hold.

• • •

Cooper punched the call button inside the car and listened as it rang, waiting for the other person to answer.

"Yo."

"We got nothing they can use. Said they've heard the rumblings, but they have bigger fish to fry or some shit. Jesus fuckin' Christ!" Cooper slammed his hand on the steering wheel.

"Coop, man. We knew this was going to be an uphill battle. We'll think of something. With what we've been doing, Saybrook has been scaling back. We all see that."

"I hear ya. Listen, get the guys together, I want to meet at the store tonight."

"Sure thing."

"Hold on a sec, Sam." Cooper hit the button and took a call coming in.

"What's up, Phil?"

"I'm going out for a tow, just inside the town limits."

"All right, man. I'm a few minutes from there now. I'll stop in case it's a two-man job."

"Yeah, see ya."

He clicked back over to Sam. "I gotta run. Phil has a call out for a tow. I'm going to stop and see if he needs help. Get the boys together. Tell 'em to bring their own damn beer this time. We'll talk more tonight."

"Later, man."

Cooper turned off the phone and ran a hand through his hair. This shit with the cops was going to be the death of him. One minute the town was swirling in chaos and corruption, terrified to even breathe for fear of the cops. The next minute, Martin "Marty" Saybrook, the leader of the dirty institution, backed off. He did it just enough to placate the masses, but that didn't mean he didn't do shit behind the scenes. Targeting people for traffic stops, planting evidence on some of the alleged criminals he couldn't arrest the legal way, forcing himself on the girls at the local strip club on threats of arrest. The man was beyond bad, but no one seemed interested in taking him down. The town council was either terrified of him, was being blackmailed, or was in his pocket.

Cooper and Saybrook had never gotten along. Saybrook had hated Cooper's dad—for what reason, no one knew, but he did. Cooper's dad had died a long time ago, but that didn't stop Cooper from being harassed by bogus traffic stops and unpleasant visits to his garage. Man was a fuckin' nuisance. But Cooper had stayed calm and hadn't gone on the offensive. After what happened to Cheryl though, everything changed.

Cheryl and Roger—Cooper and Sam's other best friend—had been inseparable. Somewhere along the way, while Roger was in the military, Cheryl had gotten mixed up in drugs. Word on the street was that Saybrook was helping one of the local crews bring in the sludge Cheryl was using, and got his rocks off often, as part of his payment. And then she was found dead, washed up on the beach.

When Cooper looked at the golden girl in her final resting place and saw his best friend unable to move, sitting vigil for the two days of viewing, never leaving her side, he knew he had to do something. Cheryl's death was no accident.

And now here he was, having spent a lot of time and effort, yet still nowhere, except for a long list of bogus arrests, affidavits from complainants, dropped and dismissed charges, excessive force complaints, and information on crimes that weren't even fully investigated, including Cheryl's death. But the feds had other priorities. They'd taken copies and smiled, saying they'd look into it when they could.

"Fuck me," he growled and pushed the thoughts from his head.

He scanned his surroundings and noticed a car parked on the side of the road. He depressed the brake a touch, and his eyes caught the woman lying on the trunk.

"What the *hell*?" he muttered to himself and slammed on the brakes just as he passed the front of the car. He threw his truck in reverse and swung onto the shoulder in front of the car. He stepped down from the truck and slammed the door. He was deliberately being loud as he did, his motorcycle boots clomping on the pavement, but the woman still hadn't moved. Considering his earlier thoughts about Saybrook and the utter joy the man found in pulling people over, especially women, he felt the muscles in his jaw tick.

As Cooper got closer his eyes moved over the woman's frame. He could tell her legs went on forever and were tanned all the way up to the edge of her skirt, even with her lying down on the trunk. A mess of long, wavy, brown hair was splayed around her. Her hips made subtle moves to music he couldn't hear. She was not a small woman. She had curves; hips that made his fingers itch to hold, not to mention one of the nicest racks he'd seen in a long time. It was clear there was ample real estate for him to grab in all the places that counted.

Him? He swore under his breath and wondered where that thought came from. Shaking it off, he bent down and spoke into the woman's ear. "What the fuck are you doing?"

• • •

Kyla's eyes flew open and she let out a scream. She scrambled across the trunk and fell off the edge as she tried to right herself, tripping over the edge of the pavement. She reached for the trunk with one hand to steady herself, the music player gripped in the other. The ear buds fell down her shoulders when she finally stood on solid ground to face the stranger.

"Quite the dismount. I asked a question." The man lifted his arm toward the trunk she'd been laying on. "I can see you aren't from here," he said, nodding to the Pennsylvania plates, "so let me give you some advice. It's not the smartest thing in the world to be laying out over a car, singing. Never know who might come up on you."

Kyla stared openmouthed at the man who had just spoken to her. He had to be six feet, four inches, and from what she could see of his arms, his olive-toned skin hinted at possible Italian roots somewhere in his family tree. His hair was a dark brown, almost black, and curled at the back of his neck indicating he needed a trim, while the top was thick, lying in a sexy, haphazard way. It looked like he had just rolled out of bed, and for a minute Kyla's thoughts were punctuated with the image of what he wore in bed. Pajama bottoms? Boxers? Maybe nothing. He had the beginnings of a five o'clock shadow on his face, which made his strong jaw more pronounced. His broad shoulders were matched by a broad chest, and his strong thighs were currently encased in faded jeans that seemed made for him. The light wash fit perfect against his waist and his t-shirt looked painted on, moving with him, accentuating every delicious detail of his form. Her eyes dipped to his feet where he wore heavy, black, motorcycle boots that matched the belt threaded through the loops in his jeans.

"Um, hello?" His voice did the trick this time, especially given the angry edge she heard in it.

Kyla lifted her eyes to find his blue eyes watching her. His look was intense, but she couldn't tell whether that boded well for her. She shifted her feet and kept her own guarded eyes on him.

"Waiting for someone. He should be here any minute."

"You're waiting here for someone? You couldn't ... I don't know ... do that somewhere other than the side of a dangerous stretch of road?"

Kyla glanced up and down the road and shrugged as her eyes came back to rest on the man. "It doesn't seem too dangerous to me. It seems kind of quiet actually."

She felt the heat of his gaze and kept her back straight, her expression blank. He was hot, sure, but he was still some strange guy, and they were the only two people on a road that she wasn't familiar with, and he apparently was.

When he didn't say anything, she cleared her throat. "You can go. I got this." Her head tilted to her car.

"Got this?" He shook his head. "What is it you've 'got' exactly?"

Kyla huffed out a frustrated breath. "What I 'got,'" she lifted her hand and air-quoted the word, "is handling my car and myself. Thank you for stopping or whatever, but you don't need to. I told the last guy I was fine. The tow should be here soon."

"So, car trouble? You're not meeting someone here?"

"Uh, yeah I am. The tow truck guy my auto club sent. That's why you don't need to stop."

Kyla lifted one hand to her hip and leaned against the trunk. She watched his eyes travel over her body, and when he smiled, she sucked in a breath. His eyes crinkled at the corners and it brightened his whole face. Hell, his whole demeanor changed. His muscles seemed to relax and the hard expression on his face was replaced with something just this side of friendly. If it was possible, it made him more good looking.

"Car trouble. See now that is something I can handle." His low voice rumbled through the late spring air, and he walked to the front of the Mustang and pulled up the hood.

"Hey, I don't want you touching my car. I want someone with experience with ... well cars, looking at her." The man didn't respond and her eyes narrowed. She watched in both horror and fascination as he bent forward and his large hands pulled and prodded at the insides. Shaking off thoughts of his hands on her, Kyla walked right up to him, and made a grab for his hands. "Stop it—you're going to break her more than she is already! Lola is sensitive and doesn't like just anyone touching her."

He lifted his head and then straightened. Before she knew what he was doing, his hands were at her waist and he picked her up, depositing her on the trunk of the car.

"Don't move."

Her mouth was agape as she watched him walk back to the front, disappear under the hood, and eventually shut it. He came back toward her, staring the entire time.

"She's nearly dead. She might be able to be revived, but for the amount of money you'd need to put into her, it might not be worth it. Though it's a '67, so that in itself makes it worth it. Least for me it would. They don't make cars like this anymore."

"Are you ... who do you think ... I cannot believe you!" Kyla's cheeks felt hot as her temper flared. She stomped her booted foot on the side of the road, her fists clenched. "You just picked me up and. . ." Her hand waved at the trunk. "Have you lost your mind?"

He seemed unaffected by her anger. Instead his eyes danced with amusement and the corners of his mouth tipped up.

She was distracted by the smile, but only for a moment. "This is not funny. Not funny at all! You just *touched* me. Just go. Just get away from me." She didn't know if she was more pissed at him for doing what he did, or at herself for not fighting him.

His head canted to the side, his eyes on her the entire time. "Did I hurt you?"

Kyla felt no pain. In fact, she felt the opposite. "That isn't the point. You can't just put your hands on someone else's car, and then on her, and then back on the car, especially when you were told not to. You need a lesson in manners," she snapped at him.

"You told me to not touch the car. You didn't say I couldn't touch you."

He flashed a cheeky grin and Kyla felt her cheeks get hotter. "What were you saying about my car?"

"You're looking at a few grand or so, with parts and labor, to get her running again."

"A what! There is no freaking way it will cost that much. How is that even possible? And how do you know that anyway?" Kyla crossed her arms over her chest. "I will wait for the mechanic."

For some reason this made him grin even wider. He leaned toward her, and Kyla stiffened. "Honey, I *am* the mechanic, only one around for about thirty-five miles. You want to walk that far to get a second opinion about your vehicle, fine. Even if you do though, mechanics there won't be near as good as me. I'm the best there is. Good with my hands."

She blinked, having no doubt a man like the one who stood before her was good with his hands. In fact, he was probably good with a lot of things. "So, where am I exactly, that there would only be one mechanic for thirty-five miles?"

He shook his head. "Jesus, you don't even know where you are? Seriously not smart." His hand swiped over his face and he sighed. "You made it to Ashten Falls, a town well north of Portland. Not much else around for miles other than a bunch of state parks, wildlife preserves, and some small towns and villages."

He took several steps closer and Kyla instinctively stepped back. It was habit. A bad one, but one she couldn't shake. She saw his brows arch but kept her face blank. She didn't respond to his comment, and kept her feet planted just in case she had to run. It was instinct. She always had to be ready to run.

"I got the call when I was coming back into town. Phil, one of the guys from the garage, is on his way with the tow. We'll have your car towed and I'll give you a lift to the motel in town. The town usually only plays host to fishermen and hunters who come up around these parts, and bikers or tourists in the summer who head to festivals in neighboring towns. But for the most part, it always has available rooms. Anyway, the owner of the motel is a doll. Her name is Rose, and someone there will help you get settled while you sort out your transportation."

She leaned on the door of her Coupe, going over her finances in her head. "I don't have ... no way do I have that kind of money. I mean, not on me." She would be lucky to have enough to get her through the next couple weeks for food and a motel. No way could she afford the car repairs.

"Well, let's figure that out later, unless you want to camp out here. I'll still tow the thing in, no charge. Worst-case scenario, I'll buy it off ya. Hop in," he said, motioning to his truck. "Name's Cooper Moretto by the way."

Kyla's jaw dropped. "I will not be selling Lola, as in. . . ever!" she hissed, reaching in and grabbing a few small bags. "And what about my stuff? I don't want it stolen while it sits here."

Cooper was dialing his phone but staring right at her, an incredulous look on his face. "Lola? Really? Good lord, woman. That's... wrong on so many levels. Who names their classic 1967 Mustang Coupe, Lola?" He stared at her, hands on his hips, and shook his head.

"It's *my* car, so I will call her whatever I want. And when I got her, I asked her what her name was, and the first one that came to me was Lola."

Cooper blinked. "You asked the car her name? Are you serious?" She scowled at the amused look on his face, though she couldn't deny he looked even better with his lips tipped up at the corners. "Babe, that's kind of. . . crazy."

"Yes, I'm serious," she snapped, getting agitated now. "My grandfather gave it to me when I graduated college, and he told me to let it talk to me. So I did." She shifted her feet, her hands squarely on her hips. "Any other insults you'd like to throw my way?"

Whoever he was calling must have answered because he didn't respond other than with his grin, which got wider. Kyla grabbed a few of her bags and tossed them in the back of the truck.

Cooper hung up and leaned against the tailgate. "Phil will be here in a few. You want anything else out of here before he rigs it up to the tow?"

She bit her lip, her eyes flicking to the contents in the back seat. "Um, this one too." She reached in to grab the biggest of the bags, stuffed to capacity, when his hand closed over hers.

"I got it, doll. You women and your shit." He grunted as he grabbed hold of the bag and tugged it out, tossing it in the back with a soft *thud*. "What the hell you got in here? Gold bars?" His hand moved to the zipper and tugged, grinning like a fool as he stared down at the mounds of lace and skimpy material, his eyes making a slow slide over Kyla.

She smacked at his hands, pushing her hip against his body, which did not budge even an inch. "Don't look in there!" She yanked at the zipper to close the bag. "Not cool."

His body shook with laughter and he stepped back. "Not like it's the first time I've ever seen a woman's panties, though usually

I'm taking 'em off when I see 'em." He kept his tone light, not hiding the fact he was enjoying teasing her.

"Classy, real freakin' classy. And who do you think you are anyway, going through someone's bag. A stranger's bag, no less. I mean who does that?" Kyla didn't even attempt to hide her annoyance. "Is your guy going to get here today or what? I've been waiting out here for what seems like forever and I have to tell you between that and your behavior, the customer service sucks."

He held up his hands in mock surrender. "I didn't mean any harm by it. I swear. It is nice to know a girl like you is hiding a wild side underneath that tank top and skirt though. And just FYI, you're cute when you blush."

"Shut up, I'm not cute," she glared at him as she huffed and leaned against her car. "And stop talking about what I'm wearing and my underwear. It's none of your beeswax."

Cooper snorted. "None of my beeswax?" He shook his head. "I can already see you're the kind of girl who'll be a handful—the good kind—and has probably driven a fair number of men into both fits of laughter, and headaches from hell, perhaps at the same time. I figure the way you wear those clothes, and the thought of what you might be wearing underneath 'em, must make up for the headaches. "

Kyla shifted her feet and blew out a frustrated breath. "Glad to know I'm so transparent." Her words were mumbled, her tone sarcastic. This conversation was maddening. One minute he was annoyed and angry for reasons she still didn't know, and the next he was flirty, insulting, and complimentary at the same time.

She glanced down at what she was wearing and shrugged. To her it was just an outfit she threw on in the morning and certainly nothing to deliberately catch attention. That wasn't her game. She wore what she wore out of comfort. From now on that would mean sweatpants and oversized sweatshirts because she didn't need anyone like Cooper looking at her like he was at that moment.

Her style was funky and laid back, and Kyla was not someone who ever paid full price for clothes, preferring to shop at outlets, sales, auction sites online, garage sales, or consignment shops. Truth was, she never bought anything retail because she couldn't afford it. She was good with putting together a style though, and accessories were key. Today she was wearing a white jean skirt, a red scarf with fringe at the ends for a belt, and a midnight blue tank top with the Rolling Stones' logo on it, in red. She was wearing flat, black, strappy sandals laced up her ankles.

She crossed her arms over her chest and turned slightly away from him. "Whatever. Why are we talking about this?"

A horn honked, and the two looked up as a large tow truck pulled over to the side of the road behind the Mustang. A very large man in greasy overalls jumped down from the truck and called out as he walked over, "Hey, Coop. This it? Man, she is a beauty!" He whistled as he got close to the car and ran his hand along the hood.

"Her name is Lola," Kyla huffed, ignoring Cooper's grin.

"Lola? Cooper, man, is she *serious?* Fuckin' A. What is with chicks doing that shit to prime pieces of American craftsmanship? Dayum! Chick is lucky she's cute. Otherwise we'd have to have a word."

Kyla visibly tensed at the stranger's words. Her eyes flicked to Cooper, who was watching her like a hawk. As his partner walked over to the front of the car, Cooper held up his hands in front of him, his eyes still on Kyla.

"I'm going to take a step toward you." He waited until she nodded and relaxed before he approached. He stayed near the trunk, his back to the newcomer, and ducked his head down. "Ignore Phil. He's a big teddy bear and likes to tease a lot. Not the kind of guy who hurts people."

Phil failed to catch Kyla's reaction. He was busy with the car. But at Cooper's calm words, she felt her body relax and nodded.

Cooper was just as much a stranger as Phil, but for some reason, the sound of his voice, the way he carried himself, made her let down her guard a fraction of an inch. He also didn't have the hard cruelty in his eyes that she looked for whenever she met someone. Of course, when she had first seen that look, she hadn't realized what it was. She had mistaken it for love, respect, caring, and most of all, protection. But it hadn't been any of those things.

"Seriously, Cooper. We need to do something about the name. If she's gonna be sitting in your garage, we need to re-christen her."

Cooper glanced at Phil and gave a small shake of his head. "We'll talk about it later. Right now, let's just get this done. I need to get Lola's driver to the motel. Park it in the lot for now. Make sure none of the stuff inside is touched, or Kyla will have us all by the balls. I'm going to bring her over to the motel."

Kyla drowned out the rest of the conversation between the two and reached into her car for her messenger bag. She was at the truck door when Cooper moved to her side and opened it. His large hands were a whisper at her waist as he lifted her up to the seat. Neither said a word. Kyla's eyes were glued to him as he rounded the truck and climbed in the cab.

"Buckle up." The words were more an order than anything, and he waited until she got the seatbelt on, even reaching over to make sure it was tight, which caused her to stop breathing since his arm was way into her personal space. Then he hit the gas. After a few minutes of silence he spoke.

"Don't worry, Phil will do as I say. Your stuff will be safe and sound within the confines of the garage, which has a locked fence around it whenever no one is around. Or you can bring it over to the motel. It's right next door." He kept his eyes straight ahead now, but when she didn't reply, he gave her a quick glance. She continued to stare out the window, her knees tucked up to her chest. Her only acknowledgment that she heard Cooper was a small nod.

Kyla remained quiet for most of the ride into the town, but as the quiet got heavier in the truck, she had to fill it with something. "So, you're a mechanic?"

"Yeah, among other things. I own the garage and another shop in town. A record store I inherited from my dad. Economy might suck everywhere at the moment, but here in Ashten Falls we're always in an economic slump. Added to that, there are ... well let's just call them issues ... in the town that keep this place from flourishing like it should. So you have to be able to diversify to make a living."

Kyla turned in the seat, her head tilting to the side. "Issues?" she asked, her tone curious. He remained silent, and she could see by the shake of his head and the way his lips pressed together that he wasn't going to spill all the town secrets to some stranger. "Are you from here?"

"I was born here, but my dad and I moved to Portland afterwards. Lived there for awhile, and then we moved back when I was ten."

"So the rest of your family is here?"

She watched his hand tighten on the steering wheel. "You got lots of questions considering you still haven't told me your name." The tone of his voice was light, but she could tell it was a subject he wasn't too keen to talk about.

Kyla stared at him a beat and was about to respond when he interrupted. "Here we are. Welcome to Ashten Falls. Look quickly or you might miss it."

Her attention was pulled from him to the buildings they were passing. She saw several people wave to Cooper, and was not unaware of a few stares in her direction.

Most of the buildings were brick and in need of some masonry work, with several beyond-the-worn stage and falling down.

The ones that were wooden, were clapboard and needed paint. However, dots of color sprang up here and there from flower boxes and half barrels outside of some of the businesses and on the sidewalks, with some flowers hanging from pots from canopies that hung over the shops. The canopies had seen better days too, but there was a certain small town charm about them, their faded colors at least proving their staying power. Other storefronts were boarded up, or seemed abandoned. She couldn't really tell. None of the buildings were overly tall, perhaps three stories at the most. In the distance she could make out clusters of what looked like warehouses, taller than the buildings on the main drag, and in the opposite direction, Kyla could see several large, brick buildings that looked like apartments.

She hit the button for the window and as the cool air hit her, she smiled. The smell of the sea was stronger here, and she could see a low fog off on Cooper's side. Although the dilapidated buildings around her didn't scream resort town, she didn't care. The beach and the salty air would make it all better.

"So was this where you're supposed to end up?" Cooper asked.

"Not supposed to end up anywhere really, or didn't plan to. But this place was definitely not on my top ten places to be. I mean, does anyone intend to come here?"

"Nope, I reckon they don't." He got quiet, pulling into a space near the office door and turning the truck off.

Kyla hopped down and rounded the back of the truck where Cooper was waiting. "The motel that way?" she asked, pointing toward a cluster of nearby buildings that made up a square. A large neon sign on the far window of a front building blinked the word "office." Between the buildings, she could see what looked to be a green area, some picnic tables, and a large pool in the center. The whole place looked like it had seen better days and could use a paint job, but whoever owned it tried to do what they could. Hanging flowerpots were scattered about, and the windows had boxes with colorful flowers in them. The parking lot that abutted the front building was close to empty, with only three cars and a motorcycle in it. She noted the front building of the hotel was separated from the garage by a narrow lot that ran the length of both properties. It was perhaps twenty feet wide and seemed perfectly positioned to break up the more industrial shop from the town's only place for people to stay while visiting. Unlike the motel, the garage had a chain link fence around it, though the effect was broken by hedges in front of it, as if hiding the fence itself. Someone clearly cared about appearances in the town, and she wondered if the hedges were Cooper's idea, or someone else's.

She let her gaze wander, trying to take in as much as she could. Across the street and about a block from the garage a group of men stood outside of a fast food joint called Seaside Fried. She could just make out a blinking sign with the words "Stan's Bar" lit up a short distance from the motel, with what looked like a parking lot between with weeds growing up through the pavement. Down the street, beyond the garage and record store, was a large, concrete block, the police shield on the front of the building over the door indicating its purpose. Next to that, the fire department doors were opened, the trucks outside. Various shops were scattered on the other side of the street, some looking like they were well kept, others with for sale or lease signs in the windows.

"Motel should have a room for you. Don't think they take fancy hotel points though. And given the amount of luggage and clothes you have, you might have to get a room for that alone," he teased.

Kyla rolled her eyes at his mention of her clothes, a laugh bubbling from her lips. "I'm sure I'll get it all in one room, but thanks for your concern. I have very few vices, clothes just happen to be one of them."

He lifted his chin towards the motel door. "Get inside. But stop by the shop as soon as you get settled. We'll figure out what you want to do with your car."

She nodded. "Thank you for the ride, Cooper. I'll be over soon as I sort things out." She fidgeted before giving him a rare, full smile. She waved again and then headed into the office.

• • •

Holy fuck, that smile. It hit Cooper out of the blue as he watched her turn the corner of the fence and make the short walk to the motel parking lot. He felt Phil's presence as he continued to stare after her.

"Hey, Coop. Who's the mystery babe? She's hot."

Cooper didn't answer. Instead his eyes were glued to that heart-shaped ass, her hips, and that hair. He didn't know which he wanted to get his hands on first. The woman certainly wasn't petite. She couldn't be at around 5'9. She had long hair that fell just above her bra strap but it was thick and shone in the sun. The color wasn't just brown but shades of brown, auburn, and lighter brown, throughout. Her eyes were a deep green and she had a full mouth which shined from whatever lip-gloss she had on. She wasn't stick thin, she couldn't be with how tall she was, and with her tits and that ass, and that was fine with him.

"Yeah she's. . . something. Keys?" He took Kyla's keys and headed for the Mustang, sitting in the passenger seat and pilfering through the glove compartment. He got her name and address, jotting it down on a scrap of paper in his pocket for the invoice. "Kyla O'Grady of Rock River, Pennsylvania." Cooper shoved the registration back into the compartment and pushed off the seat.

Phil canted his head and then shook it slowly from side to side. He whistled, chuckling as Cooper cut him a glare. "Jesus, man, what the hell? All you did was pick her up on the side of the road and you're practically drooling after her. Get a grip." He shrugged off Phil's hand clapped down on his shoulder. Cooper was a big guy, but had more muscle, not to mention was taller by about three inches than Phil.

"Yeah, whatever. Let's get to work." He turned and walked toward the garage, doing his best to ignore Phil's chuckling behind him. Yet, even as he rolled under one of the cars to work on an oil change, he couldn't get Kyla's face out of his head. She was sweet, and her big eyes and bright smile made his dick hard. But he also noticed other things, subtle movements that made him curious about Kyla's background. He had seen the way she'd fidgeted and tucked into herself when they were in the truck. He had also seen her initial reaction to Phil, when he saw a look of terror flash in her eyes. It pissed him off that someone or something had put that fear there. He wanted to know who or what had done it, and use his fists to make them regret ever hurting Kyla.

"God damnit!" He muttered as oil began dripping everywhere, including on him. He had been distracted and hadn't moved the oil pan into place.

He heard Phil's chuckle and rolled out from under the car, glaring at his friend, "What the hell are you laughing at?"

Phil shook his head, his grin getting even bigger. "You give me crap all the time about being wrapped around my woman's finger. Now, look at you. It only took a half hour for you to get distracted by a woman. So I'm enjoying this."

Cooper mouth tightened and his look turned even darker. "I'm not distracted, and definitely not distracted by a woman I don't even know." He shook thoughts of Kyla out of his head and stalked toward his office. "I got paperwork to do. Finish this oil change."

• • •

Kyla had forced herself to not look back as she moved through the office door. He was cute. No, he was hot, but she didn't like the way he had her stomach jumbling around. No. She loved it, and that made her let out a small noise of frustration in the back of her throat. The man was gorgeous and tall. He had to be six-four, which made him six inches taller than her. She always dated men who were taller than her, but with Cooper—hell she could wear heels and still come up short.

Kyla shook her head to stop those thoughts in their tracks. She couldn't afford to get lost in a man, no matter how good looking, and no matter that her body would not object if she did. She'd sworn off men, especially hot ones, forever.

The motel's office area had seen better days. The manager, Morris, was a smarmy-looking fellow with very few teeth and copious amounts of sweat dripping from his brow, and, like the office, had seen better days. Or hopefully had. When Kyla asked for a room farthest away from any neighbors he cackled, telling her that there was a vacancy sign for a reason. He handed her a key and looked her over with lecherous eyes. She snatched the key from his hand and shivered before hurrying out.

As she went up the stairs toward her allotted room, she wondered how a place like this could have such beauty in the flowers and lawn care, yet hire someone like Morris. He did not seem like he fit in at all. At least he had given her the room all the way down at the corner of the building, which meant it was slightly bigger than the others, and away from the gaggle of children she passed at the top of the stairs. They stopped, silent for about three seconds, before they resumed their game of tag. As she slid the key in the door, Kyla took notice of the wraparound, open front balcony that went around the corner to another set of stairs leading to the center quad area of the motel. There, a sidewalk wound around to meet the parking lot in front. Her eyes fell to the garage next door, an empty lot with trees scattered about in no particular design, separating Cooper's place from the motel. She saw a tire swing hung from one of the larger trees and noticed that the lot seemed well taken care of, mowed with pockets of flowering bushes and wildflowers here and there.

A large area in the back of the garage ran the same length as the motel property, half of it paved, the other half grassy and also well maintained. A selection of cars and bikes littered the pavement, along with a large grill next to the back door. There was an overhang with various mismatched lawn chairs and a picnic table underneath it. Beer cans littered the area. She snorted, wondering just what kind of parties went on back there. Beyond the garage building itself she could just make out a door to another building, connected by the lot in the back. It was the music store they had passed on the way in.

She unpacked what she could, having paid for a month in advance, and dumped the clothes she had into the dresser and small closet in the small bedroom. She kept her laptop and other important things in the case with a lock. She'd have to get a padlock for the closet door.

Kyla put that on her growing list of essentials, and then she checked the sheets, surprised to find they were clean and seemingly devoid of bugs and mysterious bodily fluids. She made a pile of dirty clothes, making a note to get some detergent, too, and finally, when her last bag was unpacked, she dropped them in the bottom of the closet. She looked around, relaxing for the first time in a long time. She had been driving for a very long time, never staying anywhere more than three nights. She didn't have the resources for a name change. Her best option had been to empty her bank account and carry around her cash. She had a little left in her account for emergencies, but even that wasn't enough for the car repairs. She worried that Frank would somehow track her down, but it had been a while since she'd heard anything from him, and her Mom had said he seemed to be settling into his life without her. He had even been seen out with some other girl.

I will cut you up so bad, bitch, no one will recognize your whore face. You will not get away with what you did.

Ice formed in her veins as his words echoed in her mind. The bastard had been confident as they stood outside the district attorney's office. The prosecutor wouldn't be pressing charges against either of them since it was a mutually combatant situation. The DA also wanted to avoid a mess, and what happened that night between Kyla and Frank was, at the very least, a mess. Kyla had been out of the hospital for only two months at that time, and hadn't seen her ex since that night in the apartment four months before. Six glorious months of no contact; it was absolute heaven. She had moved back in with her mom, finding support at home, though her brother, Mike, was not happy with her. The situation put him, an assistant district attorney in the county, in an awkward and uncomfortable position given that he had to work with the cops, who were all standing behind Frank. Mike had come to blows with a colleague trying to defend his sister, and almost lost his job. The injuries he'd sustained, and the time it took him to recover, hadn't been easy either. All of this had strained his once close relationship with Kyla and made them both unsure of where they each stood with the other.

Kyla looked for work—having gone to one of the best conservatories in the country, she wielded a dual degree in piano and vocal performance. She had wanted to put the focus back on her music, and go back to giving lessons to kids who wanted to learn an instrument or to sing. Eventually her goal was to get a Master's degree so she could teach at schools, but she hadn't gotten that chance. And hell if she'd been able to find a viable job around their hometown after the incident. Frank's friends were powerful. With no job, she couldn't afford going back to school.

Kyla had felt lost, and even with her family at her back, her frustration with her situation had grown, and she had gotten restless. Just when she thought things couldn't get worse, they did. When the phone calls started, she had tried to ignore them. But the night Frank followed her home from one of her domestic violence group meetings had been her breaking point. He forced her off the road and then handcuffed her to the car door as the rain poured down. He yelled and screamed but never touched her. He just made sure she knew all the things he would do to her when he got the chance. After what felt like hours—though it had been only about thirty minutes—he uncuffed her and drove away. She made it into her car and locked the doors, shivering as she called her counselor.

Jane didn't hesitate. She drove over and followed her home.

To say Mike had hit the roof would be an understatement. Mike had wanted to go after Frank and make him pay for what he'd done. But some of his anger seemed directed at Kyla. He wanted to be done with the drama, to not have to deal with the way the situation was dividing the town. He wasn't siding with Frank. In fact, he wanted Frank to be off the force and out of their lives. But he was sick of dealing with the gossip, the stares, the unannounced and unwelcome visits by cops and lawyers to sort through the mess. He'd had enough and he wanted Kyla to stop putting herself in situations where Frank could get to her. She had stared at him, open-mouthed. Mike had tried to make peace, realizing what he'd said was wrong and apologizing. But once the words were said, Kyla couldn't let them go. She walked away finally and started packing. Her mother tried to get her to stay. She had cried, but she knew Kyla needed to leave, not only for her safety, but because she couldn't get better while living with reminders of the past.

If you had listened in the first place, none of this would have ever happened! We told you he was bad news!

Jane hurried Kyla along, stuffed her car full and had Kyla follow her to her place. She hadn't spoken to her brother since. With good reason, given what he'd said. But dammit if she didn't miss him like crazy.

She picked up her phone, starting to dial, figuring she'd better check in.

"Hey, Mom."

"Where are you tonight darlin'? Your brother is here for dinner." She heard Mike holler a hello to her in the background.

"Tell him, uh, I said hi." Her voice was almost shy as she climbed into bed. "Um, the car died and has to have major repairs. I'm staying at this motel in Ashten Falls. It's a small town in Maine."

"Honey, how much do you need?" She felt a pang in her chest. Her mom always trusted her. Always. Even when she'd lied, threatened, raged, and nearly died. Her mom had always trusted her. Knowing that, hurt.

"It's okay, Mom. I ... I'm going to figure it out. I have to, ya know? I mean, it's not an ideal situation or town for that matter, but I have to learn to fix these things on my own."

Her mom was silent for a few beats. "I'm proud of you, honey. But you don't have to prove anything to me. Just please remember, asking for help isn't a weakness."

"Thanks, Mom. Listen, I'm really tired and need some sleep, but I'll call again soon, okay? We need to catch up on our soaps." She gave her mom the name of the motel and the town, in case of an emergency.

"Oh, we do! It's been getting juicy lately," her mom practically squealed, which made Kyla laugh. "Good to hear you laugh, love. You get some sleep"

"Love you guys." She hung up and curled up in a ball, letting the fast-approaching sleep wash over her.

...

Cooper was standing out back of the store, having a smoke and staring off toward the motel. He had watched Kyla make her way to the room at the end of the building on the second floor. Lucky for him, it was the side closest to the shop. He could see Kyla moving around, her shadow playing on the curtains. His eyes were still on the window of her room, covered by a set of sheer curtains, when the light turned off. She had to be exhausted; he could see that in her eyes when they were in his truck.

A hand clapped him on the shoulder, "Hey man, guys are all here. You want a beer?"

He nodded. "Yeah, Phil. Thanks. Let's get this over with." He made his way back inside the shop and leaned against the counter at the front of the store. A few of the guys were flipping through the bins of music, another was playing around with the drum set, and a few others were parked in front of the television playing video games.

"Anyone got any news?"

Roger spoke up first. He was tall and looked like he could break someone's neck with just a look. But his broad shoulders and thick thighs were softened by the dirty blond hair he kept short. He had the start of a scruffy beard on his face. He set his sunglasses on top of his head and crossed his large arms over his chest. "Man, when is this community protection going to stop? I mean I get it, we got a corrupt police department, but considering I gotta be up at the ass crack of dawn every morning, these night shifts are not working for me."

Sam cleared his throat from the couch. "I'll take some night shifts. The club is running pretty well with the managers I got in place, and they can always get me on my phone if something comes up. I think the better thing though is to just get the information out there and let people know we're setting up a sort of neighborhood watch. This way, if someone gets into trouble they know to call us whether it's to contact one of the attorneys in town, or get a bail enforcement agent to set something up to get 'em out. Sounds kind of simple, but I mean, if we're trying to keep people from getting beat on, just putting the word out to get in touch when they get jacked up by the cops would go a long way. Could also be a way to collate information, keep a database."

Derek spoke then. "I could set something up, we could take each person's information and description of what happened, dates and whatnot, leaving names out of course. Then we have more to hand over to ... well, whoever the fuck decides to look into this." He scowled. "Coop, what'd the feds say?"

Cooper snorted. "Some phone jockey took my information, said they would look into it, which probably means they never will." He ran a hand through his hair and let out a frustrated breath. "But Sam's right. If we have numbers, stats, something in writing to give them, they may be more inclined to get Saybrook the fuck out of here and put him in a cage where he belongs."

Roger started speaking again, but Cooper's mind wandered to Kyla. Her mouth had been one of her most distracting features, full lips and a smile that lit up her green eyes. Though when her temper flared, that was pretty fantastic, too.

"Cooper, you think that's a good idea?"

He snapped his head up; taking a second to recall what had been asked. "Yeah, that's fine with me. Whatever y'all want to do, make it work. Look, guys, I know this sucks. We shouldn't have to police our own cops. But if we disrupt the shit they try to kick up and are a presence out there to protect the people we care about, or rely on as employees, we might make a bit of headway until someone official looks into this shit."

It was Sam's turn to snort now, "Yeah, well, Saybrook is a sick fuck who gets off on hurting people—men, women, he doesn't give a rat's ass. Only thing he is going to respond to is tactics like that. We disrupt his extracurricular activities, he's going to be pissed and won't hesitate to come after us."

Roger crossed his arms over his chest. "That prick will come after us whether we stir shit up or not. I just want this over with. I'm sick of living under this cloud. I want my town back." The guys were silent. All of them had known Cheryl and all of them had been there for Roger when she was killed. They all wanted this over and were hoping, once the chief was brought to justice, Roger could find some closure. Hell, they all needed some closure.

"We'll get this done, Roger. I swear to god we will. I don't care how long it takes, we'll finish it." The other men murmured their agreement and soon the meeting started breaking up. Some grabbed another beer; others went back to playing the game system for a while. Cooper stood quietly, took a pull of his beer, and wondered if Kyla was asleep.

A few hours later when only his closest friends were left, Phil spoke up. "Cooper, you seemed distracted. What's up?"

He glanced up and glared at Phil's smirk. "I am not in the mood for your crap tonight. Not with this Saybrook shit happening."

Saybrook had a history with each, all of it involving trying to beat the tar out of them, and all of them giving back as good as they got. Saybrook hated them with a passion and loved nothing more than to interrupt their businesses, customers, and their families. He had the town council on the run, and he was getting more overt and aggressive in his power grab of late, even going after some of the women who worked at the local strip club. He was a brute who spread fear without fear of reprisal. Without fear of anything, really.

Cooper took a last drink and set the empty on the counter. "We got a Mustang in the lot, make sure no one touches that or I will find them and beat them bloody. In fact, park it in the last stall. We don't use it anyway, and cover it. Don't want it getting crap on it."

He rolled his eyes at his so-called friends, who were fighting their grins. "Shut up. All of you. We're done."

"Right, Coop." Derek shook with laughter. "Already staking your claim and protecting the girl's assets. And from what Phil said she has plenty of those."

"True dat!" Phil joined in. "She was all tits and ass and her hips … dayum, only chick I know who works it better is Sheena. Kyla is hot."

A muscle ticked in Cooper's jaw as the boys continued to rib him. "I'm fuckin' serious," he growled so low his friends stopped and looked at him with surprise. "That car is off limits."

Phil nodded, clearing his throat. "You got it. Let's get outta here," he said to the others. "Early day tomorrow. 'Night, Coop."

Roger stayed behind and once the other guys left, he spoke, "I'm leaving for a while, Cooper. I know I said I'd help with this shit, but I need some air."

Cooper looked at his friend, noticing the tiredness in his eyes. "You need me to go with you?"

Roger shook his head. "Nope. Lots of shit has gone down since. . ." He didn't say her name. "Anyway, I've been working non-stop since it happened and it's just all catching up to me. I'm barely hanging on to my control, and one of these days I'm going to see Saybrook's smart-ass grin and punch him in the fuckin' throat."

"Well that's one way to get rid of him," he replied, his tone dry.

"Yeah, it is. One that will land me in a cage, and you know I can't live in a cage, Coop. I'm sorry, man."

He clapped a hand on Roger's shoulder. "Don't need to apologize to me. I get it. So get the fuck out of here. Who's handling your projects while you're away?"

Roger pushed off the counter, hands stuffed in his pockets. "I got my two foremen handling things, and Sam is overseeing it all. That lazy fuck just has to take care of his club, so I've hauled him in to help me out."

Cooper grinned. "He is lazy, isn't he?" He shook his head because they both knew Sam was the hardest working man they knew outside of themselves. "You going to be on grid or you going off?"

Roger rocked back on his heels. "Mostly off, though I'll check in with my cell now and again. I'm thinking I need to hit the West Coast, visit some friends out there that Sam and I served with."

"Do it, man. Sam and I can handle shit here. Be sure to tell him if he needs anything, I can lend a hand or get some of the guys here to help out. Half of 'em are your part-time crew anyway."

Roger grabbed his leather jacket from the couch and shrugged it on. "Thanks. I appreciate it. Just don't take the fucker down until you give me a heads up. I want to be here when that shit happens. Take care, Cooper."

With that, Roger walked out the door to his truck. Cooper's head dropped and he stared at his shoes searching for some control over his emotions. He knew Roger had been having trouble with Cheryl's death. Hell, what sane person wouldn't? He just hoped Roger would be all right on his own. But then, maybe that was what the man needed. Cooper wondered what it would be like to just leave town. He snorted. Like that would ever happen.

Cooper walked out the door, moving across the parking lot to check the garage. Kyla had closed the heavier curtains over the sheers at her window, but he could see the flicker of light from the television between them. She was probably in bed and he wondered if she was wearing anything from that duffel bag. Groaning, he set the security alarm. He knew those were thoughts he shouldn't be having before heading home alone. It would make for a long night.

• • •

It was cold as she lay in a pool of her own blood, her broken body finding any movement almost too much to take. Was her brother, Mike, okay? Why wasn't he moving? Was he that still because he was dead? Tears stained her cheeks and she covered her mouth with her hand, groaning when she saw the spots of blood. She watched him walk toward her with one eye, her other already swollen shut. As he loomed over her, she struggled to curl into a fetal position. The air left her lungs and her body shook from the impact of his kick to her stomach.

"You will not leave me. You hear me? You belong to me and even if you get away, I will hunt you down like the worthless bitch you are! Do you hear me?"

She sobbed harder as he grabbed her hair to haul her body up toward his face. She caught a glimpse of the metal underneath his jacket, the buckle of his holster so close. She knew she would only get one chance at this. She lifted her battered face and nodded, trying to convey her acquiescence. "I'm sorry," her voice only a whisper from the earlier choking she'd received. "Please, I won't go. I swear."

Frank looked down on her and smiled as he gripped her hair tighter. He kissed her lips, covered in a mix of blood and tears. She cried out from the pressure as her hand moved into his jacket. When she felt the grip, she kissed him back to keep up the charade. She just needed to distract him for another minute or so.

"You're mine. Mine forever," he hissed against her lips.

Using what little strength she could muster, she pulled the gun into her shaking hands and shoved it into his chest. He pushed her back when he felt the barrel, his eyes wide. She remembered all those times her dad had taught her to shoot in the backyard. She tried to get to her feet, her knees wobbling. "Stay away from me or I will shoot your head off!"

He laughed, his voice like nails on a chalkboard to her ears. "You won't shoot me. You're weak, you need me. Who's going to take care of you? You think your daddy will save you? He washed his hands of you. He couldn't handle his only daughter being the drug addict that you are. I'm all you got. Now give me the damn gun!"

His words felt as bad as the earlier punches he'd given her, and in her head she was convinced what he was saying was true. She'd lost her way; everyone had washed their hands of her, everyone but Mike who was lying on the carpet in a pool of ever-expanding blood. He wasn't moving. Had all her shit gotten her big brother killed? No one would ever forgive her then. She choked on a sob, her hands shaking uncontrollably. She had nothing left. She didn't want to die, but she *wouldn't let Mike's death go unavenged. It was that knowledge that snapped her out of the pain, even if only for a brief moment, as Frank stepped toward her. She pulled the trigger, once, twice, three times, until Frank finally fell to the ground.*

"I told you to stay back. You never listened to me," she screamed. She heard the thud of the gun as it hit the floor near her feet. She was vaguely aware of sirens in the distance as she slid to the floor, collapsing from the sheer amount of pain and adrenaline shooting through her own body. She crawled over to Mike and pushed at him, but he was a dead weight. Not afraid to let the tears fall anymore, she curled up next to him, holding on as tightly as she could.

Kyla lurched out of bed, the sheets twisted around her, her hand covering her mouth as she stifled the scream she felt bubbling inside of her. She got up and splashed water on her face, staring at her reflection in the mirror. She shook her head, whispering to herself, "Please just get out of my head." She begged the demons in her mind to leave her be.

Her reflection didn't respond, and after her heartbeat slowed to normal, she sighed and made her way back to bed. She stared at the ceiling for a long while until sleep finally claimed her.

Chapter 2

Everything Kyla needed during the next several days was in walking distance, which was obviously a good thing given she was wouldn't have a car for the foreseeable future. She hadn't been back to talk to Cooper yet, not wanting to face her rapidly decreasing finances and a car that was nearly, if not mostly, dead. In her self-guided tour of Ashten Falls, she had the occasion to catch his gaze and he would nod, or give her a small smile. The look was always intense and lasted longer than someone just being polite. And that look made her insides twist, in what she remembered was supposed to be a very good way.

She walked into the bookstore and stood quietly in line as the man behind the coffee counter served those in front of her.

"What can I get ya?" The clerk was just a touch taller than she was and looked to be somewhere in his fifties. She immediately recognized him as the first man who had stopped to offer help, before Cooper. "Hey, girl. I wondered when you'd stop in. I had heard Cooper picked up a beautiful woman outside of town and had to figure it was the pretty thing I saw standing near the 'stang."

"Um, thanks." She felt a slow blush creep up her cheeks and he winked, still smiling. "Large chai, please. With soymilk if you have it. And a muffin, chocolate chip?"

"Coming right up." He moved to start making her order. "I'm Steve Donohue, I own this place. Welcome to Ashten Falls."

She offered a tentative smile, sliding cash across the counter to cover the cost of the chai and muffin. "I'm Kyla, Kyla O'Grady."

He gave her the change, watching her closely. "Nice to meet you officially, Kyla. Interesting name. I like it."

"My parents thought I was going to be a boy and had picked the name Kyle. And when I was born my mom wanted to use it, so she tweaked it a bit."

"Well it suits you. Come on over here, have a seat, I'll introduce you to some folks."

Kyla hesitated, shifting her feet as she stood with her chai in one hand and muffin in the other, not sure whether to beg off the invitation. She ran through her options: she could politely decline, saying she had to go and sit in her room by herself, proving she was the loner Frank had turned her into. Or she could stay, grit her teeth, and take the first step to going back to who she was: friendly, sometimes funny, and not an extrovert, but not a wallflower either. In a split-second decision she chose the latter, not wanting to give Frank any more power over her. He was miles away, and would get his eventually. She followed Steve to a table and sat down in the chair he had pulled out for her, smiling at the three already seated there.

"Kyla O'Grady, meet Rose Martin. She owns the motel you're staying in. This is her son, Justin Martin, local reporter extraordinaire, and his wife, Maggie. Maggie owns a local clothing store for ladies. Something you'd probably love, being you're a woman like she is."

Kyla couldn't hide her smile. "Well that's kind of stereotypical." She took a drink of her chai before adding, "Though you'd be right."

Steve laughed. "See, I knew it." He shrugged and Kyla wondered if he was always this jovial. It was like his smile was permanent and he just radiated happiness.

Rose offered her hand across the small table. "Nice to meet you, dear. I heard rumblings about a new woman in the town. Most have nothing much to do around here but talk about stuff that isn't our business." She winked at her, not hiding the fact that she was a gossip. "Word is Cooper Moretto drove you in."

"Yeah, he saw me on the side of the road after my car tanked on me."

"Not often that Cooper offers a helping hand, unless it's something he wants. Must have seen something he liked."

Kyla's eyes slid to Justin as he spoke. He was average, not bad looking, but very clean-cut, and he looked like he was born to be a reporter, right down to the Clark Kent glasses and the pencils and small notepad in his shirt pocket.

Maggie leaned over, patting her clenched hand. "Ignore my husband. Cooper is a nice man, long as you don't get on his bad side. He is a miracle worker with cars. I am sure he will help ya get it running again. What are you doing here in Ashten Falls? Was this a planned visit or were you heading somewhere else?"

"No, wasn't so much planned. Just was driving, ya know. No real destination in mind."

"Well that's serendipity then! The universe wanted you here for a reason, and here you are."

Maggie said it with such certainty, Kyla's head snapped up and she blinked. "Well, I don't know about that, but I'm here. I'm trying to settle in best I can."

Rose spoke up then, leaning forward toward Kyla. "How are things at the motel? You're being treated okay? I'm set to retire from my day job in the fall. I've worked at the power plant about ten miles from here for more than thirty years as an administrative assistant. But it's time to move on, retire, and see to my motel full-time. My husband, god rest his soul, would tell me it's about time."

Kyla nodded. "The room is great. I love the flowers you have everywhere. And the pool is gorgeous. I saw the sign that said it would be opening soon. Can't wait."

Rose was beaming at the compliments. "My husband bought all that property and the bar when we first married. There were years we've struggled, but it's all been worth it. He ran it, was everything from day manager to the maintenance man. Still have a small staff, and Justin helps out with fixing things that require tools. Roger, Cooper, and Sam are always around if I need something done. The boys in this town definitely take care of their own."

Steve had gotten up and made his way back to her with a bag in his hands. "Here are some muffins for ya. On the house. Consider it a welcome to Ashten Falls gift. Keep them in the fridge and pop in the microwave when you're ready to eat 'em. They'll be good as fresh. Well almost."

Kyla hesitated a moment before she took the bag from him, uttering a soft "thank you." She didn't know what to say to all this kindness from strangers. But then, they didn't know about her past. They might change their mind when they found out she had nearly killed her boyfriend. Self-defense or not, it had been violent and bloody. No one liked to be around people capable of that.

She lifted her eyes and shrank under Justin's curious gaze. "Cooper and I aren't best buds, but I will say, given the latest round of shit that's been going down in this town, he is definitely one you want at your back. Of all the people around here, Cooper's always had a code and he's smart. He would give you the shirt off his back, but is also someone who, if you piss him off … well, watch out."

"What do you mean, the latest round of stuff going down? And Cooper and I … I mean, he just gave me a ride. Not like we are best friends now or anything." She was trying to be funny, trying to steer the conversation from whatever it was these people were implying.

Maggie spoke, her voice soft. "You're right. Cooper just gave you a ride, and he's a good guy, tough as nails. Just go with the flow. As for the town, there will be plenty of time later to learn about that. No need to get into that your first week." She reached out and patted Kyla's hand, shooting her husband daggers with her eyes.

Kyla swallowed and was thankful when Rose and Steve changed the subject to some zoning issues. Zoning issues were a much safer topic than Cooper Moretto.

•••

Kyla headed back to the motel from the coffee shop, but as she approached the music store she couldn't miss Cooper leaning against the wall. She hadn't been inside the store yet. And even now, she wasn't interested in going inside. Her interest was on the man who stood slightly apart from the group, exuding confidence as he spoke to some of the guys she'd seen around the garage.

She was momentarily distracted as her phone buzzed. She fished her phone out of her pocket and scrolled through some texts when suddenly she slammed into a wall of chest. She stumbled to get her balance before righting herself. Standing just in front of her was Phil.

"Yo. If it isn't the girl with the hot car and the pretty eyes. How you doing, lovely?"

"Hi—Phil, right? I'm okay and thanks. For the compliment and for the tow."

"No problem. I was on call, and we don't get many of those around here, so it was all good. It gave me something to do. It got me out of an argument with my woman about my failure to mow the lawn, too." He grinned down at her. "Saved by the broken down 'stang, so to speak."

Kyla snorted. "I'm assuming a guy like you doesn't date a meek woman." She tilted her head to the side, adding, "Would it be correct to assume your getting out of that argument was temporary?"

Phil's loud, deep laughter rang out on the street. "Right on. I heard about it when I got home. Had quite the row actually, then I went out and mowed the lawn."

She laughed, finding Phil easy to talk to, despite his imposing size. "See, why can't you guys just do what you're supposed to do the first time? It would make life much easier for everyone."

He bent down and whispered in her ear, "Then there'd be no need for making up. That's the best part." He straightened and laughed again.

"Hey man, you got a woman. Save some for the rest of us."

At the sound of Cooper's voice, Kyla lifted her gaze to see Cooper's eyes on her. He looked just as hot now as he had yesterday. Dark-wash jeans that seemed made for him, black motorcycle boots, and a tight, dark gray Harley shirt that accentuated the muscles of his torso. Kyla shifted her feet, wondering if she should have chosen something other than the pair of black Capri pants, a set of tank tops—one black with a dark pink tank over it—along with pink and black flip-flops on her feet. Her small, faded black messenger bag was slung across her body at an angle. "Hey."

"Hey yourself. How you doing? You look rested."

"Does that mean I looked not rested and therefore like crap before?" Kyla surprised herself by the teasing tone of her voice, but that didn't stop her from throwing in a crooked smile.

Cooper crossed his arms over his chest, his eyes skimming over her body from head to toe and back again. "Nope. You looked beautiful before. I just didn't think you could look any more so. Clearly I was wrong."

Kyla transferred the bag of muffins to her other hand and mumbled a soft "thanks."

"You're welcome. Now, what has you wandering around a town you clearly are unfamiliar with, on your own?"

"What?" she asked, frowning at his change in tone. "I can handle myself fine. And it's none of your business."

Cooper glanced at Phil, who had his arms crossed over his chest now as well, staring down at Kyla with a similar concerned look on his face. "Phil, should we get her a bodyguard? A woman shouldn't be on her own around here."

"Problem is, any guard will want to take the whole guarding-the-body part of that job pretty damn seriously. Perhaps even literally," Phil rumbled. "You think you could handle that kind of gig, Cooper?"

"Yeah, I could more than handle that."

Kyla's narrowed eyes leveled on both men. "I'm standing right here." As if that wasn't obvious. "You guys have a habit of doing that—talking about me when I'm right in front of you. It's seriously annoying."

"I can't help it, you're cute when you're annoyed." Cooper chuckled as her brow furrowed. "Still cute, doll, but back to the subject at hand. We're trying to keep you safe since you seem intent on putting yourself in danger. This isn't Mayberry."

"No way, really? I had no idea. And here I was half expecting the good ole boy sheriff and his deputy to come present me with a key to the town and be their honored guest at lunch." She didn't hide the sarcasm in her tone.

Phil tensed and Cooper's face went to stone. "Do not joke about things you don't know about. This place has bad shit going down, and traipsing around here like you are with your muffins, half-dressed and looking at your phone instead of your surroundings, is a recipe for disaster."

"Well . . ." she huffed at his reaction. "I will have you know there will be no traipsing. I am going for a walk and then to my room. That is it. Not that this is any of your business. Now if you will excuse me. . ." She moved around them, coming up short as Cooper wrapped a hand around her arm.

"Watch your back and don't be stupid. I'm telling you this for your safety, not to be an asshole. Be smart, yeah?"

Kyla paused, her eyes lifted to his. She wrenched her arm free and stalked off, needing to get as far from the man as possible. Remembering her phone, she looked down and her stomach twisted as she read the text.

"Coming for you soon. Time you came home where you belong."

She picked up the pace and turned toward the hotel. How the hell had he found her this fast?

•••

Cooper flipped on his sunglasses and watched Kyla walk away. He kept his eyes on her, his gaze hidden behind the tinted Foster Grants, until a voice forced him to look away.

"Cooper? Hey, can we talk?"

He barely held back his cringe as he heard Marla's whiny, incessant, high-pitched voice that he swore was worse than nails on a chalkboard.

"Kinda busy right now, Marla."

He pushed himself away from the wall and started to move away. But he froze when her hand reached out and grabbed for his hand. He shook her off.

"What'd I say, Marla? I gotta go. And please, don't touch me."

"Cooper, we never talk anymore and you haven't taken me out in ages. I mean, ya know, just you and me. We need to talk about our future."

Cooper's eyes would have fallen out of his head if he didn't have his shades on. "What did you just say?" He was not even attempting to conceal his annoyance now. "Future? There is no fucking future between us."

Marla's eyes flicked over to the others milling by the door of the music store and she backed up a few paces. "Cooper, you and I are supposed to be together, like we talked about." Her lower lip quivered, but he ignored it. Marla was not the woman he knew in high school and lost his virginity to. Back then she was just one of their group, hanging around together with the rest of the kids from their small school, and it was natural the two had hooked up. What he hadn't realized was that she'd grow up to become the kind of woman who now didn't hide the fact she sold her body in order to afford expensive shoes, clothes, purses, and, if the rumors were true, drugs. Her delusions were wearing on him. The only reason she was still tolerated at the garage or record store was because of the devotion some of the guys, including Cooper, had to her older brother whom they'd also gone to high school with. Jim was dead now, killed in the Iraq war, but Cooper felt he owed it to his buddy to do what he could to keep Marla out of trouble. But that wasn't working and Cooper knew he had to stop hanging on to that excuse. Jim would have kicked her ass if he saw how she was acting, and this latest outburst told Cooper he had to cut her loose.

Cooper put up a hand, the muscle in his cheek jumped, and his voice dipped low and dangerous. "Marla, I don't know what the fuck fantasy you got in your head, but we were over about two point three seconds after our first time—you know it and I know it. We didn't work and we never will. Not to mention the fact that it was seventeen years ago. I don't know why you're still hanging on to some fucked up fantasy. It's not going to happen."

"I'm sorry, Cooper. So sorry. . ." She squeezed out from between him and the store wall but not before glancing back. "We'll talk later. It will all be okay."

"Phil!" Cooper snapped out. He waited for Phil to saunter over before nodding at Marla. "She needs a ride home." He lowered his voice then, "I don't want her around here or in my vicinity." He hissed, murmuring the conversation he and Marla just had.

"I'll take care of it, Coop. Let's go, Marla." Phil guided Marla away before he lowered his voice. "Cooper, I've been telling you that she has been off the rails lately; maybe next time you'll listen. . ."

"Just take care of it," he said, shoving into Phil's shoulder as he started to walk away. "I got to attend to something."

"To something? Or someone?" Phil lifted a brow, chuckling at the death glare Cooper shot him. "Now that one does not seem crazy … I got good vibes about her so go ahead and tap . . ."

"Don't even say it, man. Do not even," Cooper warned. "When it happens, I don't need your asinine words in my head."

"When Cooper? You said when it happens..." Phil was already walking away though. All Cooper could do was stare daggers at his back.

"Fuckin A," he muttered to himself. He climbed into his truck and swung out of the lot.

• • •

Kyla couldn't get Cooper's dark blue eyes out of her head. When she ran into him and Phil on the sidewalk, the way he watched her ... god, it was an intensity she hadn't felt in a long time, if ever. When she and Frank first began, she had been thrilled to have a cop—a decorated detective actually—want her by his side. He was sweet for about the first month, doing all the right things. He called often, took her out, bought her flowers and gifts, and stopped in to bring her lunch whenever he was patrolling nearby.

But even then, there were red flags. He was demanding and went from zero to sixty on the anger scale in one second flat. When they went out, he made sure she was dressed in a way he liked, going so far as to make her change if he thought she looked too slutty or not hot enough. He wanted her to be his perfect mate and worked on molding her into that. At first Kyla thought this was him caring how people saw them together, but it soon became apparent that he was doing it so he could show her off like a possession. He treated her not like the other half in a relationship, with respect and love, but as something that was his. This wasn't the case of a guy wanting to protect his woman. To him, Kyla was an object he owned and could use as he wished.

His borderline obsessive ownership soon turned cruel, starting with verbal taunts and emotional abuse, telling her she was fat, or that she disappointed him by working and not staying in the apartment to take care of him like she should. She'd remember the night it got physical for the rest of her life, never forgetting the horror she felt when he smacked her hard across the face. She'd never been hit before, not like that. Not with such venom and anger behind it that her head whipped to the side with an audible snap. All because she had forgotten to go to the dry cleaners. She had her head buried in a music theory book, studying for a final, and the time had gotten away from her.

After, she had stared at him, stunned into silence. Once her ears stopped ringing, she packed her books and some clothes, letting him know by her silence and her actions that she was leaving. He had begged her to stay, made a million promises, blamed the stress of his job, and swore it would never happen again. But it did. Over and over. He got smarter, too, leaving the bruises in places no one would see and making her wear long sleeve shirts when he left marks on her wrists, which was often. She would try to leave and he would somehow sweet-talk his way back into her life, promise to go to counseling, promise to never hurt her again, beg her for another chance.

Soon Kyla didn't know why she stayed, other than the fear of what he would do if she succeeded in leaving. The time before they both ended up in intensive care, she had made it to her car, keys in hand. But he ran after her, desperate and pissed off like she'd never seen him. He grabbed her by the upper arm and turned her around, slammed her back against the door. The handle dug into her back as she kicked and struggled, but he had an iron grip on her arm and she feared it would be crushed under his strength. His other hand came around to her throat and he squeezed, her lungs seizing as she tried to get air into her lungs. She heard a strangled scream and realized it came from her, right before she saw stars as he slammed the back of her head into the car door he had trapped her against.

Slow Ride

"You're not leaving, Kyla. Get this through your fuckin' thick skull, you are *not* leaving. Ever. And if you try to do it again, I won't just come get you. It'll be war, against you, your brother, your parents, those moron friends of yours at the store, and in that band you sing with. Got me?"

She couldn't answer, afraid she'd throw up if she opened her mouth. She had simply nodded while she trembled. He dragged her inside.

The worst part was, not one person who was in that parking lot did a thing to stop Frank. They all knew who he was, what he could do. Even though Kyla begged them with her eyes as she stumbled, they all looked away. That was the moment she went numb. That was the moment she gave up.

After she was finally free of Frank, after she and Mike were out of the hospital, and she was seeing her counselor, Jane, she often wondered if she would ever find someone to share her life with. She was suspicious of people now, always wondering what their true nature was, fearful of when they would turn on her. After a while she just gave up on the idea that she'd be able to have a normal relationship. Frank had worked hard at destroying who she was, and the hope she had for a good life, and he had, sadly, succeeded.

But Kyla wasn't home anymore. She was in Ashten Falls, a new town, a new start, a new everything. Frank wasn't here to remind her of what he had done, what he had taken from her. She could move on, move forward, and hope again. Couldn't she?

Chapter 3

Kyla pushed through the door to Music & Motors, or the Music half of it anyways. She'd walked by it for what felt like a hundred times in the past week, but had stopped herself from going inside. Mainly because many of those times she'd seen Cooper either outside or through the window, behind the counter, and she'd chickened out. The man made her nervous.

But Cooper also owned the car shop that was currently home to her Mustang, and he owned the music store. That right there, had her curiosity piqued. She also missed being around music. Perhaps though, the most important reason for going in was that she needed to talk to Cooper about her car. Her money was going to run out soon and she had to make a plan, or in the worst possible scenario, ask her mother for a loan.

The bell over the door rang as she stepped inside. The place was a throwback to the sixties with seventies punk, eighties hair bands, and a few of the nineties boy bands thrown in. The colors were loud, the furniture and music displays scattered, and there didn't seem to be much organization to the space. Lenny Kravitz's greatest hits CD was playing over the speakers. It was a hodgepodge of records, tapes, CDs, musical instruments, and musical accessories. One corner of the shop sported a large television mounted on the wall. At the moment, three teenagers were hunkered down on the couches and chairs, yelling and shooting at monsters and zombies on some video game.

Kyla's eyes moved to the counter, which was sparse and sat across from the front door. She didn't see Cooper, or anyone, working in the store. As she was about to leave she caught sight of a piano in the far corner. She walked over and ran her fingers over the ivory keys. Until she heard the soft sound that escaped from the light touch, she didn't realize just how much she missed playing. She slid onto the bench, not caring about the dust on the seat, and began to softly play Canon in D. It wasn't a hard piece, it was something she'd learned early on in the piano lessons she'd taken as a child, but it was still one of her favorites.

Kyla was so focused on the piece that she hadn't heard the teenagers stop playing their game. She hadn't sensed them move either. A glance over her shoulder told her that they were behind her, mouths agape as they watched her play.

As she finished the piece one of the teenagers spoke. "Whoa. I haven't ever heard anyone play that thing. Ever. And I've never heard anyone play like that. You're really good."

Kyla smiled, "Thanks. I've been playing all my life so I've had a lot of practice."

The boys chatted with her a bit more and then, after she played another piece for them—this time a rock piece from the early nineties—Kyla found the courage to ask the question weighing on her mind.

"Um, have you guys seen Cooper, the guy who owns this place and the car shop?"

One of them guffawed, "Women are always looking for Cooper. He's got a line of women in town that follow him around. Never catch him though."

Kyla rolled her eyes. "I'm not looking for him to ask him out. He's fixing my car and I need to talk to him about that."

The teenagers didn't seem to believe her by the looks they were giving each other. "Sure, lady, you need to talk about your car. I saw him leaving earlier in the tow truck, so who knows when he'll be back, but try the garage. Phil will know when to expect him."

Kyla sighed as the boys wandered back over to their video game, and the store was filled again with the sounds of zombie heads being blown off and the boys' high-fiving. Kyla considered going to the garage, to talk to Phil, but decided against it. Instead, she turned back to the keys and played some more, feeling more at home than she had in a long time.

• • •

On her third visit to the store as she flipped through a box of old records, someone approached her from behind, stopping so close she could feel the heat. She whirled around, her hands up in front of her, and started to push at whoever intruded into her space, only to look up into Cooper's blue eyes.

"Hey there, Ms. O'Grady." He didn't attempt to move. "What do you think of the place?"

Kyla blinked. "The place?" She furrowed her brows. "Oh, here. I like it. It certainly has character. The fashion sense is a bit scattered though. I mean, a poster of the Cure next to New Kids on the Block? I think that might be against the law."

He chuckled. "Yeah? I'll get right on fixing the interior decorations of this place when I have a free minute. How's that?"

She shrugged. "Fine, but the punk gods might rain down some serious hellfire if you don't fix that, and soon." She liked teasing him and found it came easy.

Cooper shifted and pressed forward, forcing Kyla to press her back into the table behind her. "Find anything you're interested in while in the shop?"

Her gaze dropped to his mouth and then lifted back to his eyes. Her tongue darted out and licked her lips. It was mostly an unconscious move on her part, but the effect was a low growl from Cooper. "I don't know. Maybe. I'm sort of a try-before-you-buy girl."

Cooper blinked slow and then smiled, his white teeth flashing. "I doubt that, honey. You look exactly the opposite of the kind of girl who takes it for a test drive before knowing what she wants. I'd say you're a careful consideration sort of woman." His head dipped, his mouth at her ear. "'Course we could try the test drive thing. Sometimes it's nice to switch things up."

"We need to talk about my car." Kyla whispered, trying to stay focused and not think about kissing the man whose lips were so close to her skin.

"You're right we do. I tallied the labor and parts cost. It's going to cost a mint to get her fixed and take time for the parts to come in. But I've been thinking, since you're here in town, maybe you can work off some of the cost?"

Kyla felt her eyes widen and she pushed at Cooper's chest. "Are you kidding me? I cannot believe you would think I am that kind of girl!" Her voice was rising, along with her temper.

Cooper grinned, shaking his head. "I like seeing you all riled up. Who knew there was a temper lurking inside there?" Kyla scowled but Cooper kept right on speaking. "Seriously, Kyla, what kind of guy do you think I am? I meant working at my shop, not sex. I need to hire someone in the front office and you need your car fixed. I figured it's a win-win situation."

"Mr. Moretto! I need to go before I'm late getting home. Can you cash me out?" came a voice from somewhere near the front.

Cooper touched Kyla's hand, his fingers brushing over her palm. "Just think about it and get back to me in the next day or so, all right? Otherwise, I'm going to need a down payment to get these parts ordered and on their way."

Before Kyla could answer, Cooper was gone. Literally one second he was there, the next Kyla was watching his backside as he sauntered over to the counter. She missed his heat instantly, but she took the time to get her breathing under control. After that, he was moderately busy at the counter as kids gathered their things and headed out for the day. Kyla slipped out the door, seemingly unnoticed, and headed home for a cold shower. And a nap, though she knew it wouldn't be a good one unless Cooper was starring in her dreams.

• • •

Kyla watched the crowd of people in the motel's pool area celebrating the opening of the pool. It was decorated like a tropical paradise, with cardboard hula dancers, bright lanterns and lights hanging from the posts and trees. Despite the slight chill in the spring air, between the decorations and the people, the atmosphere was warm and cozy. Kyla saw Rose holding court at a table with Steve, the owner of the bookstore. Kyla had gotten to know both of them better since she'd been staying in town, and liked them both. They were kind, caring, and great listeners, yet they didn't pry into Kyla's past. Kyla giggled as Steve stood up and she saw the grass skirt he was wearing over his khakis. Kyla was starting to fall in love with Ashten Falls, and it had a lot to do with the people she was meeting.

"Kyla, I'm glad you came. It's nice to see new faces sticking around town." Kyla smiled as Rose called out to her. She headed over and sat in the chair Steve pulled out for her.

"We have visitors," Maggie piped up from the nearby lounge chair she was laying out on. "They just don't stay. The town has to work on its marketing campaign, otherwise we're never going to move forward."

"C'mon, people, let's start eating," Steve hollered and set down a plate full of grilled meat on a nearby table filled with bowls of macaroni and potato salad, fruit salad, and chips. A nearby cooler overflowed with beer, water, and soda. "And just in time for the food, here come the boys from next door."

Kyla looked up at that moment to see Cooper and Phil head their way, each carrying a cooler. There were other people following whom she didn't recognize.

Rose handed her a plate filled with food. "Well-done cheeseburger. Just how you like it." She was smiling and followed her gaze to the group now gathered around the food table. "I invite the local businesses to the pool opening every year. The town is pretty small and we all have to stick together. Cooper has a similar block party in October, kits out the backfield and plot next door with Halloween decorations and a haunted trail. Kids love it."

Kyla eyed the plate in her hands with trepidation; mounds of mayonnaise-laden salads abounded. At least there was a scoop of fruit salad, but she was pretty sure that was bathed in what looked like marshmallows. "Thanks. It's nice, everyone coming out and supporting each other. Don't see that too often."

She was settling on the bench seat when someone was suddenly next to her, leaning in and pushing her gently with his big shoulder. "Long time no see." She chewed, her eyes flicking over to Cooper before giving him a small smile.

Cooper settled on the seat next to her and dug into his food, chatting with Rose and the others as he did. He pushed the plate away when he was finished and leaned back a bit, casually laying the arm closest to Kyla on the back of the bench. Though she tried not to, she flinched, which drew his curious eyes. He didn't ask her about it, instead adjusting his arm so his hand was more on her shoulder. And then he squeezed. It was a gentle, warm touch that she felt all the way to her toes. When his hand slid just as casually down her arm to rest on her hip, his fingers moved just as lightly and gently. Kyla stared at her plate, her mind unsure what to do with it all.

After a long moment and forcing her nerves back, she relaxed. She wasn't going to let Frank in here. Even he couldn't reach that far unless she let him. Kyla stole a look at Cooper and smiled again. It was shy, but it was a smile.

"Told ya." Maggie grinned.

Kyla stuck out her tongue at her and went about eating.

"What?" Steve looked between the two women as if they'd fallen off their rockers.

Cooper spoke up, unfazed by it all. "Don't even try to understand it, man. It's never a good thing to try to figure out what women communicate about, especially when they're doing it without words. Whatever it is, at least they aren't talking about clothes, shoes, or sex. And trust me, given the amount of clothes Kyla had in her bag when she rolled into town, Maggie and Kyla could talk for hours about that subject. Right?"

"Sure, because women are so shallow those are the only subjects we talk about." She rolled her eyes and shook her head. "'Course when we talk about sex, just so you're aware, it often involves us talking about performance issues and what, uh, improvements that can be made in that regard."

"Ain't that the truth," Rose muttered from a nearby chair. Kyla and Maggie met each other's gaze, then looked to Rose, the three of them collapsing into gales of laughter.

Kyla was wiping at her eyes and felt Cooper dig his fingers into her hip. She looked down to find her own hand, the one she wasn't using to eat, was resting on his thigh. How the hell had that happened?

Cooper's head ducked down to her ear and he whispered, "Don't have any negative performance issues to talk about, babe. As for improvements, if you let me in, you'll like how creative I can be."

Kyla lifted her gaze to his and saw an intensity radiating from his eyes, directed right at her. She felt her body warm from his heat. All of which made her snappy comeback come out breathier than she'd intended. "Sure of yourself much?"

"I was sure about you the minute I walked up to your car and heard you singing. The header you nearly took off the trunk was an added bonus." He winked, clearly amused at her stellar performance the day they'd met.

Kyla's mouth dropped open. She pushed her plate away. Maggie and Rose watched her with knowing looks. They'd heard what he'd said. Suddenly her stomach was doing gymnastics.

Steve thankfully started gabbing, talking to the guys and dragging Maggie and Rose into the conversation. "So, Kyla, what are you going to do about your car?"

Steve's question snapped her out of the thoughts churning in her head. She glanced at Cooper, then back at Steve. "Um, Cooper said the Mustang is in pretty bad shape and since I don't have that kind of cash laying around, he offered me a job at the shop."

"Are you taking me up on my offer?" Cooper asked.

Kyla nodded. "We still have to talk details but yeah, I think that could be a good thing. I need to get Lola fixed, so the sooner that can get started, the better."

There was dead silence at the table before Steve finally spoke. "You named the 'stang Lola?"

She felt Cooper's body vibrating with laughter and she shot him a glare. "I hate you."

He ducked his head and whispered into her ear. "No you don't."

"Cooper!" An annoyed voice came from somewhere behind them. A bleach-blonde, sickly-thin woman was standing behind them in a skirt that showed her ass and a top that nearly showed her nipples. She couldn't have been more obvious unless she wore a neon sign that flashed the words "open for business." "Derek said you're DD, can you give me a ride home? 'Fraid I had too much to drink, baby. You know what that means. . . ."

Kyla felt Cooper tense next to her, his jaw clenched tight. He turned to catch Derek's eyes and communicated something that could only be described as a promise of an early death. He gripped Kyla's hip tightly one more time and turned to the group at the table. "I'll be back later. Food was great as usual. Rose, we need to talk about dates for the Halloween gig. Maybe convince Kyla to sing at it. She's got an amazing voice." With that declaration he stood and ground out to the stranger, "Let's go, Marla." He disappeared around the corner of the motel with the woman struggling to keep up with his long strides.

"Skank," Maggie muttered, letting out a huff. "I don't know why Cooper hangs around that."

"Maggie," Rose chastised softly. "They've known each other a long time. Leave it be."

Kyla fidgeted, uncomfortable that she'd been practically cuddled with a man who apparently had something going with another woman. She sighed, picking at the fruit salad on her plate.

"So, Kyla, you're into music, huh?" She would be grateful for Steve's change in the subject until the day she breathed her last breath. She pushed thoughts of Cooper and Marla out of her head and focused on getting to know her new friends and letting them get to know her.

...

Marla stood in the doorway of her apartment and watched Cooper pull out of the spot in front and head back the way he came. He barely spoke as he drove her home, no matter how much she tried to get him to engage. When she had lifted herself into the truck she slid to the center seat, but he gently pushed her over to the passenger side. His silence and distance bothered her. She'd been hanging around Cooper and his friends forever, even when her brother was alive.

Marla turned and shut the door, her mind spinning at the memories of her brother. She missed him. The day she found out he died, when she opened the door to two men in Army dress uniforms, her world had shattered into a million pieces.

But she knew everything would be okay, because eventually Cooper would remember the magic of their time together. He would come to her when he realized he couldn't live without her and beg for her forgiveness. She wouldn't hesitate and the two would get married and have babies and live happily ever after. That was the way life was supposed to be.

It wasn't supposed to be about funerals with military honors or men who used you for one night and left the next morning. It wasn't supposed to be about needing to sell yourself for the best things in life.

She just had to be patient.

Marla knew Cooper was going to that party to see the new woman in town, Kyla. Her nose wrinkled. The new girl wasn't his type. She was all hips, and her ass was big. Her hair was dark and long and everyone knew Cooper liked petite, thin blondes with big boobs. Women like her. Not women like Kyla.

But clearly Cooper wasn't ready to settle down yet. She would have to give him more time. He needed time to get this dark-haired whore out his system. Then he'd come to her again. Marla could give him that. She'd let him have his fun one last time and then. . . and then they would start their forever.

• • •

Cooper had gone back to the motel after dropping Marla off at home, intent on finding Kyla. Maggie told him she'd gone off to the pier. He could not believe she had just walked off, at nightfall, to the pier. It wasn't in the best part of town, and at this hour, who knew what kind of trouble she could get into. Scratch that, he knew just what kind of trouble she could get into and to say it freaked him out would be an understatement. He walked quickly and hit what constituted the boardwalk in town.

As his eyes adjusted to the coming dark, he saw Kyla at the end of the pier. He spoke only when was close behind her. "It's nice out here in the early morning and just at sunset, watching the boats coming in from their day. Wondering what they got in their hold for the market. That curiosity hasn't gone away, not since I was a kid and stood here watching 'em."

His eyes flicked down to her face. "Sorry about having to leave—I was on duty, getting the girls home who need rides. And Marla always needs a ride." Cooper moved his hand around her waist. "I didn't want to leave though."

Kyla relaxed and raised her eyes to his face. "Apology accepted, though you don't really have to apologize to me for being a good guy and making sure people get home safe." She paused and then asked, "Is she your girlfriend?"

He grinned. "Nope. And if I had one, I am not the type of guy who would have his arm around another woman in front of her. If you ask around, that'll be confirmed."

He dropped his eyes to her mouth as her teeth nibbled at her lower lip.

Kyla seemed to hesitate again before he felt some of the tension ease from her, though she kept her eyes on the water. "I don't need to ask around; it's not something I need to be concerned with. She likes you, that much I could tell." Her tone was slightly aloof, uninterested, and it pissed him off.

Cooper pressed his fingers into her hip and turned her so her chest was pressed against his. He dipped his head, a breath away from those pouty lips of hers. "If you could tell she liked me, then I'm guessing you can tell the difference in how I act with someone I'm interested in and someone I'm not."

Kyla shrugged and tried to push away. "Cooper, this is … fast. You, the way you are. . ." She looked down at his hands that were on each hip now, "and I don't know if I can. . ."

He cut her off. "I'm not asking for anything other than a chance to get to know you better, Kyla, and see where this goes. Unless you got a man at home or something. 'Cause if you do, I'll step aside. I'm not the kind of man to horn in on someone else's woman."

Cooper watched the emotions on her face: shock, fear, pain, then anger.

"I'm not anyone's woman," she bit out as her body went ramrod straight in his arms.

"Hey, Kyla, it's okay. Just didn't want to mess with your head if you were tangled up with someone else." His words seemed to soothe her as he felt the tension ebb away from her again.

"I'm not tangled up with someone else. It's just ... complicated. My ex is not a good man. He never was. I don't make good choices and I have a tendency to screw things up."

"It sounds like you blame yourself for shit." He cut her off as she opened her mouth to say something. "You don't have to tell me about this guy right now. I already can tell he did you wrong. And really, there isn't a need to rush this, Kyla. I'm a patient guy. Kind of. Why don't we just get to know each other better and see what happens?"

He watched her nod but could see the topic of the two of them getting to know each other made her nervous. So he changed the subject. For now. "Are you comfortable in Ashten Falls? It seems like you're making friends: Maggie, Steve, Rose. . ."

"I met them at the bookstore a few days ago. Steve introduced me. They were all so nice, they invited me to the party. Maggie invited me to her shop."

"You might want to head over there then. She sells a lot of that underwear you had stuffed in your bag," Cooper quipped.

Kyla's cheeks turned pink. "You're obsessed with underwear," she muttered. "Let's talk about something else, like why you stopped to help me."

Cooper chuckled. "Because I own a garage and it's my job?"

Kyla rolled her eyes. "Phil was working that night. You didn't have to stop."

Cooper lifted his shoulders in a shrug. "I offered to help Phil and then as I drove up I saw this hot chick on the back of the car. That pissed me off and got me interested, in that order. The rest, as they say, is history." He leaned in and kissed the tip of her nose quickly, and then gave her a light squeeze before turning his head to observe a fishing boat coming in for the night.

"But why me? You don't even know me, and I'm not from here, and you want to get to know me? Why?"

Cooper didn't answer right away, taking his time to form a response. "I don't know for sure, Kyla. I saw you, heard you singing, and something clicked. I have no idea where it's going but I know we both feel an attraction to each other. And since you're going to be in town for a while, why not you? You're beautiful, intelligent, funny, and have an attitude that I like. What more could a guy ask for?"

"Thanks." Kyla's voice was soft as Cooper pushed her back against the railing. "You're not trying to save me, are you? You don't see me as some challenge to conquer or anything?"

"No. Kyla, listen to me." He lifted his hands to her cheeks. "I don't let a lot of people in. I just do what I do, for me, for my business, for my friends and family. But I don't look for challenges or take on causes. At least not more than one at a time. The problem is because I don't always communicate every fuckin' move I make to people in this town, they get it in their heads that I've got ulterior motives. I don't play games, or try to hide my motives." Cooper glanced down and was struck by how close Kyla was listening to him, her lips parted. She seemed almost interested in what he was saying. That certainly was a change of pace from the women he usually dated.

"Okay, so what is this cause you say you've broken your rules to take on?"

Cooper sighed and dropped his forehead to rest it on her shoulder. "I got a friend, his name is Roger. He had to get out of town recently, but you'll likely meet him someday—anyway, he had a girl. Beautiful, sweet, heart of gold. But when he joined the army after 9/11, which he did so he could provide a future for them, she lost it. Turned to drugs, got hooked bad, and started turning tricks to pay for her habit. It was killing her dad. No one could pull her back from her vices, and we all tried."

Kyla must have sensed his difficulty with talking about this. She reached up and her fingers wrapped around his arm as she pressed herself against him.

"Roger was in Special Forces. There wasn't much he could do. When he could get home, he did, and she'd live straight for a while, but then he'd leave and Cheryl would lose it again. It was awful. Finally, about two years ago, Roger had enough with the war games and decided to come home for good. He set up his construction company, got Cheryl cleaned up as best he could, and they were ready to get back to good. But they never got that chance."

Kyla burrowed into Cooper, shivering from the cold and, no doubt from what he was telling her.

"I watched my best friend's girl self-destruct and I never thought she'd get clean. And after everything she'd done, I never thought she and Roger would make it. But they were determined and so fucking in love. Cheryl had decided to give some information she had about the Ashten Falls police chief to the feds that would have cleared him out of this town for good, and then she and Roger were putting the past behind them. But instead of having a future together, someone killed her. Coroner said it was a drowning, but it wasn't. That jerk did something to Cheryl. Roger was, and I think still is, broken. Sam and I, we had to do something. I'll be damned if I let Marty Saybrook and his goons get away with shit. It's why I'm trying to stop his reign of terror, by collecting information and passing it on to the feds. They aren't doing much with it, yet, but I'm still doing it. That man has already taken too much goodness from this town."

"Holy heck." Kyla buried her face into his chest. "That is horrible. But, Cooper, if this is true, this cop is dangerous, and dangerous cops, especially ones who have something to hide, have nothing to lose. You could get hurt."

Cooper tightened his hold on her. "Don't worry, we got that under control. I'm not telling you this to scare you. I'm telling you this so you get why I act the way I do. I do what I fuckin' well want to, or because something in my gut tells me it's the right thing." He paused, his eyes meeting hers. "And this is the right thing to do. Just like getting to know you is the right thing to do."

"All right." Her voice was breathy as her eyes locked on his. "I just don't know if we're a good idea. You don't know me." She started to turn her head until his right hand cupped her jaw and he held her eyes to his.

"Well then, I'll be getting to know you." His thumb traced circles over her skin. "You intrigue me, Kyla, and you're by far the most beautiful woman I've ever seen, so seems kind of natural we see where this goes."

She finally shook herself out of her thoughts and with a glare asked, "Do I get a say in this at all?"

He watched her a moment and then laughed softly, his thumb moving to her lower lip. "Your body pressing up against mine right now, the way you're staring at my mouth, that breathy response you just gave ... you've already said it."

Her eyes narrowed and she tipped her chin up. "Thanks, Mr. Know It All."

He leaned his forehead against hers. "I'm just reading your body language."

Kyla watched him closely. Cooper tried to read what was going on in her head, but other than more flashes, this time of uncertainty, shyness, and a different kind of fear than before, he couldn't figure her out. Finally Kyla lifted on her toes and brushed her lips against his, letting her tongue dance along his lower lip before settling back on her feet. His body went still at the kiss but only for a moment. Seeing the chance before him, he took it and grabbed her tightly to his body, his mouth settling back over hers. Cooper took more than the taste she'd given, and he didn't give a fuck. His tongue slid into her mouth and he swallowed the sound of surprise he heard in her throat.

The surprise didn't last long though. Soon, Kyla's body melted into his and she seemed to be participating just as much as he was. Finally, Cooper pulled back and laced his fingers into hers. "I'm gonna walk you home now, Kyla."

That wasn't an offer, it was an order, but Kyla, seeming a bit dazed, didn't protest. In fact, she squeezed his hand as he led her off the pier.

When they reached the parking lot of the motel they could see the party was over and everyone had scattered. Kyla turned toward him at the bottom of the stairs and tugged her hand free of his. He let go, reluctantly, surprised when she settled it on his shoulder. She was on the second step, he was on the ground, making them almost the same height. His hands went to her waist and then around, his fingers splayed across her back. She leaned in until her lips touched his. When she pulled back she whispered "goodnight" against his ear and hauled that sweet ass up the stairs. He moved only so far as the back of the garage, his eyes on her room until the curtains in the front window were shut and the lights turned off.

Chapter 4

The next three days were a whirlwind, to say the least.

First, she got three more text messages, all of them run-of-the-mill threats. She forwarded them to her brother to deal with. Kyla didn't have the time or the inclination to do so. She was starting over. Things were going good.

That didn't mean she wasn't confused.

And most of that had to do with Cooper.

After their conversation on the pier and a sleepless night of worry, she talked herself out of starting anything with him. No way would she kiss him, or let him kiss her again. No matter if every part of her body was telling her they were not in agreement with her brain. She had to steer clear. She had to keep her head on straight. Her sanity depended on it.

Cooper didn't get this memo though, as evidenced by the knock on her door the next morning.

It was 9 A.M. when the banging started. She dragged herself to the door, still in the shorts and tank top she'd worn to bed. Her hair was out of the headband she'd had in it last night, and she didn't stop to untangle the wild mane on her way to the door.

Instead she just wrenched open the door and snapped, "What?"

All she saw was a wall of chest in a Moretto's Mechanics shirt standing in front of her and heard an amused "Mornin'."

She swallowed. Cooper Moretto standing in her doorway with two to-go cups and a box in his hands.

"Are you going to let me in?"

She stared a fraction of a second longer than she should have before the words registered in her brain. She mumbled something and stood aside. Cooper pushed in, heading for the counter.

"I'll be right back," she muttered. She went to the bathroom, took care of her teeth and hair, and walked back out. Cooper was leaning against the small breakfast bar.

"I got you a chai. And some muffins. Steve said you liked soy milk in the chai and chocolate chips in your muffins."

Kyla stopped again, just out of reach, and blinked at him. "Thanks. I do. Wait, why are you here?"

Cooper flat out grinned. "You're cute in the morning. I had to go to the bookstore and needed a coffee. Figured I'd grab something for you and stop by. Is that okay?"

Kyla wasn't sure. Was it okay? Last night she had decided this was not going to happen. That nothing would ever happen again. But now, he was there, in her room, buying her chai and muffins. That wasn't in the plan.

"Kyla?"

She started, heard the uncertainty in his voice, and saw it in his eyes. She didn't like seeing that.

"Yeah, it's fine. It's good actually. Thank you."

She watched in awe as his face softened and he reached an arm out. "Come here." His voice was low and rumbly and sent shivers from her head to her toes.

She went to him and without him even touching her she wrapped her arms around his middle and pressed in tight. She closed her eyes as Cooper's arms closed around and folded her into him.

"I'm not very coherent in the morning." The words came out mumbled against his chest.

She felt his body shake. "I can see that."

His head dipped and the side of his nose slid along her cheek until her face turned to his. He found her mouth with his and didn't hesitate before he plunged his tongue inside. His hands slid, feather light, up and down her sides. Her hands came up to his chest and she gripped his t-shirt tightly in her fists, her tongue seeking his out. When she finally pulled back for a breath, his eyes were liquid heat.

"You kiss me like that and I swear I forget my name."

It was Kyla's turn to laugh now. "Must be you, because normally I'm not much into it."

The look on his face was one of surprise. "Seriously?"

She squirmed under his gaze. "Yeah. It's kind of, well, personal. And I don't ... I don't like getting close or personal. And kissing is personal. Scary personal, even." She paused before she said too much. When things had gone bad with Frank, she stopped kissing him and did everything she could to avoid him kissing her. Kissing was giving someone all of you, letting them in to experience all that was you. It was hard to be disinterested or hide that emotion in a kiss. At least for Kyla it was. She bit her lip and looked up at Cooper. "Sorry. I know I'm weird."

She backed off, or tried to, stymied by his hands at her back.

"You aren't weird. You're guarded, I've figured that out. But you aren't weird." His head bent again and he touched his mouth to hers. "I like how you kiss me. You mind keeping that up?"

She tilted her head to the side and thought about that for second before answering. "Sure, as long as you don't piss me off."

Cooper's body shook and then she heard his unrestrained chuckling. "All right, I will try not to piss you off."

When his arms loosened she moved just to his side, still keeping her body close enough to his to brush up against, and drank her chai.

"I have to get to work. When you get the sleep out of your eyes, come by so we can get you started working in the office."

She had muffin in her mouth, so she nodded and then swallowed. "Yeah. Um, do you sell those t-shirts in non-hulk size by chance? Maybe in a women's fit or a tank?"

"You want a tee?"

"Yeah. It's awesome. I mean, you got the whole dark red lettering and the bike in the background with the skull on it. It freakin' rocks."

He slid behind her, his hands coming around to her belly. "I'll see what I can do. Maybe someday I'll get a look at you walking around my house in nothing but the tee I'm wearing and some of those panties from your bag."

"Oh my god" was all Kyla could breathe out as her hand trembled.

Cooper kissed the skin along her shoulder and then her neck, all the way up to her jaw. "That's something you might look forward to."

"Yeah." Dang it! There was that breathy voice again. She shook her head. "I mean, maybe, I don't know. At some point. You're taking advantage of my sleep-addled brain. This isn't fair."

"All's fair in love and war, remember that." He said this on a chuckle and kissed her quickly on the lips. "I have to go but see you in a bit."

And with that, he grabbed a muffin and was gone, leaving her breathless and in need of a cold shower.

That was the kind of morning she'd had.

And now, several hours later, she was once again with Cooper, arguing about how to get her car fixed.

"We seem to be at an impasse here," she mumbled as she stuffed her hands in her pockets. "I don't have the kind of money it's going to take to fix her. Or anywhere near that for that matter. I can see about having it stored somewhere until I start making some money."

"Kyla, you're not storing the car in some random storage shed on the outskirts of town until you get enough dough to fix it in one shot. Yeah, you're right, it's going to take time and money since this isn't an easy fix, and some of the parts are special order. But I don't use the last bay in the garage. It can sit there and when you get the money for a part, we'll get it and I'll fix it. I won't charge for labor."

Kyla gritted her teeth. "You are not fixing this car for free, Cooper."

"It's not free. I just am not charging you."

"No! I won't be indebted to you or anyone else. I won't owe anyone anything ever again. I won't have it thrown in my face later that you did this for me."

Her fists were clenched at her sides. The air was thick in the cramped office and she was hot. She needed air.

"I need to get out. I need to go." She lurched toward the door as she fought the rising panic.

Cooper moved as she went for the door and stopped her with a gentle hand on her shoulder, the other held around waist. "No, you aren't running, Kyla. I get it. We had already decided, you'll pay for the parts. That was the easy part. We'll figure something else out about my labor costs, though I'm telling you I really want to do this for you. And Lola, working on her. . . Christ, you should be paying me for that privilege."

"I'm sorry, Cooper. I just ... this is something I need to do. You, my mom, my brother—you all want to help me by giving me money or doing something for free, but this isn't just about my car. I need to find a way to fix her and pay for it myself. I'm not trying to be difficult."

He lifted his hands and placed them on either side of her face. "I know you aren't. I just am trying to make this less of a hit on your wallet. I can't help it; I want to take care of you. Especially since we're doing what we're doing."

Kyla scowled. "Cooper, this isn't the Dark Ages. It's not a man's job to take care of his woman, and we aren't even *near* that stage anyway in whatever is between us, so just ... god, why are you such a pain in the ass?" She stomped her foot, her hand slapping at the top of the desk. Some random files and paperwork went flying. She mumbled a "whoops" and bent over to pick them up. When she stood she noticed Cooper grinning at her before his face got serious again.

"First of all, whatever stage we are at means you are my woman, Kyla. And I'm all for women's lib, but there are times when a man needs to take care of things, when we *want* to take care of things for the person we care about." Despite her narrowed eyes, he pressed on, "Most men today don't do it, but that doesn't mean they shouldn't. It's probably one of the reasons the world is going to hell in a hand basket."

She arched a brow as the corners of her mouth tipped up. "Whoa, what do you have here? Cooper Moretto, world philosopher?"

He flashed a sinfully sexy grin. "I'm a man of many talents." He waggled his brows in an overly dramatic way and she burst out laughing.

Kyla was getting her laughter under control when she spoke. "Cooper, stop flirting. We need to deal with Lola."

"Slave driver," he teased and then did get back to the subject of her car. "I'll get a price list for the parts. When you got the money for one, we'll cross it off the list and order it. When it comes in, I'll get to working on it. It'll be piecemeal and probably take a while, but it'll only be me who works on it. I can't have the guys doing it. First, because it's your car and I don't want them touching you or Lola. And second, I'm swamped here and need them focused on the rest of the customers."

She opened her mouth, but he held up a finger as his phone rang for the millionth time since she'd arrived.

As he took the call Kyla glanced around the lobby of the shop, noting that it had seen better days. A glance into the attached garage area said the same thing. The place looked like a grease bomb had hit it, repeatedly and without mercy. She started to sit when Cooper grabbed her upper arm to stop her, nodding at more grease, or something, on the seat. "For god's sake, this place is a mess," she muttered, standing in the middle of the room away from anything that could possibly leave a stain.

"Yeah okay, Chuck. I'll get right on it when you bring it in. I'm swamped though, and Phil had to head to Portland, so with everything going on, you're looking at a couple days. You cool with that?"

After a few more minutes he hung up, tossing the receiver on the cluttered desk. And then picked it up as it rang again. And then two more times after that.

Kyla was biting her lip by the time Cooper hung up the phone for the final time.

"If I work here, instead of paying me, why don't I just work off the labor you put into the car? And then I will figure out another way, a second job or something, to pay for the parts. I could work mornings to early afternoons, and then get another job working nights."

Cooper's face softened as he considered her offer. He moved closer and placed his hands on either side of her waist. "Intriguing offer. That would be a lot of hours though at minimum wage. It could take a while."

Kyla turned her head toward him a fraction of an inch, her lips just a touch away from his. "Well, it'll take me a while to get money for the parts. So if we do this piece by piece, I can keep track of the parts and your hours on a spreadsheet or something." Her eyes hit the fairly new computer, which was the only thing that wasn't covered in grease and dirt. "And I'm here until I'm not, ya know? I mean, I can't go anywhere until Lola is fixed and it's not like I'm on a schedule or have anywhere to go anyway."

She watched, fascinated, as he tilted his head to the side and then brushed his lips against hers. He nipped her lower lip before pushing back. "How 'bout a few days a week, like six to four?" He looked over her shoulder, his eyes falling on the chaos around him. "I'll pay you for anything over five hours. The five hours every week I don't pay for you will go toward the labor cost for the car."

"Six, as in the morning? Seriously? How about eight?"

Cooper snorted. "We get started at six. . . how about seven-thirty to five? Can you handle that?"

She sighed. "Fine. Seven-thirty to five, Monday, Tuesday, and Thursday?"

"And Saturday at nine, but we usually close by one those days. Though maybe once you get this place straightened out, you can migrate over to the music store. Seeing as you sing, I'm assuming you like music." At her nod he continued. "That place is mostly dead, like your car, but I have to figure out what the hell I'm going to do with it. It's languishing." His thumb traced her cheek. "Oh by the way, I don't require uniforms, but when you're here, I'll expect you to deal with the customers when they come in. Make sure to wear something that will keep 'em from freaking out over the bill." He grinned as his eyes drifted to her cleavage. "We don't have any tanks, but I'll be ordering some. Tight fit."

Kyla rolled her eyes and crossed her arms over her chest. "When do you want me to start? It's a Tuesday."

He shrugged. "I'm just being honest. I'm a man, so I know what distracts my fellow men, and your rack ... well it's more than distracting." He hooked a finger in her tank top where her ample cleavage was on display, chuckling as she swatted at his hand. "As for a start date, if you want to you can start today. I got some things to do next door. If anyone comes looking for me, holler out the door or call my cell."

Kyla watched Cooper saunter out the door and then turned her attention to the stacks around her. She rolled up her sleeves, hunted down some cleaning supplies and boxes, and then set to work.

•••

Several hours and a very sore back later, Kyla stood up to survey her work. She had piles of papers and mail she still had to go through and put into folders on the desk, but she'd at least been able to give the place a good cleaning, including mopping the floor and removing the cobwebs in the corners. The room smelled citrusy and the windows were open to let in the soft, June breeze. She could now take a breath and not choke on dust and grease. The computer gleamed and Kyla had put a protective cover she found, unopened, on the keyboard and screen to keep them that way should any greasy mechanic ever touch the thing. A stack of cash and coins sat on top of the desk. She had come across the random money as she went through the papers, sorting them into various piles: bills, personal, invoices, junk mail. She'd go through the rest of the piles later and organize them by date and subject.

Wiping her brow, she headed out the front door, put some change into the soda machine, and grabbed a cold drink. She had found a brand new Keurig machine, also unopened, and set that up, and even placed an order for a delivery of K-cups. She probably should have checked with Cooper first, but given the state of his office, he probably wouldn't know the difference.

After taking a drink and going back into the office, she lifted her shirt, tying the bottom in a knot just above her belly button. She was about to tackle one of the piles of invoices when the bell above the door rang. She had expected it to be Cooper, but instead it was a cop. She froze when she saw him and her stomach flipped painfully. The man was a few inches shorter than Cooper and had blonde hair and dark eyes. He was staring at her and after a beat she cleared her throat and pasted a smile on her face.

"Hi. Can I help you?"

"Where's Cooper? I brought in one of the cruisers for him to look at."

Kyla reached for a clipboard and invoice, "He had to run out for a minute. He should be back soon. Are you dropping off a vehicle for repair?"

"Yeah. One of the department's cruiser's was in a fender bender." Kyla shifted as the man's eyes moved down her body, "You must be the new girl in town, the one he found on the side of the road with the Mustang? He's a lucky bastard."

"Yeah, my car broke down and Cooper's helping me out with a deal on the repairs."

"Yeah sure, I bet he's helping you with the repairs." He smirked and tossed the keys to the cop car at her. "I'm Jackson Murphy, by the way. You got a name?"

Kyla crouched down and lifted the keys, handing him a clipboard with a form on it for him to fill out, not responding to his comment. Heading back behind the desk she covered the cash with a nearby stack of papers. Given her conversation with Cooper by the pier the other night, she didn't know if this cop was one of the chief's lackeys or not, and she wasn't going to take any chances.

"I'm Kyla." She glanced over the form, not having any clue what the complaints about the car meant, but she figured Cooper could call him if he had questions. "Want us to call before we fix it or just go ahead with the repairs?" She remembered when she was living at home in Pennsylvania, her mechanic always asked her that so she figured it was the right thing to do.

"Just go ahead. Cooper and the town have that contract, so he just fixes it and they do whatever. Politics." He grinned at her as he tried a softer approach. "So, Kyla, when did you get into town, and is this an extended stay?"

She nodded, sliding the form next to the door to the garage for Cooper before turning back to Jackson. "No. I mean, I don't know. No long-term plans." She was thrown off by his question, unsure of the answer herself.

"Sounds like you might need some convincing to stay. Maybe I could take you to dinner, and introduce you to the finer aspects of life in Ashten Falls." His eyes twinkled as he leaned over the counter toward her.

She felt her shoulders tense and shook her head slowly just as she caught movement at the door. Cooper.

"I don't ... I don't have much free time. I'm pretty busy here and um. . ."

"That's Kyla's nice way of telling you there ain't no way in hell she'd go anywhere with you," Cooper finally spoke up from just inside the doorway. Jackson straightened, his face hardening.

"Picking up women on the side of the road now to get your fix, huh? You already go through the women around here and need to branch out?"

OK, this was not going to end well, and she didn't have the mental energy to watch two bulls lock horns. Going into retreat mode, she stepped back ... straight into the bookshelf behind her. She threw her hands up to protect her head from the avalanche. "Such a klutz," she muttered as she bent down to retrieve the books, her way of avoiding whatever man-measuring was going on between Cooper and Jackson.

Cooper headed around the counter to pull her up, holding her close to his body. His hand moved down to her lower back, his fingers skimming along the exposed skin there before resting on her ass.

"So, Jackson, thanks for dropping off the car, but if you'll excuse us, I brought lunch for the two of us to enjoy before I get back to it." He said, dropping a bag with the logo of the sandwich shop on the table.

Kyla should have been mortified at what was happening, but instead she leaned into him and hooked a hand around his waist. She moved her hands under the back of his shirt, desperate for warmth as the stress began to set in. But as her fingers ran over his smooth, muscled skin, reality slammed back into her. There had to be a rule against groping the boss on the first day of work, especially in front of other people, and on that thought she started to push away, until his hand tightened on her ass. Her breath hitched. Cooper caught it, which she knew by the way he folded her into his front and she *felt* his reaction.

Kyla turned her face in Jackson's direction. "Like I said, officer, I've got things to take care of, so. . ." she trailed off, shrugging and trying to let him down easy. "It was nice meeting you, and I will be calling you as soon as the car is ready." She smiled brightly at him, her tone friendly.

Jackson's jaw clenched. "Well, thank you, Kyla. I'll be seeing you around soon enough then. And I look forward to it." He let his eyes linger on her chest longer than was polite before banging out the door.

"What the hell was that?" she asked, trying to push out of Cooper's grasp. Her attempt was unsuccessful as Cooper kept her tightly to his front. "I don't need you putting me in the middle of a dick-measuring contest with a cop—a freaking *cop* of all people!"

He canted his head to the side as he watched her with concern. "I was making a point, so he'd stay away from you. I was staking my claim—letting him know should keep him at bay." He sighed when he saw her eyes flash. "What I'm saying is that the cops around here can be bad news, like I told you. Can you promise me you'll stay away from him? Please?"

"Staking your claim? Could you be more of a Neanderthal? I am not a piece of property that you can just 'stake your claim' to, Cooper." Cooper opened his mouth to speak but she continued her tirade. "Besides, I can take care of myself, thank you very much. I didn't ask for some white knight to rescue me." She was annoyed, that was for sure. But a part of Kyla had to admit that no matter what Cooper said about claiming here, he wasn't treating her like a piece of property. Not like Frank had. Instead, it was like Cooper wanted to take care of her, to protect her, not possess her.

A flicker of amusement crossed Cooper's face as he leaned down, whispering in her ear, "I ain't no Prince Charming, I can guarantee you that. But that guy has done things that make me look like I am. Stay away from him. And you might want to untie your shirt so the whole place doesn't get hard looking at your midriff and imagining what's underneath your top." He nipped her earlobe and then met her eyes, the muscle in his jaw jumping. "Eat your lunch. I have work to do. We'll talk about this later."

Kyla was left standing there, wondering what the hell happened. She glanced down at the counter and remembered the cash sitting there. She grabbed it along with the order form Jackson had filled out and followed Cooper.

"Hey! Are you pissed off at me?"

Cooper stopped short, his eyes flashing with anger. "Not at you, no. But am I pissed? Hell yeah. I walk into the office to find that douche hitting on you, his eyes all over your chest falling out of your top and your bare stomach."

She shook her head. "Men," she muttered as she stalked toward him. He was pissed because she attracted the attention of a customer who he didn't like? "Could you be more confusing? You told me to look nice and distract your customers when I was working for you. So I do and then you get mad when a guy looks at me. And yeah, I had to tie my shirt, but that's because it's hotter than Hades in the office and I was ... hot!" Kyla planted on a hand on her hip, her foot tapping on the cement floor. She didn't care that some of the other guys were staring at the two of them. She didn't care if they could overhear their conversation, which they likely could, given the way they were all avidly watching the show. She pointed a finger at Cooper's chest. "So make up your damn mind. And fix the air conditioning!"

"Looks like I might have to rethink my directive," Cooper muttered. "I don't want you looking like that and giving him a show. Or anyone for that matter. Now, do I have your permission to get to fixing this car so that hemorrhoid can get the hell off of my ass as soon as possible?"

"You're a smartass. And a jerk. I only came in here to give you this." She held out the order form for him to take. "And I wasn't sure what you wanted me to do with this money, either. I found it all over the desk and drawers. You really need to keep better track of your cash." She held out the open envelope so he could see it.

Cooper glanced at the form, placing it on a nearby workbench before taking the envelope from her. He flipped through it, counting it before taking out a good chunk and handing the rest back to her. "Put it in the safe, combination is in the fridge, just inside the door. This way if ever I'm not here and you need change or need to order something, you can." He stuffed the money he'd taken in the pocket of his jeans. "And thanks."

"Fine," she clipped and watched his head jerk up, not caring when his eyes narrowed on her, "Oh, and I ordered some K-cups. For the coffee machine."

"Whatever. Just don't turn this place into a Starbucks. I need people to work here, not socialize."

Kyla looked around at the garage. "I'll do my best to keep the socializing to a minimum." She didn't even attempt to hide the sarcasm in her voice.

"Kyla."

She waved him off and was already marching toward the office. "Fix the freaking cars, Cooper. I got things to do."

She banged through the door and stuck the sandwich in the fridge, having lost any semblance of her appetite.

• • •

On her second day at the garage, Kyla was still annoyed with Cooper, having done everything she could to avoid the motel on her day off, so she wouldn't run into him.

She could tell when she came into the office Thursday that he was annoyed by this. But she didn't go in the garage and apologize. He was the one who got mad for no reason and acted like it was her fault Jackson had come on to her.

Whatever.

She put her bag under the desk and looked up as Phil wandered in.

"You tell Cooper you're putting that up?" He nodded to the flat screen TV still in the box that Kyla had found.

"He's going to freak out if the guys are in here watching TV and drinking fancy coffee instead of working." He had an amused look in his eyes. "See, I'm the laid-back one here. Cooper is a bit more serious, likes to be in control. Which I can understand, since he invested all his money into it when he bought it. He's built a great business, though the record store could use some magic. That was his dad's, so I doubt he will ever let that go, despite most people getting their music online these days."

Kyla pushed the box out further into the room while he chatted and, box cutter in hand, started carefully opening it, pulling out manuals and wires as she went. She was only half listening, but her head popped up, her eyes catching Phil. "I still can't wrap my head around him owning a record store. It just seems not Cooper-like to me."

Phil sidled over and took the box from her, easily lifting the television out on a small table nearby. "Be right back." He disappeared into the shop, but soon returned with some tools and a bag. "This goes with the television. It mounts it on the wall there so it's out of the way. Least the cable he pays for won't be wasted now." He went to work and continued talking, Kyla leaning back against the front counter. "As for the store, like I said, it's been in the family forever. His dad opened it in the late seventies or early eighties. He was friends with Steve. They each bought the neighboring buildings and did their thing, and then when Cooper was back from college and setting up shop, he bought the garage from the prior owner who was retiring. Problem is Coop just doesn't have the time to market the music store or do anything else with it, really." He turned his head to look at her over his shoulder while screwing in a bracket one handed.

Kyla fidgeted, the toe of her shoe kicking at the ground. "The store could be so much more than what it is. Kids love hanging out there and he has all those musical instruments. He could add lessons, some more modern merchandise, t-shirts of bands and other products like that, gift cards for iTunes and whatnot."

He grunted. "I don't think Cooper can carry a tune, let alone teach a kid how to play do-re-me on the piano. The musical gene skipped our boy." He went back to working on the television. "Those are good ideas though, you should let him know. Maybe he could find someone to give lessons and do all that other stuff."

"Maybe. I could help out, too. I went to college on a music scholarship."

Phil arched a brow, "Really? You went to one those fancy-ass music schools in New York City or something where all the ballerinas and piano geniuses go?" He grinned at what she assumed was her blushing, "So what kind, that classical and new age stuff, huh?"

She bobbed her head to the side and she stared a minute. "No, I wasn't ever that good. As for what I play, I like everything. I basically stick to music where the lyrics kick ass just as much as the notes. It could be anything from rock and roll, punk rock, alternative, or rap—as long as it's good quality, I like it. For example, last night I was listening to Johnny Cash and then some Alicia Keys. See, eclectic." She flashed him a smile

A deep, rumbling laugh bounced around the office. "Definitely got some good taste then darlin'. Cash is a classic and Keys, she's just plain hot. Love her voice. You need to meet my mom and sister. They are all about music, sing in church and everything." He had his back turned to her as he finished putting the bracket up, and turned to pick up the TV. "My mom raised the lot of us. Well, not Cooper. Cooper and his dad moved here from Portland when Coop was ten. He lived with his dad until college and then, after his dad passed, Mom unofficially adopted him. She made him stay here during breaks and stuff. She said he wasn't old enough to leave the nest and our nest was his until he was ready to fly. He just had to follow her one rule."

"What rule is that?" Kyla was enjoying this conversation with Phil for several reasons. Not only was she learning more about Cooper, but she was also becoming friends with Phil, who was a really nice guy.

He stepped down from the bench he'd been standing on, his eyes meeting hers. "No back talk. Anything else she'd talk it out with you. But back talk earned you a possible smack upside the head, then silent treatment until you smartened up to apologize. Her silent treatment is the worst. I'm telling you, the worst criminal in the world would break when she pulls that out." He shuddered. "Glad my torture is amusing," he teased her as she laughed. "Sounds like my mom. If my brothers or I messed up, she just gave us a look and walked away, not saying a word. That look and her silence were enough to have us trying to make it right."

Phil grunted. "See, moms are clever like that. It must be built in female DNA or something. My woman, Sheena, does it too. She does it to me so I know she will pull it with our kids. Hope they are fast learners." He nodded in her direction as he pulled a wire from behind the desk, running it along the ground behind the bench seats. "You'll probably be like that, too, I bet, being a woman."

"Doubt it," she said, her voice just barely audible, her nose scrunching up. Kyla had no expectations of ever having kids. "Anyway, thanks for doing this for me."

Phil opened his mouth but thankfully shut it at the change in subject, "No problem. It will be good for downtime, though there isn't a lot of that here. Not for us mechanics anyway. Just remember, Coop's going to be all moody about it. Flash him a smile, or flash him anything really, and he'll get over it." She ducked her head as Phil winked at her, "Hey by the way, July fourth, my mom has a huge picnic over at her house. Food, friends, family, football, all the guys and their families come."

" July fourth? Well, I don't have any plans, and I assume I will be stuck here unless I win the lottery to get my car fixed. But, I don't really know anyone."

She heard a chuckle from the doorway and saw Cooper standing there. He jerked his chin towards Phil, "Yo, Phil, the television, huh?"

Kyla interrupted, taking a step away from the counter and toward him. "Cooper, it's more for the customers when they're waiting for their cars. Or for whoever is working out front, if it's quiet. I like to have background noise, and I'll make sure the guys aren't sitting around not working. I promise. Cross my heart." Her finger traced an X over her heart.

Cooper lifted his eyes to hers, his tone gruff. "Work starts to suffer, I'm going to cut the cable. Got it, Phil?" Although he was asking the man, his eyes stayed on Kyla.

"Got it, man. Won't see me in here on my ass—I got enough on my plate with the cruisers AFPD keeps busting up. I swear those fucks can't drive worth a lick." He shook his head. "Anyway, I'll be sure to tell the boys. Oh, guess what? Kyla is coming to the

Fourth of July picnic at Mom's. Good way for her to meet some more of the folks around here. The good ones anyway."

Kyla saw Cooper's jaw clench. "I mean, I don't want to intrude," she said hastily. "Like I said, I don't really know anyone here, and it sounds like a family thing."

"No, that's a good idea, all the guys will be there and some of their women and kids. It will be good for you to get to know who might be coming in and out of the shop. Besides, it's weeks away. By then you'll know a lot more people. I'll pick you up at one, so pencil me in."

She stared at him, her mouth agape, but before she could respond, Phil stood up and slapped his big arm around her shoulders.

"Good, Mom will like that. She likes to meet new folks and you're good folk. I can tell." His eyes crinkled and he tapped her on the head as he passed. Phil was just a big teddy bear.

"Yeah, well, we'll see." She busied herself at the desk and then grabbed for her purse. "Don't you two have some cars to fix?" She waved her hands at the door. "Shoo."

"Told ya, Phil. Slave driver."

Phil barked out a laugh as he disappeared into the garage and it was Cooper who caught Kyla's eyes.

"Kyla, we good?"

Kyla sucked in a breath and hesitated as he came close to press himself to her side.

"I don't like you avoiding me."

Kyla sighed, "Cooper, I wasn't avoiding you. God, I just needed some time alone. It's not all about you."

His voice cut her off. "That's the last thing you needed. When we fight, we talk it out. There are going to be times I get pissed about something you do. And I'm sure you'll get pissed at something I do. When that happens don't walk away from me and slam the door." He tucked a piece of her hair behind her ear.

"I'm not trying to be in your face all the time, I just don't want arguments getting twisted 'cause we let them fester. You want to argue with me, have at it. I prefer that, than you walking away."

"Well, I needed to cool off, Cooper. I have a temper and I didn't want to lose it." She decided then to take a chance. If Cooper wanted to talk things out, then fine, she would. "And yesterday you really made me mad. You got pissed because someone you don't like thought I looked good, or whatever he was thinking. I'm not sure, I really want to know." She shivered before continuing. "But the point is, you said you wanted me to entice people, then you got pissed and you took that anger out on me by being all moody and doing exactly what you're telling me not to do, and that's walking away."

Cooper's jaw clenched. "Kyla, I said yesterday that I shouldn't have asked you to do that. What more can I say?"

"It's the point of it, Cooper; that you asked me to do it in the first place. No one, woman or man, should have to dress to impress, or in this case distract, in a sexual way. It's demeaning. You were basically telling me you wanted me to dress like a whore at work."

Cooper gritted his teeth. "I didn't want you to dress like a whore..."

"Well, lucky me. You might be evolving then, Cooper." she shot back.

Cooper moved quick, positioning himself in front of her in an instant. His hands moved to her hips and he leaned down, his mouth close to hers. "Kyla, listen to me, please. I didn't realize what I asking. You're right, it was wrong of me to ask that you use your body to distract the customers. I didn't even think of what I was asking until I saw the way Jackson was looking at you and I thought I was going to kill him. I shouldn't have done it and I'm sorry I ever did." His hand slid over her cheek and tucked a strand of hair behind her ear. "Wear what you want, what you're comfortable in. I have no right to say, or ask you, to do otherwise and I was an idiot for thinking I did."

Kyla focused on his eyes, trying to gauge his sincerity. She didn't know him well but he didn't seem to be blowing smoke. She leaned her forehead against his. "I accept your apology. Thank you."

His lips brushed her cheek. "See how easy this was? Talking it out instead of walking away and trying to avoid me is definitely better. We good?"

Kyla rolled her eyes. What had she gotten herself into with this guy? She wasn't about to tell him that he was right, even though he was. She had been avoiding him, a technique she'd learned with Frank. Having a conversation with him always meant fists flying. But Cooper wasn't Frank, and it was unfair to herself and to Cooper to react in the same manner she had in the past. She'd have to work on that.

She pressed her palms to his chest and lifted on her toes to touch her lips to his, and then she pushed him toward the door. "Whatever. Now get to work."

Cooper shook his head and pushed through the door. "So fuckin' cute."

Kyla hollered after him, "I'm not cute!"

Chapter 5

Martin looked down at the woman writhing underneath him and knew from past experience she was close to finding her release. He thrust into her, hard, as he gripped her hair and yanked her head back. After three more thrusts he emptied his release into the condom and pulled out. He didn't care that she was left panting and unfulfilled on the mattress while he pulled on his pants.

"Martin. . ."

"Shut it, Marla. I need to go."

"But I thought you could stay for a little while. And I need … I need your help," she whined and crawled toward him.

His lip curled, a sadistic smile on his face. He was the chief of the Ashten Falls Police Department and the last thing he was concerned about was some whore's pleasure. "Marla, how many times do I have to tell you, I don't care if you come. I got shit to do. So get yourself off or find some other cock to do the job. I don't have time for this."

Marla sat back on her heels and pouted. He had to admit the woman was gorgeous: slim, blonde, blue eyes. As he looked at her now though, his eyes moving over her naked body, he realized just how much she looked like the other bitch he'd had wrapped around his finger. Until she betrayed him. He'd had her taken care of just before she blabbed all his secrets to the feds.

He grimaced at the memories of their time together, at his weakness when, after they fucked, he'd stay in her bed and talk. Like they were some sort of couple. God, he had been an idiot. He knew, deep down, that the whore was hooked on Roger and there'd be no changing that. But he let himself think, for a moment, that he cared for Cheryl. He thought that he could finally be himself around her and maybe be happy. But she had ruined that. It was her fault he had to do what he did. It was her fault he had to make her pay.

Dumb bitch.

"Martin, can't you just touch me, please? I was so close. . ."

He clenched his jaw before jumping up from the bed. He was tired of women like Cheryl, like Marla, thinking what they wanted mattered. He moved fast and before Marla could crawl away he backhanded her. He felt her blood on his hand, but he didn't care. He yanked her by the hair again, this time dragging her off the bed and onto the floor. She was on his knees, the way he liked his women. He lifted her head so she was looking up at him. The blood was trickling from her nose and lip down her chin and neck. He smiled. "I told you to take care of it yourself. Now stop being a whiny bitch and shut the fuck up. No wonder Cooper doesn't want you around."

"He does want me around! And don't you ever say otherwise," she snapped at him and for the first time Martin could see a little of himself on her angry, pinched face and hear himself in the tone of his voice. It was sort of a turn on.

He released his grip on her hair and pushed her away. He reached for his jacket. "Good. Now, speaking of Cooper, what are you doing about him? You still hung up on being with that prick? I've heard he's going after that new woman in town, Kyla." He'd heard about her from one of his officers and had seen her walking around town. She looked good and definitely piqued his interest. Unfortunately he had too much on his plate to take a taste when he saw her. He'd get around to that, though. Eventually. He always did. "It's all just another clue that Cooper doesn't want your skank ass."

"I'm not a skank!" she hissed, her hands clenched at her sides. "I just want to be with Cooper. I don't know how to do that. He thinks I'm trash, but I don't know why."

Martin shook his head. "Look in the mirror, Marla. You fuck around, you do drugs, and hell, you've had sex for money in the back alleys of this god-forsaken place. You think a man like Cooper wants to tie himself to someone like that permanently? Especially when your competition is a woman who looks as hot as she does."

"She is not hot! And he only wants to fuck her; he'll tire of her and come to his senses soon enough!" Marla screamed and all Martin could do was smile.

"Sure, whatever you say, Marla. Now get your ass over here."

Marla was still screaming as she moved to him. "I am going to beat the hell out of that bitch. He won't think she's pretty after I do that. He won't even recognize her. She's not going to take him away from me."

Martin tugged Marla against him when she got close. "I love it when you go off, screaming and cussing." He was unsnapping his slacks again. "See, it made me fucking hard. Again. Now, get on your knees and suck me off before I leave you, crazy bitch."

He grinned as Marla dropped to the floor before him and looked up at him with her big eyes. "What will you give me if I do, Chief?"

"That solicitation charge of yours, well let's just say it'll be taken care of. Now, get to it." He grunted as she wrapped her lips around him.

God, he loved his job and this town, he thought, as he buried his cock deep in her mouth.

• • •

After a week of working for Cooper, Kyla was starting to get settled. Getting the garage organized was quite the task, but it was slowly coming together and she spent her spare time reading, hanging out in the music store, or turning her room at the motel into a home. The feeling of being home was something she hadn't had in a while, so even the little things, like buying her own towels and groceries, made all the difference in the world.

On Sunday she woke up relishing the fact she had a day off. She changed into a skirt and tank top, her bathing suit underneath so she could catch some sun, and threw her messenger bag across her body. Sliding into her flip-flops, she pulled the door shut behind her and made her way down the back stairs. The garage was quiet, but she saw the gate was open and Cooper's truck was in the lot.

Kyla made it to the chain link fence, only to have someone grab her arm and tug her back hard. It was instinct to turn her body toward whoever it was. She yanked and struggled against him, kicking out with her foot. "Let me go!"

The hand on her upper arm loosened but didn't let it go. "Kyla, relax, it's me."

It wasn't Frank. When that registered she let her arms go slack and sagged against him. "I am so sorry, Cooper."

"It's okay. Not your fault. I shouldn't have been so quiet. You've got quite the fight in you, though. Jesus, you can kick."

She closed her eyes and felt the blood drain from her face. She straightened, but Cooper remained close enough that she felt the heat of his body against hers.

"Did I hurt you?" She heard the thickness of her voice as she struggled to keep it together.

"Hurt me? No. How could you hurt me? Come here."

Cooper's arms were around her right there in the middle of the sidewalk. For all Kyla knew, there were a hundred people around them, but all she could focus on was the man who held her tightly.

"I saw you heading for the street. Looked like you were ready to cross and seeing as there isn't a crosswalk here, I was trying to get your attention. Cops like to give out shit tickets like that."

He kissed her at the spot where her neck and shoulder met, his tongue touching her just enough to make her tremble against him. "I'm the one who is sorry. I shouldn't have startled you like that. Forgive me?"

Frank always asked her to forgive him after he beat the shit out of her. Always expected her to go along with it, be his meek little mouse. But Cooper wasn't Frank. He hadn't done anything to hurt her. She knew that. There hadn't been anger in the act, and it wasn't like he hurt her, physically or otherwise. It had only startled the hell out of her.

She didn't have to live in fear anymore and flinch when someone surprised her. She lifted her chin to rest on his chest and looked up into his face.

"You have to be patient with me, Cooper. I startle easy. I react wrong. But I'm working on it."

She loved it when his face softened and his eyes brightened with warmth. "I'll keep that in mind, Kyla." Cooper kissed her mouth, a quick, hard kiss that set the fire inside Kyla burning. But he pulled back before it could get out of hand. "Crosswalks, Kyla. Use 'em."

"Anyone ever tell you that you're bossy?" She tried to muster a similar tone, but it didn't seem to work as well, seeing as the corners of his lips were twitching. "Are you laughing at me?"

"Not at you." He winked, his dark blue eyes roaming over her face. "Between you wandering around town on your own, and now confirming you have a clear disregard for your safety by not following the rules of the road, maybe you do need that bodyguard. And I have just the person in mind."

She sucked in a breath, a hand pressing against his chest. "Cooper, I don't need a bodyguard. I'm fine. I was just going to walk to the beach." She mustered all the attitude she could at the last minute and huffed. "Not that it's any of your business. I'm not going to do the whole 'tell the guy I'm kinda sorta seeing everything I'm doing' scene."

He held that amused smile on his face as he stretched out his hand. "There's the attitude," he said with a chuckle. "Kinda sorta seeing, huh? I can dig that description of us. For now."

Kyla rolled her eyes and then sighed, "Whatever." She started to move across the street, surprised as he walked alongside her. She didn't say anything, stealing a glance every now and then. "You really don't need to follow me; I can handle it from here."

Cooper shook his head. "Kyla, look I get it, you want to be independent and not need anything from anyone, but you're new to this town and don't know the first thing about the place. Shit is going down and given my recent, and now well known, interest in you, I don't want you getting caught in the crossfire. So humor me, yeah?" He didn't say anything for a moment, letting her guide them in the general direction of the beach. "Besides, you need a crash course on this place, and I'm feeling generous today, so I'm going to give it to you in the form of a personal tour."

Cooper being nice and protective, bringing her chai and muffins, kissing the daylights out of her ... it was all too much. She was terrified and didn't know what the fuck to do about it. Except protect herself.

"Oh, lucky me," she muttered.

Cooper lifted a brow, annoyance flashing on his face. "I'm not going to apologize for wanting to keep you safe, Kyla."

She turned to face him, crossing her arms over her chest. She could see he was pissed, and she was annoyed for being angry at herself for pissing him off. It was all very confusing. "Well, you being nice can feel like you're trying to control me, Cooper. I can't change who I am or what I'm trying to get through. I've never had this before without it turning bad."

"Kyla, we don't have to analyze everything we do or say to each other. Christ, I wanted to walk you around town. It lets people know we're together, it keeps you safe, but more important, it lets me spend time with you. Is that such a fuckin' crime?"

She bit her lip, her eyes trained on her toes. She'd snapped his head off, assumed he was trying to control her when all he wanted to do when take a walk to the beach with her. Freakin' Frank.

She closed her eyes and then opened them, lifting her head as she did. "I have issues separating what happened before and now. I see things that aren't there. I shouldn't have jumped to the conclusion that you're a controlling asshole."

Cooper's head jerked. "Christ, Kyla. I like you because you are your own woman. You work hard, you're good at what you do. Hell, since you've worked for me, the guys and I have been more productive than ever, getting shit done and able to take in more business. I even got a few orders for some custom paint and detailing work. I'm able to take 'em because you've organized that freaking office and even me to some degree. You keep me on track, not to mention you're pretty persuasive. After all, no one before you ever convinced me to put that TV up." His lips tipped up at the corners and she could tell he was teasing her. At least about that last part.

She smiled. "Yeah, I had such a persuasive argument."

Cooper grinned, backing her up toward the wall of a nearby building. "Well, it wasn't just your argument. It also had to do with how gorgeous you looked in that top." He dipped his head down and his lips skimmed her jaw and down her neck. "And speaking of tops, I got a woman's fit tee and a tank with the shop logo on it for you."

She was breathless. "You don't know my size."

She felt his tongue slide over her shoulder. "You can try 'em on and I'll let you know if they fit. Or not."

"Cooper." Her voice was shaky and so was her body. The last thing she could think about was trying on clothes in front of Cooper. Or maybe that was exactly what she wanted to think about.

"I'm not going to hurt you, Kyla." Cooper lifted a hand to her face, his thumb sliding over her cheek. "I don't know what's going on with you and I. Something about you caught my interest and I'm exploring that. I don't know where this is going to lead, and I can't make any promises especially with recent events. For all I know, I could end up in jail or worse, given the corruption me and my guys are up against." He took a breath and continued, cutting off her response. "Maybe because of that I should back off. But I can't. I'm a selfish bastard, and with you that's upped to the nth degree. I wanted to get to know you as soon as I heard you singing on top of that car. And if in getting to know you I can help you fix whatever the fuck some asshole broke, then I am going to do it." He skimmed one hand down her cheek and pressed his palm into her chest, right over heart. "I want in there, Kyla. But if you aren't ready for my help, then tell me to back off. I'll walk away. It'll be the hardest thing I've ever done. But I'll do it. For you."

Cooper was giving her an out. But as much as the idea of being with him scared the hell out of her , she didn't think she could handle him walking away. The ball was in her hands now. And Cooper had no idea how important that was to her. He was giving her the control, the ability to decide whether they were moving forward or not. She would never be able to show him how much she appreciated that. Kyla swallowed the tears that threatened to clog her throat, happy tears for a man who wasn't trying to make her into something she didn't want to be.

"I don't want you to end up in jail or worse." She pressed her palms against his chest and his muscles tensed underneath as her fingers curled into his shirt. "The corruption we talked about before, other than what the chief did to Cheryl, what else do they do? What else do I need to be afraid of?"

Cooper inched forward, pressing her tightly against him, his hands sliding along her torso. "Have you been afraid of something in the past, Kyla?"

She shivered. She always did whenever he used her name. It seemed to rumble out of him, lower and deeper than when he called her babe or doll. Normally she hated such endearments, but coming from Cooper she didn't care. Kyla didn't trust her voice. Instead she nodded.

Cooper's eyes held hers for a beat before speaking again. "Town hall is a mess, corrupt politicians who take what they want without regard for the town or the people living in it. Saybrook is the worst. He's run this town with an iron fist for way too long. And when I say iron fist, I mean almost literally. He doesn't mind using excessive force to get confessions, or just to get off. He is a sick bastard and his violence has no limits. Men, women, teenagers, he doesn't give a fuck. The problem is, he's been running the place for so long, and so many are afraid to say anything, no one investigates him. Those who do complain … well, they usually meet other fates that are much worse than getting the shit kicked out of them."

Kyla's eyes widened. "And here I thought I was escaping one corrupt cop only to find myself in a town run by another." Was sticking around Ashten Falls a good idea? But where was she going to go? She had no car and no money to pay for the repairs. And besides, wherever she went, Cooper wouldn't be there.

He tucked a strand of hair behind her ear. "Corrupt cop, huh? That the guy who hurt you?" He didn't wait for her to answer.

"Some of the other guys in town, mostly business owners, we got together and are trying to force the issue. We've made reports to the state and the feds, carefully and anonymously. We've tried to get some information from inside the force, but so far that's been hard to come by. It's not like anyone really wants to go against their boss. Not to mention the fact that too many people in town think the chief is a god. He keeps the crime rates down by messing with the stats, and honestly some don't care about him beating the crap out of criminals. Problem is that some of those he considers criminals aren't, or at least haven't been found guilty yet."

Kyla sucked in a breath, her hands wrapping around him and hanging on tight. He gave her a soft smile and continued.

"I get pissed when I see good people getting hurt and worse 'cause of some moron on a power trip. Sam, Roger, Tommy, a few others, we're all trying to change shit around here. We've become a thorn in the side of the top cop by making ourselves known on the street, befriending some of the victims of his violence and being in the way when he and his cop friends try to bring a beat down on people. This puts me on his radar." He squeezed her waist. "And since you're on my radar, I don't want you getting on his. Ya know?"

"So that's why you're protective and joking about the whole bodyguard thing."

"Yeah, well that and I'd really like to guard your body." He winked at her. Kyla laughed at his deliberately cheesy joke. "Why would he come after some chick whose pants you want to get into? I'm sure I'm not the only one who's been that kind of target on your radar." She was teasing him, though she surprised herself at the pang of jealously she felt in her gut at the thought of another woman being on Cooper's anything.

"You're the only one who's mattered though. And you're the only one I've ever thought about so much, I see you in my dreams." He dropped his head down and covered her mouth with his, not hesitating to taste her.

He sucked on her tongue and pulled back, his eyes watching hers. "Get it now?" His lips brushed hers before she could answer.

She blinked, trying to find her focus and the words she needed to answer his question. "Yeah."

He gave her that smile she couldn't resist. "Good, looking forward to more of this." He kissed her again and then straightened, tugging at her hand. "You fit nicely against me."

"Wow, that's kinda, well sweet, Cooper. You better hope I don't tell anyone that underneath that rough and greasy exterior there's a romantic at heart." Kyla laughed, teasing him now.

Cooper gave a look of mock horror on his face. "What, a guy can't tell a woman how he makes her feel? Do I lose my man-card for doing that?"

She shrugged. "I don't know. I'm not a guy, so who knows what the rules are? Just haven't seen it often where a guy would admit something like that. The last guy I was with wasn't exactly one to talk about feelings. Or care about them for that matter."

They reached the corner of West Street and Beach Drive, and he tugged her by the waist. The traffic was heavier at this time of day, though it was by no means bustling. For the first time in a while, however, she didn't care whether there was anyone around or what they would say.

"So this guy who didn't care about your feelings, was he the cop?" She dropped her eyes to his shoulder. "I'll take your silence as a yes."

Cooper lifted her chin with his finger, "I can't promise you anything, Kyla, or tell you where this is going, but I can promise I won't ever intentionally hurt you. If you get confused, want to talk, need to get something off your chest, we'll talk. I won't hide anything from you. Take a chance on me, on the possibility of us, and I don't think either of us will regret it."

If this were any other man, she would have tried to back away, but his words burrowed into her head and mixed with the sounds of her mother and brother, urging her to live her life and not let her past dictate her future. Her therapy sessions filtered through her mind. The therapist had told her over and over again that she had a right to a happy life and deserved it just as much as the next person. For once, she let herself fall, following the advice of the people who'd stuck by her through the last years she'd spent in her own personal hell on earth. It was high time she stopped letting Frank control her life.

"Okay." She breathed out and tilted her head just to the left. "Can I go to the beach now?"

"Yeah, let's get you working on that tan. I'm going to want to explore those tan lines, all of 'em, soon enough." He kissed her quickly and walked with her across the street, stopping at the top of the steps.

She glanced over to the rock wall that lined the street and saw the stairs that led down to the beach. It was nearly deserted, but then it was still early. "Are you coming?"

"That an invite?"

"Yeah. I mean, I just figured you were here. . ." God, she sucked at this flirting and being coy crap. "And I thought you didn't want me wandering around town, alone."

Cooper didn't say anything for a minute and then finally spoke. "You're being cute again. As much as I'd love to spend all day looking at you in nothing but a bikini, I got to get back to the shop to do a few things before dinner at Phil's place. I will take a rain check, though. And don't worry about being alone. One of my guys will be keeping an eye on you when I can't be around." Cooper slid his hand into the pocket of her skirt and took out her phone. He punched some buttons, a lot of them, and then slipped it back into her skirt. "Now you have all my numbers. The house, shop, music store, my cell, even Phil's cell number. You need anything, you call me. And you keep calling until you find one of us." He kissed her nose before starting to back away. "Phil will know I gave you his number and won't mind. So do not hesitate."

"You're being bossy again." She narrowed her eyes, but the force behind it was lessened substantially. "And I'm not cute," she reiterated her point from the other day, though it came out more breathy than she intended.

Cooper bent down. "Yes, you are. By the way, I'm taking you out two days from now. You got a dress and heels to wear to dinner?" he asked as his lips hit hers, a combination of soft and hard that took her breath away. He smiled against her mouth as she melted against him, his fingers sliding up the skin of her back to the tie of her swim top. She pressed her chest to his, her hands dropping to the waistband of his pants and tugging him closer. She laughed as she heard him growl low in his throat, both sounds muffled by what their lips were doing.

After what seemed like an eternity Cooper stepped back, those intense eyes watching for her reaction. A knowing smile tugged at his mouth. "Later, Kyla."

Chapter 6

"Hey there, mind if I throw my towel down here? I hate laying out by myself, makes me nervous."

Kyla opened her eyes and looked up at the woman staring down at her through her dark shades. A quick glance around the beach showed there were still only a smattering of people about at this time of day and plenty of real estate available. Still, she nodded at the woman. "I don't own the place, so have a seat."

"Thanks a bunch! I'm Sarah. You new around here? I know just about everyone in town it seems, and haven't seen you before."

She sat up on her elbows and took off her glasses. "Yeah, kind of. I wasn't too far outside of Ashten Falls when my car died. So it's in the shop while I figure out a way to pay for it. I'm Kyla."

"Nice to meet you, Kyla. So where are you from?"

"Pennsylvania, small town outside Pittsburgh." She always used Pittsburgh as the benchmark since most people knew where that was.

"Cool. I've never been farther south than Boston. That was the last vacation I had, too. Hmmm," she paused as she seemed to consider that. "Well, what are you doing here? Have you found any work yet? What do you think of Ashten Falls?"

"I like it. The people I've met so far have been really cool. It's nice to be in just one place instead of driving around."

Sarah slathered herself with sunscreen and settled back on her towel. "So are you planning on staying here long-term?"

Kyla paused before answering. That was the question, after all, wasn't it? Was Ashten Falls just somewhere she'd pass through, and once her car was fixed, she'd head off somewhere else? Or was the town a place she could stay, maybe put down roots, and stop running. There were definite benefits to staying here—her job, the people she'd met and become friends with so far, and of course, Cooper. "I don't know," she finally said, "I'd like to stay here, and I have a job at the garage now so I'm making a little money while paying for the car repairs, but I haven't really thought of anything beyond that. I'm just taking it one day at a time, I guess."

Sarah waggled her eyebrows. "Working with Cooper must be interesting. That man is hot and one of the nicest guys I know. Are the two of you. . . you know, together?"

"We have a date day after tomorrow, Cooper and I. He's taking me out to dinner. I'm petrified and have no idea what to wear." Kyla blurted out this information. She bit her lip, tearing her gaze from the water to Sarah. "I hate dating; it's so stressful. What the hell do we talk about? I don't know why he'd be into someone like me, and not with the women who hang around the shop, bringing in their cars that don't need fixing just to check him out." The spike of jealousy at that thought surprised her. "They are all so thin and have great hair. What if I say something stupid or fall on my face in heels?"

She was close to panicking and Sarah chuckling next to her wasn't helping.

"Kyla, listen. Cooper's a couple years older than me, but I've known him forever. Like I said, he's a nice guy who treats women well, from what I've seen. He also cares about the town and looks out for the people in it, even the ones who work at strip joints, even though he doesn't have to. Can he be overprotective at times? Yeah, but he has the best intentions. As for you, you're gorgeous, real, and fun to talk to. You aren't going to do anything stupid or fall on your face, and even if you did, I doubt Cooper would care. If he asked you out and wants to spend time with you, then Cooper likes you, Kyla. So just go with it. See where the night, and the date, take you. There's nothing wrong with having some fun after all, unless you aren't attracted to him. Is that is?"

She shook her head. "Oh no, that's not it at all. Cooper's great, heck, he's beyond great. But it's complicated. He, uh, kissed me. Well, I kissed him first, but then he kissed me and now we seem to be kissing and touching all the time and it's really distracting. And I don't know what to do 'cause, we work together, and I really do *not* need complications right now and I swore off men."

Sarah blinked, then threw her arm around Kyla's shoulder in a sideways hug. "No wonder he likes you. Making the first move. You go, girl! I don't know much about his personal life, but I can tell you Cooper hasn't dated the same woman twice in like, five years or something. He was engaged and from what I've heard, his fiancée slept with a college friend of theirs. He was livid, and it fucked him up big time 'cause he'd sacrificed a lot for her, but … well, she was always a cheating whore. He just refused to see it."

Sarah's arm tightened around her. "Congrats, Kyla, you got the eye of one of the biggest, most bad ass men in town, in what, a week or so? Whatever your secret is, you have to share with the rest of us."

"Oh great, two messed up people who swore off the opposite sex. Hell," she muttered.

Sarah chuckled and moved back on her towel, lying down to catch a few more rays. "Chickie, seriously. Cooper is just a guy, but he is one of the good ones, and trust me, there are very few of those left.

"Take a chance with him. So you kissed him, and he kissed you. You guys flirt. It's part of life, so enjoy it. It's not like you two need to declare your love in the paper or anything. So relax." Sarah giggled, then grabbed Kyla's phone to punch in her numbers.

Kyla laid back on her towel, placing her sunglasses over her eyes. She needed to get the topic off of her relationship with Cooper, and fast. "So, Sarah. Have you lived here all your life?"

"Yep. Born and raised right here in Ashten Falls. I went to the local community college for a year after high school, but then I transferred and moved to New York City for a few years."

When Sarah didn't explain further, Kyla pressed the matter. "You moved to New York and then came back here? Did the city and you not mix or something?"

She glanced over in time to see Sarah shrug. "I was there for almost five years. I went to culinary school, worked in several restaurants. I could have stayed, but my mom got sick and I wanted to be close to her while she was going through treatments."

"Sorry about your mom. Is she okay now?"

Sarah turned her head and grinned. "Yeah. She just hit five years of being cancer free. She and my step-dad moved down to Florida last year actually. I could have moved then, but they offered me the house, so I took it." She lifted her chin slightly, her eyes shaded by her sunglasses. "I'm saving up to open my own restaurant here, someday. For the moment I work at Felicia's as a waitress and over at the diner as a cook and server."

"Sounds like you have a great mom and step-dad."

"Yeah, they're pretty great. I think they knew if they sold the house, it would either be torn down for something new, which would break my mom's heart, or whoever bought it wouldn't take care of it. By having me take it over they can be reassured that her roses aren't going to be torn out of the ground. She loves those damn things."

Kyla sighed as the sun warmed her face. The two continued to talk as the afternoon ticked away. At one point they both grew silent, dozing in the warm sun.

It was a cool breeze that jerked Kyla awake and she looked around, confused until she got her bearings. She was on the beach, talking to Sarah. They both fell asleep, "Sarah." she called and watched as Sarah lifted up on her elbows.

"Crap. I was out, but now it's frickin' cold," Sarah griped. Kyla nodded and stepped into her skirt and top, though this didn't make her any less chilled.

"So I'll pick you up tomorrow, Kyla. Noon, outside the motel."

"What? Why?" She didn't bother to hide her confusion. Had she agreed to something while she was half asleep?

"Because you need an outfit for your date with Cooper. We'll go the mall, it's about thirty minutes away and we'll grab lunch when we get there."

She tossed her bag over her shoulder, hesitating as she debated whether to go or not. She had clothes to wear, but Sarah was right. This was a date with Cooper. She wanted something to really wow him. She could afford to splurge, just this once, to make a good impression.

The two walked up the stairs to the road above. Sarah squeezed her bicep gently. "We'll talk more tomorrow. Later!" And with a wave, she headed for her car in the beach lot nearby.

Everything felt a little surreal. Sarah was right: Kyla deserved a little fun and flirting and admiration from a hot guy, no matter how long it lasted. She was determined to go with the flow and see what happened.

• • •

Cooper ran a hand through his hair as he stared down at the insides of Kyla's car. They had ordered some of the parts and today he finally had a chance to actually get started. A part of him didn't want fix the vehicle too quickly. He knew it was selfish and that he couldn't stop Kyla from leaving town if she wanted to go. But he hoped she'd stay. There was something happening between them and he wanted to explore it.

That thought alone scared him a little. Whatever was happening was something he hadn't felt before. His ex-fiancée—he'd thought that was love. But when he walked in on her and one of his best friends naked in his bed three months before they were supposed to get married, he was hurt. And he was pissed. But he didn't feel like his world was ending. In fact, when the wedding was cancelled and her stuff moved out of his old apartment, he only felt relief. He'd felt like he could breathe.

That breathing got even easier when he met Kyla. He'd been dealing with this mess with the cops in Ashten Falls, while at the same time burying himself in his work at the shops. He had forgotten what it felt like to be attracted to someone for more than what they looked like. To want more than just a quick fuck. When she smiled and let go of the pain he saw in her eyes that she tried to hide, he saw something he knew he wanted and wouldn't give up without a fight.

Cooper's hand clenched around the edge of the car as he thought of Kyla's reaction to him. She had flinched and he saw fear in her eyes before realizing it was him. He didn't want to push too hard. She had to get comfortable and trust him enough to open up to him. He could be patient. But what he knew so far, he didn't like. Kyla's ex, the cop she mentioned, did a number on her and Cooper had to fight the urge to force her to tell him who the guy was so he could deal with it.

"Hey, Coop. I'm not as good with cars as you are, but I'm thinking that glaring at the engine won't make it work. Just sayin'."

He twisted his head to the side to greet his visitor. "Hey, Sam. Yeah, I'm finding that out the hard way. If she wasn't such a beauty, I'd toss her out of here."

"You talking about the car or the car's owner?"

He straightened and closed the hood. "Don't start, man. Seriously not in the mood."

Sam grinned, "I love this. Who would have thought you, who refused to get serious with anyone since that ex-bitch of yours proved to you she was in fact a cheating bitch, would fall the first time Kyla batted her lashes. Get used to the ribbing." Sam clapped a hand on Cooper's shoulder, "And from what the boys tell me, she's hot. So when do I get to meet her, or are you keeping me out of the way in case she realizes I'm a much better catch?"

At that statement it was his turn to laugh, the sound echoing through the garage, "The day a woman catches you, Sam Martin, will be the day Phil finally gets off his ass and asks Sheena to marry him. Not going to happen."

Sam tilted his head to the side and looked contemplative. "Never know. The right woman might persuade me. Speaking of Phil, when is he going to ask Sheena to get married? They've been together since high school and steady since college. What the hell is taking him so long?"

Cooper shrugged, "No clue, man. Better do it soon or else Sheena and his mom are going to pick a date and drag his ass to the church." He walked to the long bench in the back of the garage and started cleaning up. "So what brings you by the garage, Sam? Aren't you usually at the pub on Friday afternoons? Or are you leaving again?"

Sam, when he returned to the States and was discharged from the army, had come back to Ashten Falls ready to settle down and start a business. He had money socked away from his time in the Rangers and used it to buy two of the abandoned warehouses on the edge of the industrial district. It was sketchy territory and everyone wondered what the hell Sam was up to with this project of his. Before their eyes, he poured all his efforts into the first building, restoring it into an entertainment hot spot known as The Warehouse, but still kept the industrial look. It wasn't anything fancy, but it was good food that didn't break the bank. It was someplace to take a woman on a date, and that date could then expand to the dance floor and stage, which covered the other two-thirds of the space.

Opening The Warehouse wasn't the only iron Sam had in the fire. Cooper knew he still did some work for a security contractor as needed and had only just returned from doing something he couldn't talk about. He only cared that his friend came home alive.

"Nah, not going anywhere for the next year or so. I needed a break, and working as an independent I told 'em to take me off the rotation. If they need something that is in my area, they might call, but if it's overseas, no way. Reason I'm here is about Saybrook."

He tensed and leaned against the bench. "Shit. What'd he do now?"

"Nothing major, at least not for him. A guy was coming in from Portland. One of Saybrook's guys stopped him, just inside the town limits. Beat 'em pretty good. The guy has some serious head trauma. Maybe this is something we can leak to Justin. He could run a story to put the cops on notice that people are watching."

"Who the fuck is going to care about a dealer who gets his face rearranged by a cop? They'll just be glad he's out of commission. And Justin would run with this story, but I don't want to get him caught in the middle. Last thing he and Maggie need are the cops targeting him. Shit." Cooper wiped his hand over his face, "Any other trouble, maybe with a credible victim?"

"Nope. Like I said, Saybrook is being careful. He knows we're watching him. How could he not? Wherever Saybrook goes, one of us is there. Gotta be honest though, I'd rather have him stomping around and being an ass than laying low and quiet. Gives me the creeps."

"Yeah. I know what you mean."

"So seriously, what's going on with this woman of yours? You two tight or what?"

Cooper lifted his shoulders in a shrug. He liked Kyla, for a lot of reasons. Not only was she beautiful, but she was also smart, funny, had a smile that knocked his socks off, and if the kids who hung out at the store were right, had a whole mess of musical talent. Kyla also brought out his protective instincts though. Whenever he saw that look of fear cross her face he wanted to wrap her in his arms and shield her from whoever put it there. "Don't know.

Things are new and I don't want to push her into something. She's in a fragile place from what I can tell, had an asshole ex who really fucked with her head. I don't know the full story, but it seems pretty bad. I'm going to do what I can to get in there."

"Careful, man. You sure you want to take on something you need to fix?"

"I don't need to fix anything. She'd not a broken clock. Whatever happened to Kyla threw her for a loop, and I know that 'cause if you startle her, she jumps a fuckin' mile and tries to kick and fight like her life depends on it. I can be patient with that. And being patient isn't the same as me fixing her. That's just me knowing that she's worth getting through whatever shit we have to until she's clear on the other side."

Sam blinked and didn't even try to hide the surprise on his face. "Well, it's good you see it that way. If she has the power to reel you in, she must be pretty amazing. Though I guess she has to be, if she has the patience to put up with you. I can't wait to meet her. Now, are you done for the day or what? I want a beer and figured we could go to the club for some dinner."

" I'll meet you there in, say, thirty minutes. I need to shower and change."

"Sounds good to me."

He watched Sam leave and closed down the garage for the night. As he made his way out the back door, his eyes drifted up to Kyla's window. He wondered where she was tonight, since it was early and the lights were off. He shook off that thought and the desire he felt to go find her, and instead got in his truck and headed home.

Chapter 7

The morning started out with Kyla working in the office, her back to the door of the garage as she went through a filing cabinet.

"Kyla."

She heard Cooper's voice but didn't turn her head when she asked, "Yeah?"

"Come here."

"Coop, I need to get this done; your filing system is serious crap. Things were just thrown in here, with no system, no folders, not even in alphabetical order. I need to finish this, it's making me twitchy."

He moved up behind her and swept her hair off her shoulder with his chin, his arms wrapping around her waist.

"You have issues. It's just filing."

She twisted her head to look up into those fabulous blues of his. "You'll have issues if things aren't in order and you need to find something at some point. A little organization can go a long way. . ."

She trailed off when she felt Cooper's lips on her neck and one hand snaking up the front of her shirt to stroke along the side of her breast. "Cooper, we're at work." Her statement didn't hold much protest though. She was too distracted by the way he was making her body feel with just his lips.

"Relax, no one can see. Even if anyone is looking, they'd just see my back. But no one is, 'cause I shut the blind when I came in here."

She closed her eyes and tried to resist but failed, and instead melted against him and tilted her neck more to give him better access. "Well next time lock the door."

Cooper nipped her soft skin and laved the spot with his tongue to soothe the area. His murmured words filtered into her brain slower than they would have if he wasn't driving her body to arch back against him.

He brushed his hand over her breast, his thumb and forefinger moving over her nipple. Kyla arched up into his hand and sighed. "Kyla, I gotta cancel our date. I have to head to Portland, as in now. I am so sorry." He pulled her to him and leaned his forehead on hers. "I won't be back until after ten, but I can stop over after if you want."

She twisted her head toward him and lifted on her toes kiss him, a light and sweet kiss. "And is this why you're trying to get to second base with me right now? Soften me up when you stand me up?" Her tone was light. "Work is work, Cooper. I understand. If you aren't going to be around, then I will head to Felicia's, that strip club Sarah works at, to hang out with her. She wants me to see the place she works at, or one of them."

Cooper squeezed her tighter against him. "If these kinds of distractions work, expect many, many more in the future, babe." He winked and slid his nose down her cheek. "If you go out, be careful. I will try to come by when I get back. And our date will happen, just not tonight. Got it?"

Kyla nodded and kissed him, her lips pulsing over his and she took the initiative, plunging her tongue into his mouth to dance with his. She sucked on it and pressed her hips against his.

He groaned and pulled back. "I have to go."

"Then go, before I take your clothes off right now. Just, go!" She pushed him toward the door, "And hurry back." She turned and shut the door, leaving them both grinning.

•••

When Kyla had locked up the office for the night, she headed back to the motel to change into a black jean skirt, high heeled sandals, and tank top, with a light, see- through sweater over it that had a wide neck and slid off her shoulder showing enough skin to be sexy but not slutty. Sarah had assured her that, although there would be half-naked women at Felicia's, it wasn't sleazy at all.

Kyla confirmed that the moment she walked into the place. The décor was warm and inviting, with shades of greens and blues on the walls and tabletops. The lighting was low, but accented by fairy lights scattered over potted trees that were placed on the edges of the room, around the bar, over the archway that led to the private rooms, and near the stage. The high-backed booths and round tables weren't crowded together, but were instead strategically placed to give the patrons and the dancers privacy when needed. The stage itself was built to give everyone a view of the entertainment and allow enough walking space between it and the seating areas so people weren't falling all over each other. Sure, the waitresses were wearing tight shirts, short skirts and high heels, but it wasn't any worse than your average sports bar. And the dancers themselves had gorgeous costumes they started out in, slowly taking them off as they moved their bodies to the music pumping through the sound system. And the dancing was good. The women who worked the stages had real talent in that department and that talent almost made you forget they were naked by the end of each song.

It didn't take Kyla long to settle in and start having a great time with Sarah, Maggie and some other women Sarah worked with.

There was only one hiccup the entire night and that was when Marla finished her set and came up to the bar, topless and in only her thong. She'd pushed through the crowd and ordered a drink. Instead of leaving to go into the back room like most of the dancers did, she stayed and glared at their group. Kyla tried to ignore her, but that was nearly impossible when Marla, after her third drink, pushed into their huddle.

"Well, look who's decided to slum it tonight. How are you girls doing? Looking to join the other team for the night? Maggie, you want a lap dance?"

Maggie snorted. "Fuck off, Marla. You know I come here to hang out with Sarah. Now what is it you want?"

Kyla kept quiet, as did Sarah, which might not have been a good thing, since this gave Marla the opportunity to speak again. "So, Kyla, how are you finding the town of Ashten Falls? Cooper finished with your car yet so you can get the fuck out of here?"

She blinked at her. "Sorry, but I don't know you, and I don't really want to talk to you given your earlier comment. And whether Cooper is done with my car or not is none of your business anyway."

Marla snorted, something totally not attractive coming from her. "Of course it's my business. He and I are together. Well, not officially but you know, he's got to sow his oats before we settle down and get married, have babies, and all that."

Sarah choked on her cranberry vodka while Maggie laughed. Kyla just stood there, dumbstruck at Marla's pronouncement.

"It's not funny, Maggie! You know he and I are meant for each other. I don't know why you bitches don't see that. No one ever fucking sees that."

Sarah finally got herself under control and moved between Kyla and Marla. "You are so unhinged, Marla, it's a wonder you haven't floated off this planet. Cooper is not yours. Everyone knows you two fucked, when you were both in high school and then it was over. But you can't seem to get it out of your head that the two of you are meant to be. So let me give you a clue, some friendly advice. He does not want anything to do with you and only lets you hang around because he feels bad for what happened to your brother. Now get your drink and move the fuck out of our air before I find Felicia and tell her you're acting crazy and harassing paying customers."

Marla's fist balled at her sides. "You whore! Mind your own business, Sarah, and stop lying. Cooper and I will be together and trust me, honey, the chances of that happening are way higher than Tommy ever taking back your skanky ass. So watch your mouth."

Kyla saw Sarah pale even in the dim light of the bar, but it was Maggie who stepped in. "I'm telling Felicia about this, Marla, so you might want to look for another job. Now get out of here."

Marla threw one final glare at the three of them and stomped away, stumbling in her heels as she did. They were silent for a few minutes before Kyla finally spoke. "She's a few fries short of a happy meal. Holy hell, what is *with* that woman?"

Sarah and Maggie started giggling, which lifted the veil of tension that had descended when Marla rolled up. Soon the three had almost forgotten about the incident and were well on their way to having a good time again.

Around eleven fifteen Kyla noticed Cooper and his friend Tommy had come in. But other than flashing his devastating grin at her and raising his beer bottle, he hung out with his friends, apparently letting her have her girl time. If it had been Frank, he'd have been all over her and not let her out of his sight. He also would have called her a whore for the outfit she wore.

After hours of dancing, laughing, and drinking, she was finally on her way out the door, having outlasted Cooper's stay by quite some time.

"Hey," a voice called to her from the mouth of the alley.

"Cooper?" she breathed, taking a tentative step toward him. She didn't pull away when he tugged on her hand, instead she curled her fingers into his. "I thought you left."

"Not letting you walk home this late alone. I had to go outside and talk to Tommy about something. Besides, didn't get to spend much time with you tonight, but I liked watching you. The other guys did, too."

She arched a brow as she glanced over at him, a smile on her face. "Is Cooper Moretto jealous?"

He snorted but avoided her eyes. "I don't get jealous. I know what I got right here in my arms. As long as guys are just looking, I can handle that. If they were touching, well, then I'd have to punch people in the throat." His eyes burned with an intensity that made her insides go all liquid. "So don't make me have to punch anyone in the throat."

"Cooper. . ." She started to pull back but didn't get anywhere. "I wouldn't do that. I'm not that kind of girl at all. Even if my head wasn't all over the place, I would never do that."

Cooper squeezed her hips and dipped his head down, his dark blue eyes pinned on hers. "Your head is fine, Kyla. Beautiful, in fact. I think you're scared of you and me and what we could be, but I don't think that makes you fucked up. I'm scared too, 'cause I've never had anything this real before."

"Cooper, we should probably talk. I should tell you about my past so you know what you're getting into. It's kinda bad." It was more than kind of, but she didn't elaborate. Not yet.

He shook his head. "I love that you want to do that, but not tonight. And if it's bad, when we talk about it, I want you to be sure you're ready. Because I don't want you more haunted than you already seem to be. I'm not going to run just because of something you have in your past. It's probably not half as bad as you think it is."

It was her turn to snort. "It's bad. I let down my friends, my family, everyone I ever cared about, Cooper. But I let down myself most of all. And I'm scared that I can't ever undo the damage."

"But, if you did something bad, or that you think is bad, that doesn't make *you* bad. I already know whatever happened, it involves a corrupt cop, and I assume he was a boyfriend. You mentioned he didn't care. You flinch, or your body gets tight whenever I get angry or startle you. So, I've already got an idea."

Kyla bit her bottom lip and took a breath. She could continue to hold off from telling him about Frank. Or she could just get it over with and rip off the Band-aid. Avoidance sounded good to her, to continue to hide, but a bigger part of her just wanted to get it out and be done with it. She chose the latter. "I was with Frank a long time. Everyone tried to get me to leave him. I didn't. I was too scared of what he'd do, of what he'd done already. I figured he was the best I was ever going to get. I mean, I *let* him hit me, punch me, heck, I let him beat me over and over again. I let him control me, tell me what to do, what to wear, who to talk to and be friends with. And I never tried to leave. Not until the last time and when I did that. . . ." She shook her head, eyes closed, as she paused to collect her thoughts. "I thought I could get all this out. I thought I could just tell it all to you right now, all about Frank and the fight, and me trying to leave. And what happened to my brother. But this is harder than I thought. Can I have a couple more days to get the rest of this out?" Her voice was barely a whisper and she leaned her forehead against his strong chest.

His hands slid up and down her bare arms. "Kyla, thank you for telling me. It doesn't have to come out all at once." He bent down and kissed her deep before tucking her against him and moving out of the alley and down the sidewalk.

"Ya know, I gotta say, one of the other things about you that I like is that you're the perfect height for me. Not too short, not too tall. Not many women who can fit that requirement."

She let him lead her toward the motel in a daze. It had been a long day, she was exhausted, but holy hell she was enjoying this and wasn't going to pull away. It felt too good. "Glad you can check that requirement off your list, Coop."

He grinned down at her. "Tits, ass, attitude, your height, the way your eyes get soft and fire up all at once when I've got my arms around you. You're the total package."

She rolled her eyes but laughed. "Lucky me."

She was silent the rest of the way to the motel, stopping as he started toward the stairs by the office. "No, wait, not those. I go up the ones farther away but closer to my room . . ." she trailed off and saw his jaw clench as he followed her gaze to the office. The light was on and Morris was in there, staring out at the two of them.

Cooper guided her back on to the sidewalk.

"He bothers you, you call. Hear me?" He pulled her tightly to his side, sending a scathing glance at Morris when they walked by. When they reached Kyla's door he took her key, not letting her go as he unlocked it. "I want to come in tonight, but I have something to take care of. And I don't think you're ready for that yet, Kyla. But soon, I will. So whatever you gotta do to let me in, do it fast."

She stared at him, stunned at his bossiness, which by now she should have been used to. She opened her mouth to respond, but before she could Cooper's mouth covered it. "Don't forget about our date. Now get inside and sleep sweet."

...

Kyla's dreams were not sweet that night.

"You will never be able to leave me. Ever. I will always find you."

She squirmed as she felt his breath on her ears, tears rolling down her cheeks as she struggled against the solid mass in front of her.

"Kyla ... Kyla. . ." The voice was sing-songing her name. *"Stop fighting me. It will be so much better if you just would stop fighting me."* She blinked away the tears, unable to wipe them from her face as she heard someone else enter the room.

She heard a soft voice in the distance, a whisper almost, the word "no" repeated over and over. As it got louder she twisted and turned, pulling hard against him.

Kyla's eyes flew open she found herself crumpled on the floor next to the bed, the bed sheet twisted around her legs, soaked through from sweat and tears. The lamp had fallen over, the glass from the shattered light bulb scattered on the floor. She stared at the pieces for several moments as she took deep breaths to get herself under control. That had been by far the worst of all the dreams she'd had since that night. But she remembered what Jane had been telling her during her counseling sessions: she had to put herself out there, to go with her gut and trust people.

Shaking, she picked herself up from the floor and glanced at the clock, groaning as she saw it was only three in the morning. The messages she was getting were creeping into her subconscious, invading her dreams now and bringing back that night in Technicolor it seemed. Would it ever end? She had no idea but she was determined to not let them stop her from moving forward. Knowing she'd likely not fall asleep anytime soon, Kyla changed into workout gear. She hoped a yoga routine would settle her mind some. Maybe then she could get some sleep before she had to go into work.

...

Kyla's lack of sleep the night before was making the screen fuzzy. She reached for her nearby glasses, pushing them up on her nose. Or it could be the fact that Cooper was standing close behind her chair and leaning down, his cheek right next to hers as he looked over the accounting software she'd convinced him to buy. "Babe, I don't have time to be working on a computer, so this is your deal. You get it, that's fine. But make it worth me spending my money on it, yeah?" She had agreed and set it up so it tracked invoices, payments, and receipts and she could use it for both the garage and the music store since the computers were networked.

Her eyes were on Cooper now, staring at his mouth and the small grin there. She sighed, thinking how good he looked when he smiled like that.

"Thanks, Kyla," he said.

Kyla slapped a hand over her mouth, not realizing she had said that aloud. She sat frozen as he straightened and pulled her up from the chair, his hands circling her waist, and then stuttered out, "Sorry." He didn't pull her tightly against his hips, he didn't have to. He only grinned wider when he felt *her* settle against him.

"Don't apologize. I like knowing you think I look good. Makes my work day that much better." Cooper ducked his head down, his nose sliding along the side of her cheek to her earlobe. "I better get in there and help Phil. And speaking of Phil, he mentioned to me your ideas for the music store. We need to talk about that soon. Until then holler if you need me."

Kyla was almost disappointed as he pulled back. Scratch that. She was completely disappointed. She couldn't deny she liked him near her, the way he smelled, the way he looked at her, and how his hands felt on her skin. It hit her hard in the gut—she wanted to kiss him again, slow and deep so she could explore and savor every moment. When she realized he was staring at her, his eyes burning with an intensity she hadn't seen before in him, she felt her cheeks warm.

"Will do, boss," she murmured, ducking her head but only for a moment since his finger was under her chin and lifting it up to look at him.

"If there weren't a garage full of men a few feet away, I might have to do something about what I'm feeling right now. As it is, I don't have the privacy to do just that. Not now, but soon." He stepped back, the front of his jeans straining against his erection. "I'll be in at one to take you to lunch. We'll go to the diner to see Sarah, best food in town."

Kyla sucked in a breath, hearing the determination in his words and not taking any offense to it. She fought the urge to start tearing his clothes off right then and there, but not with an audience. Instead, she focused on his offer to take her to lunch to keep her hands to herself. "Okay." She grinned at the surprised look on his face. "I don't say no or give attitude about everything, Cooper."

His hand was on the door, but his eyes were searing into her. "Good to know. Can't wait till you say yes and my name, over and over again." With a wink he was through the door, leaving her to pick her melted self off the floor and try to work until lunch.

Chapter 8

Lunch was amazing. Sarah seated them in a secluded booth in the back and took their order. Cooper made sure to keep close, sitting on the same side of the booth as she, his hard thigh pressed up against hers. He had one hand around his drink and the other was in her lap, his fingers gliding across the skin of her thigh. It was an intimate gesture and felt comfortable as they talked about family and life in general. The food arriving meant he had to lift his hand from her leg but didn't stop with the gestures that were making her stomach do gymnastics. He would swipe the hair from her face or squeeze her hand when she had it resting on the table. At one point he lowered his mouth to hers and licked off the ketchup from her bottom lip, taking a quick taste of her mouth before resuming his lunch. She could see herself getting used to this.

Even after Cooper paid, they remained in the booth. Kyla lifted her leg and hooked it over his, her foot dangling between his thighs. "Don't we have to get back to work, boss?"

Cooper's gaze was hot on her leg and in one swift movement his hands were around her waist. He lifted her as if she were a ragdoll and settled her on his lap. One hand slid to the back of her neck and his mouth covered hers, alternating between hard kisses and gentle nibbles. The high back of the booth in front of them would hide them from view of anyone who happened to be in diner, unless someone walked right up to the table.

"Working lunch, employee relations, and all that." She felt him smile, the words muffled against her mouth. Cooper parted her lips with his invading tongue and swiped at the roof of her mouth, goose bumps rising on her skin in response.

Lightning hit when he sucked her tongue and he swallowed her soft moan quickly. She adjusted her body, her knees pressing into the bench seat as she straddled him, her pelvis pressing into his. Kyla could feel that he was hard and ready through his jeans and there was no doubt from the grinding of her hips against the hard length of him that she was telling him she wanted him, too. Cooper tore his mouth from hers and buried his face in her hair. He nipped at the sensitive skin of her neck and then pressed his tongue there, licking and sucking. One hand sifted into her mass of hair and held the back of her head, his other reaching under her tank top. He didn't stop until he found her bra, sliding along the side of her breasts, his thumb swiping over her nipple. "Kyla, we need to get out of here. Now, before I lose control and take you right here."

"This is you in control?" Kyla joked but was cut off by her barely stifled groan when his hand moved between her legs and pressed. She had already felt the dampness in her panties from his kiss, but when his hand touched her center, even through the fabric of her clothes, a rush of heat scorched through her. It was that moment, with Cooper looking into her eyes, touching her, being gentle with her, that she knew. She wanted this, and she wanted Cooper. Not just in the physical sense, though that was certainly the case. Kyla wanted him in every way possible, even if this just lasted a little while. And, looking at him now, having gotten to know the kind of man he was, she had to tell him that. She had to tell him everything. "Cooper. . ." she whispered.

"Jesus, Kyla. We need to go."

Cooper set her on the bench next to him again and got up. His hand was around her waist and his fingers were tracing circles under her shirt, making her shiver with excitement as they exited. He had opened the door of his truck for her when all hell broke loose.

"Cooper!" It was Jackson and another cop walking toward him. "We need to talk."

Cooper's face had turned to stone. "Can't, Jackson, got plans. Find me later."

"No, Cooper. Now. We can talk here if you'd prefer, in front of your woman. Or we can talk somewhere else without an audience. Either way, we're talking now."

His woman? Kyla opened her mouth to contradict Jackson's assertion, but the look on Cooper's face told her that might not be such a good idea.

"Fine." He turned and climbed up to stand on the running board of the truck, scooting her over and handing her the keys. "Kyla, drive back to the garage. Do not hesitate, just put the keys in and go. Do not stop until you get there, and tell Phil that Jackson wanted to talk to me. You tell him I'm talking to him here. Do you understand?" When she nodded he leaned in to kiss her hard on the mouth. "It's going to be fine, I promise. Leave the keys in the top drawer if you don't see me before you leave. I'll come by when I can."

She opened her mouth to speak, but he cut her off with a kiss before leaning back. "I gotta go, babe." Her eyes moved over to Jackson and the other cop who were standing several feet away talking, never taking their eyes off the truck.

"I know, I just. . ." She bit her lower lip. After what the she'd heard about the cops in this town, she didn't want to leave Cooper alone. But she wasn't going to get all clingy either. He was a big boy and could handle himself. Right now she had to hold on to his promise that things would be fine. She lifted her eyes to his and nodded, whispering, "Be careful."

She was already putting the keys in the ignition but his eyes were still on her. "Always am, doll." Cooper dazzled her with his smile and jumped down, slamming the door. She looked in the rearview mirror as she pulled out of the lot and noticed he was waiting for her to leave before he went over to Jackson. The urge to throw the car in reverse and run over the cops was overwhelming, but she figured that might be a bit extreme. So she did as Cooper asked and went to the garage, screeching into the lot like the wheels were on fire. She ran into the garage looking for Phil.

"Jesus, Kyla, what is wrong?!"

"Two cops, Jackson and another, asked to talk to Cooper outside the diner," she told him exactly what happened, minus the part where Cooper got to second base in the diner booth, and watched Phil slam his fist into the nearby wall. Kyla must have gone white as a ghost because he was suddenly in front of her, his hands on either side of her face.

"It's all right. I got this. I'll get Sam and we'll head down there and keep an eye on things. Just hold things down here, okay? You need to go anywhere, use Coop's truck. Do not be walking anywhere alone and if you go back to your room, you go out the back door and through the gate back there." He dropped a key in her hand.

"Phil, what is going on?" Her voice and her hands were shaking, her eyes darting between the dent in the wall and Phil. She knew he'd never hit her, but still the force of his anger surprised her.

"Just bullshit. I can't go into details, Kyla. Especially not now—I gotta see to Cooper."

She watched dazed as he walked into the garage and bark orders to the guys before getting into his truck and pealing out of the lot. Jack meanwhile made a point to come into the office regularly throughout the afternoon, asking for coffee and making small talk. He basically kept her occupied so she didn't freak the hell out. Or at least any more than she already was.

・・・

That evening, Kyla relayed the details to Maggie, who immediately called her husband, Justin. But Maggie was also determined to get Kyla's mind off where the hell Cooper was and dragged her to Felicia's so they could hang out with Sarah. It didn't help. Kyla was jumpy. Her eyes kept moving to the door, hoping Cooper would come in. He didn't. Adding to that, she received a few more text messages from a number she didn't recognize. The text messages were getting more graphic and this made her want to vomit.

"You think your injuries last time were bad? I can't wait to see your face when I plant my gun in your cunt. Yeah, the one you shot me with. I got it back, bitch. How do you think that will feel? I can't wait to see it."

She was sure it was Frank now. Kyla's hands were shaking as she put her phone away. She just wanted to go home, to be inside her room, safe behind the locked door. Exhausted both physically and emotionally, Kyla called a cab and went home. Her mind whirled with her fears, about Frank finding her, about him hurting her again, but they all came back to her worry for Cooper. Where was he? Was he okay? He was out there somewhere after a shadowy meeting with corrupt cops. No matter how many times she repeated Sarah's mantra in her head—everything was going to be all right—Kyla knew better.

• • •

Sarah, Maggie, Rose, and Kyla sat at the table on the patio of the bookstore. Sarah was looking relaxed, and she had reason to be. It was a day off from both her jobs and those were rare. Kyla was leaned back in an iron chair, one leg tucked under her as she sipped on her iced chai. She wore her hair thick and loose, tumbling over her shoulders and back, comfortable in her khaki shorts and a hot pink retro Jem t-shirt with the words decked out in glitter, and matching hot pink flip-flops. She may have looked relaxed on the outside, but inside she was feeling the opposite. Her insides were churning as they had been for the last couple days.

"So tomorrow is the July fourth picnic, the one Phil invited you to. You're supposed to go with Cooper, right?"

At Sarah's question she looked up and wrinkled her nose. "I haven't talked to Cooper since we were at the diner. Phil stopped by, told me Cooper was fine, and that he got caught up having to take care of a few things. Phil assured me he'd call." She shrugged. He still hadn't called. This bothered her on a few levels. That day in the diner things between them had been getting pretty heavy, frustratingly so. But here she sat, no contact from him since his ominous departure, three days ago. She thought they were getting somewhere, she'd started opening up to him and was prepared to tell him everything about her past, to let him in. How could he say he wanted to explore their relationship and then dump her like she had no business participating in his life?

"I'm sure he is fine, Kyla. Phil would tell you if something was wrong. He knows how much you care about Cooper. He wouldn't lie to you or placate you with untruths."

"Whatever." She waved off Maggie's reassurances and ignored the soft look from Rose. Sure, she was trying to play it cool and trust Phil, but with her history, she was scared, worried sick in fact. To deal with it, or more like avoid it, she focused on work. Going into the office, keeping busy, and then going home.

When the second morning following the incident rolled around, her worry and concern turned into anger. She didn't expect Cooper to tell her his every move, but it wasn't like everything had been exactly normal the last time she saw him.

Maggie reached out a hand and squeezed Kyla's, jarring her from her thoughts, "Kyla, seriously, he's fine. Cooper can handle himself."

She leaned forward and addressed her three friends, "I'm not worried anymore. I'm pissed. I get that Cooper can take care of himself, but what happened at the diner scared the crap out of me. He's only told me bits and pieces about the troubles with the cops in this place and all of it makes me uneasy. I left a corrupt cop at home. It's why I was on the road. I know what they are capable of at their worst, and Cooper knows I have issues with this." He might not know all of it, but he should have known enough to check in with her. "So this is just hitting a little too close to that home and freaking me the fuck out." Her eyes flicked to Rose and she mumbled, "Sorry, Rose."

"It's all right, love. I understand your anger. Hold on to that. It will get you by the fear until you see him and can give him a piece of your mind."

Maggie giggled. "Wish I could be a fly on the wall when the two of you go toe to toe."

"Yeah, well, that may not happen. I've lined up Jack to take me to the picnic since Cooper can't be bothered," she dropped her news. The other three women stared at her, silent as the grave.

"What?"

Sarah shook her head. "Cooper's head would explode if he knew Jack was taking you."

"Well it shouldn't," she retorted. "I know I'm new to the whole 'normal relationship' thing, but seriously, he hasn't even fucking called. Who gets carted off by the cops and then doesn't call for days and days. It's not normal!" She cringed when she realized she'd sworn again and shot Rose an apologetic look. "Sorry again, Rose. I never swear like this."

This time it was Rose laughing. "You're right, it's not normal. And when he comes to pick you up tomorrow, he'll learn that lesson real fast."

"No lesson needed. I don't even like him. It doesn't matter that when he kisses me my toes curl. Cooper is a thoughtless jerk." She huffed and sat back in the chair, her arms crossed over her chest.

Sara arched a brow, her head shaking. "Keep telling yourself that, but no matter how many times you do, it's not going to make it the truth. Sure, be pissed, you have the right to be and definitely give him a talking to. But don't deny what is written all over your face. Not to us."

"Whatever," Kyla mumbled into her chai and took another drink while her friends grinned.

Chapter 9

A drop of water landed on the skirt Kyla was staring at and she moved quickly to brush it off. Her current quandary was what to wear to the picnic at Phil's mom's house. She still wasn't sure if Cooper would remember to pick her up. Maybe he'd changed his mind. Or maybe whatever came up was still, well *up*. She'd wait until one thirty and if he didn't show or call, she was calling Jack. Or maybe she wouldn't go at all.

There was nothing she could do about it now so she sighed and went back to look at her clothes. There was the skirt with the short sleeve top and flip-flops, or the capris with a double tank and converse sneakers. Settling on the capris, she started to get dressed, her back to the door.

"Knock, knock," she heard from nearby. She twisted her head and saw him watching her, leaning casually against the doorway to the bedroom.

Cooper grinned as his eyes moved over her curves covered only in a bra and her still unbuttoned capris. In two steps he was behind her, one hand around her waist and pulling her against his chest.

"I need to get ready, Cooper." She kept her tone cool, detached, and went back to the clothes on her bed.

"We have time. I came early to spend some time with you."

She didn't respond, instead moving toward the small closet and rooting around for a pair of sneakers.

"Kyla."

"Yeah?"

"Look at me."

"I'm kind of busy. We're going to be late and that would make a crappy first impression."

"Please stop talking to the closet and look at me, Kyla."

"Jesus, Cooper, what? You can't just walk into my life and suddenly the world stops. It's not all about you. I have stuff to do, and the last thing I need is to deal with your bossiness!"

Cooper was at her back in a flash and touched her arm. It was light, not threatening, but something about it made her knees wobble.

"I thought we were past this, you avoiding me."

Kyla went still at his tone. She knew he wasn't mad at her. It sounded more like annoyance. But something flipped inside her head. A memory came slamming back, hard and fast, and she couldn't stop the trembling that started. Soon her entire body was violently shaking. She shook her head. "Cooper. Please let me go."

She couldn't process the look of concern on Cooper's face. She was in another place, another time. "Kyla. Baby, I'm not going to hurt you. I just need your attention."

When Kyla spoke her voice was barely above a whisper. "Let me go. I need you to let me go. Please. I won't talk back. I'm sorry." She was terrified, caught between what was happening now and the memory that was gripping her like an iron band across her chest.

Instead of letting her go, he pulled her into his chest and wrapped her in his arms. One hand sifted through her hair, the other slid up and down her spine. "Talk to me."

The words tumbled out before she could stop them.

"Just a memory. A bad one. I couldn't fight it. It's not you, it's me. Sometimes they just happen and I can't stop them from overtaking me, bringing me back to that place."

Cooper didn't say anything. He just continued to hold her and wait.

"He'd gotten so mad at me. I was taking too long to get ready. He came in as I looked for a pair of heels in the closet. I knew he was angry, but he had told me an hour before we had to leave. It was like he wanted me to mess up, to fail his test. And I did.

I thought I had five more minutes. But I didn't." Kyla pressed deeper into Cooper and his arms tightened. "He pushed me hard and slammed my forehead into the mirrored closet door. The glass shattered everywhere. He'd forced me, right there, I said no, Cooper. I swear, I said no." Her breath hitched and she felt Cooper's arms convulse around her. "When he was done he dropped me down hard on the glass. The shards had cut my feet." She shivered in his arms. "The only good part was that it was the one time he let me stay home from a social function. There was no way to explain away the bruises and cuts on me. There was so much blood to clean up."

"Jesus Christ. Kyla." He buried his head in her neck. "The fact that you saw not having to go somewhere with him as an upside is, in and of itself, fucked up."

She swallowed back the shame. "I know. I wasn't strong enough."

Cooper pulled back and looked down at her. "No, you aren't weak, Kyla. You survived what sounds like a living hell. Not many would be strong enough to do that. You did what you had to, but that does not make you, in any way, fucking weak. And I don't ever want to hear that crap from you again. Not ever. Do you understand me?"

Kyla lifted a hand and wiped at the tears on her face. "All I can do is try, Cooper. Frank was my only real relationship. So I kinda suck at this stuff."

Cooper grinned. "Well, then let me lead the way. I won't steer you wrong. I promise." His hand lifted to trace along the lace of her bra cup, dipping down to her cleavage and going along the other. "I've missed you something fierce."

His admission had her softening against him, but that didn't mean she wasn't still pissed. "Cooper, we need to talk. What the heck happened the other day? Where have you been and why didn't you call me or come over? I've been scared out of my mind!

Jackson took you away and Phil just said everything was fine. But it wasn't fine, Cooper. What is going on?" She pushed against him but stopped herself when she heard him suck in a breath. Her gaze flew to his face and she gasped. "Oh my god, what happened?" Her fingers were tentative as they grazed over the fading but still angry bruises on his jaw, on his cheek, and the cut over his eye. "Are you okay?"

"I'm perfect now, Kyla. No need to worry." His head dropped forward and he leaned his forehead to hers. "You did good the other day. Phil said you were a real trooper. Thanks for doing that." He kissed her quickly, but she didn't let him pull away completely, instead gripping his shoulders tighter than she had ever had before. She was trying to say a lot with just that kiss—it was urgent, full of desire, and relief that he was okay.

"Babe," he started, the corners of his mouth tipped up. "I'm okay, I promise."

She continued to stare. For the first time since she could remember she realized what it must have felt like for her family and friends to see her, to see the bruises and not be able to do anything about it.

"Your face." The tremble in her voice was the first indication that her whole body was in fact shaking beneath him. "I shouldn't have left you there."

"Kyla, listen to me. I'm fine. I swear to Christ I am. I wouldn't lie to you about this. As for leaving me there, I asked you to do that. I would have been pissed if you hadn't 'cause I'd have had to worry about you. I knew if you went back to the garage and got Phil things would be fine. And they were."

After another long look she called up her courage enough to straighten and narrow her eyes at him. "Don't ever do that again, Cooper Moretto."

"Kyla. . ."

"No. No you don't get to talk. At the diner you asked me to leave you with a bad cop and I did. Stupidly, I did. And now ... now look at your beautiful face."

"Kyla, Jackson came to me and yeah it was bad. He had a job to do, but we came to an understanding, just let me. . ."

She cut him off. "No, Cooper! Listen to me. I had to drive like a bat outta hell to get Phil, worried out of my mind. Then I didn't hear anything. Not one thing. For days. And the guys were acting weird but wouldn't tell me anything. And I can't deal with not knowing, Cooper. I am not the naggy, clingy girlfriend type, I swear to god I'm not." She stopped and shook her head as the anger ran out. Her voice cracked, "But you could have called. I was terrified, Cooper."

"After the picnic, we'll talk. I'll fill you in. I shouldn't have left you like that. I just wanted to be the one who talked to you. I am so sorry."

Her breath hitched. "I thought you wouldn't be coming back."

She felt his body still against her.

"I'll always come back, Kyla. You got me wrapped up in you so tight, it'd be impossible for me to not come back." He tipped her chin up and kissed her. It was sweet and soft and reassuring. "Now, let's go back to one of your earlier statements. You're my girlfriend? A non-clingy and non-naggy one, which is good because I don't deal with that shit, but you said it all the same. You mean that?"

She needed a five second delay button on her mouth. The truth just kept spilling out without a filter. But it was too late now. "Yeah."

He grinned and she squirmed, which made his grin bigger.

"Good." Clearly he thought this whole scene was amusing, and he owed her more than that. Their relationship should mean more than an easy laugh.

"Shut up. I'm still mad at you."

"Are you going to tell me why?"

"No. Yes. I don't know. It makes me sound even more clingy and naggy than I already did."

Cooper threw his head back and laughed. Hard. When his body finally stopped shaking from her apparent hilarity, he spoke again. "Just tell me. I can handle it."

"Because I don't want to mess this up with you. And if what happened with Jackson is a harbinger of what is to come, you have to know I will not ever leave your side when my gut is telling me to stay. I don't care what happens, or what I hear or see. I won't do it and don't you dare try to make me, Cooper."

As she was speaking he moved them to the bed and sat down, pulling her with him as he leaned against the headboard. Kyla cuddled against him, her palm flat to his chest. She felt his strong heartbeat beneath it and used that strength to open up to him. When he didn't answer for what seemed like forever, she started to pull away. "Sorry," she whispered into his chest.

"Don't say sorry for talking to me, Kyla. Don't apologize for telling me where you're coming from with all this. I fucked up by not calling you. I should have known that sending Phil to talk to you wouldn't be enough. I could have texted you. I didn't. That's on me." He ran a hand through his dark hair and sighed. "I was going to tell you this after the party but might as well get it out there now. But what I say is between you and I only, Kyla." When she nodded, he continued. "Believe me when I tell you this will not happen again. Jackson's been Saybrook's lapdog for a while now; I always thought he was in his pocket. At the diner, he was there for Saybrook, who apparently doesn't like all the observation we're doing of him and his guys. He asked for volunteers to give me a message and Jackson took it. We came to an understanding. He is not liking his position in the department, nor does he like seeing what is going down. So he's going to feed me info, all anonymous of course, and hopefully keep the pressure on Saybrook." He ran his fingers along Kyla's cheek. "But he still had to make it look real and deliver that message. It could have been a lot worse. So when I left, I immediately headed down to Portland to talk to some contacts. I am an idiot for doing that. Never fucking again, will I not contact you. Ever." Cooper's lips thinned and the muscle in his jaw jumped. "And I will not startle you. I swear I am working on that."

She sensed the steely resolve in his voice but also the pain he felt for her.

"Cooper, don't be mad at yourself. It's getting better. It's just sometimes I forget or get lost in a memory. I trust you enough to know you aren't intentionally freaking me out. I just have to learn to not let the fear trap me inside myself and confuse you with Frank."

"Damn straight 'cause I am not that motherfucker." His hands went to the sides of her head.

"Cooper, kiss me again?"

He did and it didn't take long for things to get heated. One hand slid to her ass, the other to her breast. They both squeezed and he added a thumb swipe over the fabric of her bra, her nipple hardening. His teeth nipped her neck and he whispered, "Go get dressed so we can go eat before I decide to eat right here. And then we won't be getting to the picnic at all."

"Cooper!" Her cheeks heated as she covered them with her hands. "Go get a Coke or something from the fridge and I'll be right out."

"Will do. Gotta call Rose and Jack, too. I don't like the look of your lock. I'm going to have a new one put in, a dead bolt."

She wrinkled her nose as she tugged on her shirt. "Ugh, bossy!" she accused, shaking her head when she heard him laughing. She rolled her eyes and finished her make-up and hair while Cooper made his calls. She knew there was no sense arguing with him and if she got some additional security while she was here, who was she to complain?

When she came out of the bedroom he was holding the photo of her and her brother when they were kids in his hand. "You were a cute kid," he said. "Does your brother know about me? Threaten to do me bodily harm if I hurt you?" When she nodded, he laughed. "I already like 'em. Jack is putting a new lock in later. I'm not letting anything happen to my best female employee."

"I'm your only female employee," she grumbled, letting the tension slide from her shoulders. "So are we going?"

"Anxious to not be alone with me?" he said, his voice low. His fingers played at the bottom of her tank top and his lips twitched as her breathing increased.

"I don't ... no." She tried to step toward the door, but his arm stretched out to pull her back to him.

"Then you want to be alone with me? 'Cause we can skip the picnic, or at least show up late." He bent his head, his nose and lips barely touching the skin along her neck, moving to her jaw, and finally finding her lips.

She thought her heart might explode out of her chest as he kissed her in that way that made her want to jump out of her skin, or at least jump all over him. Her hands grabbed the waistband of his jeans and she tugged him closer against her while Cooper slid his hands underneath her top. As he moved up her back, he stopped when his fingers reached the fabric of her bra before continuing higher.

Kyla didn't want him to stop. She did not want him to ever stop touching her. She nipped at his lower lip, her eyes twinkling as she watched his face as they kissed. But as his hands slid higher and skimmed the scars on her back, she froze. "You're right, we are going to be late, which would make me look bad." She pulled her tank top down.

Cooper adjusted his jeans. "One of these days we'll finish what we start. No interruptions. Just you and I. Are you going to be able to handle that?"

"I'm trying to get there, Cooper, and I honestly cannot wait until I am."

His hands glided to her ass, squeezing lightly as he kissed her forehead. "I know you are. Let's go. You've got a bunch of people to meet and Edith is going to hand me my ass if we don't get there." He guided her through the door, shutting and locking it behind them.

When they reached the parking lot he handed her a helmet, waiting patiently as she put it on. "Coop, I've never ridden a motorcycle before."

"Glad I'm your first then." He chuckled at her scowl. "C'mon, let me help ya over." He got on and helped guide her on behind him. "Hold tight, doll, and get close."

Kyla scooted forward, sliding her hands around his waist and linking them in front of him. "This better be better than my actual first time, 'cause lemme tell you, that sucked. As it usually does for the girl, apparently."

Cooper stilled, turned his head, and lifted his visor. "Don't worry, this first time will get you going in all the right places. Just squeeze me tight if you need to make a stop to take care of things." He winked at her before turning around and starting the bike.

She held on tightly as they roared off to the picnic, itching to squeeze tight but using every ounce of self-control she had to stop herself.

• • •

She felt like she walked into the biggest family reunion she could imagine as Phil's mom, Edith, introduced her to the guests. This wasn't a reunion though, just the family Fourth of July picnic with family defined as "everyone we know."

Most of the guys from the shop were there as were their significant others. Edith's house was on the edge of town and deep in the woods. When they'd arrived, Cooper had shown Kyla around and took her over to the edge of the property that sloped down into the bay. The waves were light with very little wind, which made the sea shine like rippled glass. They stood in silence, Cooper's arm around her shoulders. His fingers grazed her skin, sending a shiver through her body. Kyla loved that he could affect her like that with just a touch. She tucked herself into him, despite the heat, and he didn't mind at all.

"So what do you think?"

Kyla kept her cheek on his chest. "It's breathtaking and so peaceful. I mean, all the chaos of the party and then you walk down this trail and it's like another world."

"Glad you like it because my house isn't far from here and is a similar set up. It's closer to town and with a few less trees between the house and the water. I've planted a bunch more, so eventually, maybe in fifteen years, I'll have an identical set up."

"You want trees blocking your view?"

"From the second floor I can see the water. But it's nice to have that buffer, especially in the winter when the wind whips up. I could have bought a piece of land just like this when I was looking, but my place has a very private beach. It cost a fortune, but it will be worth it."

Kyla scrunched her nose. "What will be worth it?"

"You, naked on that beach, working on getting rid of any tan lines you might have." His fingers poked under the strap of her tank top, a teasing touch.

Kyla's laugh floated on the wind. "Is that all you think about?"

"Babe, I've wanted inside you for awhile now. The fact that we haven't gotten there is killing me." His forefinger touched her cheek and moved down to trace the outline of her lips. "I'm patient though and I know it's worth the wait."

"Cooper. . ." she started, but before she got anything else out they were walking down the path toward the party.

"Let's get back before Edith sends out a search party. We need to eat, too."

She nodded and let him lead her over to the food table and then she sat down at a picnic table set up in the semi-shade of several large trees. Kyla pushed her sunglasses onto her forehead and was happy for that shade, given the heat of the unusually hot day. Edith and Sheena, Phil's girlfriend, were sitting across from her. Kids were running around, shouting and playing. Teenagers, some that Kyla recognized from the music store, were lounging on the grass and beach towels. Groups of men and women stood around, drinking beers. It was a friendly, laid back atmosphere Kyla knew she could get used to. Heck, she already was used to it and she'd only been there for an hour. Cooper's friends had embraced her like they had known her for years. She felt at ease, laughing and joking, collecting new recipes and invitations for coffee or to hang out on the beach. While it scared her, it wasn't scary. It was the kind of change she knew she could live with ... maybe even forever.

"I gotta say I was quite surprised to find that Cooper hired someone, especially a woman, to work in his shop. That hasn't happened in ... well ever." Sheena laughed as she said it. Kyla had taken to her sunny personality right away. "Even Phil was surprised and it takes a lot to surprise him."

"Now, Sheena, Cooper knows a hard worker when he sees one, I'm sure. I was in there yesterday. Place looks divine, at least in comparison to the last time. I love the new coffee pot, too. I might have to stop in more often."

Sheena snorted. "I'm sure they wouldn't mind as long as you brought some fried chicken and potato salad, Edith. Spoiled brats."

"Sheena's right. They don't need any more of that," Kyla chimed in. The guys already were getting used to her ordering and picking up lunch for them. She needed to break them out of that habit and fast, or she'd be stuck doing it forever. And there was that word again, forever.

"I'm afraid it's too late for that. But they're as good as they come and would do anything for anyone, especially the ones they care about." Edith gave her a knowing look and nodded over in Cooper's direction. "Be careful with him. He might look tough, but he is still in many ways fragile like the day he came to live with us."

Kyla smiled. "Phil mentioned Cooper came to stay here for breaks from college after his dad passed. I'm glad he had someone to look out for him."

Edith's face got soft. "I've always had a soft spot for Cooper even before he and his dad moved away when he was little. So when they came home, I was ecstatic, as was Phil. Those two became partners in crime right away, tearing through town. Cooper's dad or I, were always having to go out searching for 'em to rustle them up for meals. Usually they were found by the water. Those two were like fish as kids. They'd come out of the bay all pruny and shivering, but they kept at it 'til we hauled their butts home."

The three laughed at the image of mini-Phil and mini-Cooper whining about wanting to stay in the water longer.

"When his dad died, Cooper was in college, but I insisted he stay here, let me take care of him until he was ready to buy the shop. Thankfully Jack had left him a bit of money and he was able to do that right after graduation. Set up his shop and well, now the rest is history as they say."

Kyla's eyes drifted to Cooper and she watched as he grabbed some beers from the cooler, handing them out to the group of guys he was talking to. A younger boy came over and tossed a football to him, and she couldn't help but smile as he threw it a pretty far distance, the children running after it. She noticed a woman nearby practically drooling over him as she laughed at something he said, clearly flirting. She recognized her, even from here. Fucking Marla. What the hell was she doing here and why was she flirting with her Cooper?

Her Cooper. *Oh fuck, where did that come from?*

Kyla heard Sheena make a strangled noise in her throat. Edith pursed her lips in disapproval.

"What the heck is she doing here?" Sheena bit out, clearly no more thrilled about seeing Marla as Kyla was.

Edith sighed. "You know she is always invited and I can't just take that away. She has nothing else. And I know. . . ." Edith put up her hand and Sheena clamped her mouth shut. "I don't want her trying to get between you and Phil or go after Cooper. I don't want her near any one of my boys frankly, but I have to hope that one day she will get her head out of her patooty and straighten out her life. For her brother's sake." Edith's eyes slid to Kyla. "Her brother was killed in Iraq and had been buddies with Cooper and Phil in high school. Marla was seventeen when it happened and her mother couldn't deal with her son's death or her daughter's grief. I don't approve of what she does or how she acts, but I have to try."

Kyla felt a pang of sadness for Marla but even more for Edith. She was a woman who wanted to help others, to fix people. She just hadn't figured out that Marla was not looking to change or turn her life around.

She exchanged a look with Sheena, but said nothing before concentrating on eating.

Kyla finished her food and pushed her plate away only to notice Cooper watching her. His head was tilted to the side and he had that sexy half-grin on his face. God, he looked so freaking *hot* when he smiled like that. She smiled back, turning her head quickly as she felt her cheeks flush.

"I can't believe he grew up here because your house is so tidy and I don't know if you've noticed, but Cooper has no organizational skills whatsoever," she said to Edith. "He has a serious hoarding issue."

"Or you have a touch of OCD." Kyla stilled as she felt him standing behind her, Cooper's hands resting casually on her shoulders.

Edith beamed like a proud mother. "I was just telling Kyla here about how great the office looked and that I might need to come over for coffee more."

"Well you're welcome anytime," he said as he leaned over and kissed her on the cheek.

Kyla stood and turned into Cooper, leaning against him as she untangled her feet from the bench. Her eyes flicked to Marla against her will—she'd just as soon ignore her.

"She was invited awhile ago. Edith couldn't rescind the invitation even though she wanted to," Cooper said softly.

She shrugged. "Edith explained. It's fine. I can be civil. I just hope she can."

"Football time!" Phil yelled as he began handing out flags that people were strapping around their waists.

She lifted up on her toes and kissed Cooper on the cheek and then hollered to Phil. "I'm in!"

Cooper was surprised and tucked a strand of hair behind her ear. "You sure you want to play? I've seen you fall all over your own feet just walking." He slid his hand to the small of her back, his thumb tracing circles and sending shivers from her ears to her toes as they moved toward their other teammates.

"I'll be fine. Someone had to play receiver at the Thanksgiving pre-dinner games at home."

She missed those games, and she had been damn good at them. Her brother had made sure she could run and catch along with their cousins and friends.

"This is touch, Kyla," Phil said as he handed her a flag. "You're on Coop's team. Be prepared to get your asses kicked."

"It's okay, Phil, no need to reassure me. Just remember, all's fair in love, war, and football, right?" She smiled, giving one of the other players a high five as she passed by to get into the huddle with Cooper and Tommy.

The first few plays went well. Cooper threw her the ball at one point, which she fumbled when she saw Phil barreling toward her. The man was a commanding figure on the field. Cooper took every opportunity he could find to smack her ass, and even though she pretended to be offended and to swat at his hand, she really didn't mind. She wanted to win more than anything.

"They are so cute together."

Kyla heard Edith's comment as she ran down the side of the field and tripped over her own feet. She hit the ground with a thud and somersaulted awkwardly.

"Ugh," she groaned, pushing herself up on her hands. "That was spectacular."

"You okay?" Cooper asked as he grabbed a hand and pulled her up.

"Yeah, I'm fine. Let's go. This is third down." She limped over to the line of scrimmage, sore, but she knew she could shake it off; she'd taken harder hits before. And she could pick up some ice bags at the convenience store later. Getting into her stance she found herself face to face with Marla.

"Better watch out, klutz. It's easy to break something out here." She rolled her eyes at Marla's sneer but the woman continued. "I've tried to give you the benefit of the doubt, 'cause you're new and you might not know Cooper and I are a thing. I thought letting him have his fun, working you out of his system, would be enough. Because that's what he does, Kyla. He fucks 'em and leaves 'em. He never dates the same woman more than a few times." She leaned in and hissed, "So back the fuck off. You're only going to get a broken heart."

She lifted a brow. "Well if he only dates someone a few times, then you have nothing to worry about. And I guess you'd know since, from what I hear, he had you once and hasn't gone back in for seconds."

She ignored Marla's glare, and the rest of her muttering, and glanced back to Cooper, who was in the quarterback position. Was Cooper one of *those* kind of men who saw a challenge and sought to conquer it before moving on to the next? No, he told her this was real. That he wasn't into her because she needed fixing. And she believed him with every part of her being.

Besides, Kyla had survived the mess with Frank, barely. Like her mom said, she had to move on and whatever happened in the future, she'd be ready for it. She wasn't going to let the likes of Marla or Frank run her out of town and away from the new life, the new home, she'd found. She wasn't giving that up.

Tommy was next to her on the line and apparently overheard just enough. . "Shut it, Marla," he ordered before it could go any farther. "Just play the game. The game is tied, Kyla."

She nodded. "You're right. Let's get this game done."

Kyla heard the snap from Cooper and did the only thing she could, which was dart around Marla and run for the end zone, turning her body to look for the ball. She reached out and felt the leather hit her hands, tucking it into her body as her feet came down and hit the ground. She heard a huge cheer go through the crowd of players and onlookers, but her joy was short lived as a half second later someone slammed into her. She felt the air fly from her lungs before her head smacked the ground, hard.

In her daze she could hear yelling around her, and Kyla winced as she opened her eyes. All she could see were legs and sneakers before her eyes closed again.

She flinched and tried to squirm away, groaning at the pain pulsing through her body, as hands and fingers skated over her extremities.

"It's just me and Tommy, Kyla." The sound of Cooper's voice and his reassurance made her relax, but even that hurt. "Everyone get the fuck back! Someone get some ice. Jesus, Tommy, tell me she is going to be okay."

"I'm fine," she mumbled. She tried to lift her head but it felt like it was the weight of a bowling ball. "Holy crap, that hurt. Was that a good score though? My feet hit the ground before I was hit."

"Yes it counted, Kyla. Now, don't move until Tommy checks you out, you hear?" Cooper moved away while Tommy crouched next to her. She watched Cooper stalk—*yes stalk*—over to Phil, Sheena, and others who were yelling at Marla. Odd how Marla just stood there, her expression blank except for the few times her gaze shifted to Kyla. Marla's face went soft when Cooper approached before it turned blank. Before Cooper got to Marla though, the woman screeched something unintelligible, turned and ran for the front of house, leaving everyone staring after her.

"Hey, Kyla, let's make sure you don't have any broken bones okay? Now tell me what hurts."

She peeked out from behind the arm covering her eyes to look at Tommy, catching his for a moment before she covered them back up. She had learned from Cooper earlier that Tommy was an EMT with the fire department. "The better question is what doesn't hurt. And the answer would be my pinkie." She moved her pinkie. "Nope, that hurts too. But it's fine. I've taken harder hits. I just need to catch my breath." She was putting on a brave face, of course, but she had no other choice.

"I'd imagine everything hurts," Tommy replied, but he continued the examination. "No broken ribs but some bruising probably." His eyes met hers for a moment. "You've made an enemy, Kyla. You need to be careful. She might be a moron, but she grew up here, and Cooper and Marla . . ." He sighed. "They have a history."

She held up a hand, blinking rapidly. She heard what Tommy was saying. She closed her eyes, her head turning to the side as she tried to get her breathing back to normal.

He moved away as Cooper stalked back, this time alone, to help her up. She let him help her, but once she tested out her feet and could stand on her own, she put some distance between them and ignored his questioning look.

"Well, this is embarrassing," she mumbled to no one in particular as she took the ice someone offered. She applied one to her face and flinched as Cooper slid the other discreetly under her tank top, holding it against her ribs gently.

He bent his head to her ear. "Let me take you home."

She shook her head, her eyes focused on the rest of the players, who had all started moving toward the backyard. She dropped her head, her voice quiet. "No, it's fine. I can go, you stay here. They are going to do the fireworks and I don't want to take you away from the party. These are your friends and family, Cooper."

He looked confused. "I have no idea what that means, Kyla. I am not staying here and letting you go back to the motel alone after the hit you took 'cause some bitch can't get it through her head I am not hers." He turned her toward him, tipping her chin up to look at him. "I'm taking you home."

She started to smile but even that turned into a wince. "Fine, let's go then before my legs give out." She cursed softly as she tried to take a step, but before her other foot hit the ground, Cooper scooped her up in his arms. Edith and Sheena were staked out by the side of the house holding Kyla's purse and a bag of leftovers Edith had packed.

"Make sure she gets some rest, Cooper, though I think she should see a doctor," Sheena insisted.

Kyla shook her head. "No, it's okay. Tommy looked me over, I'll be fine. Especially since Mr. Caveman here won't let my feet touch the ground."

Cooper was grinning. "I'll call you later, Edith. Sheena, you might want to check on Phil. He's pissed."

Sheena nodded and peeled off to find her man while Cooper deposited Kyla near a truck. "What about the bike?" she asked.

"Phil will bring it back later and get his truck."

The ride home was silent, but it wasn't tense. Cooper held her hand the entire time, his thumb making small circles on the back of her hand. She was almost asleep by the time the fifteen-minute drive was over. "Tommy says I have to wake you up often to make sure you're all right. You sure you don't want to head to the hospital?" he asked.

Kyla nodded and carefully climbed down from the truck before Cooper made it around. She chuckled at his annoyed look, hobbling next to him as they made their way to the stairs. "I'm fine. I'm sore, not paralyzed."

"Everything all right over there?"

They stopped at the edge of the stairs near her room. Morris was standing at the base, his eyes on Kyla. He looked greasier than ever and his smile revealed the fact that he likely hadn't brushed his teeth in ten years, if not longer. She shivered and pressed closer into Cooper's side. Morris wiped his grubby hands on his overalls. "Didn't think you beat your women, Cooper, but I guess we all gotta keep 'em in line somehow."

Kyla sucked in a breath too quickly, and that added to the pain in her ribs. She loosened the grip on the ice bag at her side and felt Cooper crowding closer to her. "I don't beat women, Morris, but I got nothing against throwing a man around. Now get the fuck out of my way."

The hotel clerk laughed, a sneering, high-pitched noise that didn't fit who he was. It made the man go from gross to scary in about one second flat. "Don't worry, Cooper. Your secret is safe with me. Damn whores never listen and sometimes they deserve it."

She felt Cooper start to move and grabbed onto his shirt. Not only was she in need of some ibuprofen, but she also did not want Cooper to pay for some shit this creep was mumbling about. "Cooper, please, I need to get inside. I hurt everywhere and I can't deal with any more chaos tonight. That includes trying to get your ass out of jail for beating the pulp out of this guy." Her fists clenched the fabric beneath her fingers. "Please, Cooper," she said, her words a whispered plea only he could hear.

He grunted, then shot a final glare at Morris as he sidestepped the man and carried her up the stairs to her room. There, he set her in the bathroom to change into something more comfortable while he made a few calls. She took a shower, and as she dressed she heard Jack in the other room. Pulling on shorts and a t-shirt, she hobbled out into the living room. Both he and Cooper turned and looked her over.

"Jesus," Cooper breathed and was at her side. "You're black and blue." His hands skimmed her arms.

Kyla shrugged. "I've always bruised easy. Jack, what are you doing here?"

"Fixing the lock. I was just about to leave. Get some sleep, all right?"

"You left the party for this?"

Jack shook his head. "Nah, I got a date so I was leaving anyway and wanted to get this done before that. Might be tied up for the weekend." He winked as Cooper barked out a laugh. Kyla merely wrinkled her nose.

After he left, Cooper sat on the couch and pulled her onto his lap. "How you feeling, baby?"

She shrugged. "The shower helped. This helps, too." She ran her palm over his shirt. "I was hoping tonight would end differently."

"Yeah? How did you want it to end?"

She glanced up, her eyes feeling heavier than usual for six o'clock. "With you, and I wearing a lot less clothes. Naked would have been preferable."

Slow Ride

Cooper's lips pressed into her temple before he trailed soft kisses on her cheek, jaw, chin, and then up to her mouth. He was careful as his hands and fingers roamed her body, testing how she felt. "When I take you, I don't want to be afraid of hurting you. But I won't be leaving tonight, Kyla, so we can definitely get rid of the clothes, or most of them."

She tucked her face into his neck and sighed, happy despite the hit she took from Marla. "Sounds good to me." Her voice sounded sleepy even to her. "I didn't like taking that tackle from that bitch, but I am glad I went to the picnic. And even more glad I was with you."

She felt Cooper relax underneath her and this made her body melt even further into him. "I'm glad too, baby. Now go to sleep. I'll wake you up to check on you in a bit."

"All right, honey." And with those words Kyla let sleep wash over her.

Chapter 10

She woke up the next morning and felt hard heat pressed against her back. She remembered Cooper waking her up several times. For a while she been tucked between his solid body and the back of the couch, a blanket tucked around her. He had been watching some old movie on television. Later she awoke as he carried her to the bedroom. She was awake enough that time to strip off her shorts and slide under the covers. Kyla had watched as Cooper stripped out of his shirt and jeans, leaving only his boxers.

When Cooper came back from the bathroom, he tugged the covers over the two of them and Kyla turned and curled into his front. His hand feathered down the thin fabric of her tee, stopping on her hip.

"You always just wear a t-shirt and panties to bed? I figured you'd have some fancy nightie from that bag of yours."

"You don't approve?" She arched a brow. "My nighties are in the drawer. This was in the laundry basket. Pulling open a drawer wasn't going to happen."

She saw him press his lips together. "It's okay, Cooper. I'm okay. I've had to deal with worse from . . ." She stopped, refusing to say his name. "Honey, after a couple days I'll be good as new."

This didn't seem to make him feel any better, but his arms loosened.

"Go to sleep, Kyla. We'll talk more tomorrow."

Kyla nodded and tucked herself against him. "Night, Cooper." It didn't take long for sleep to find her as his heat enveloped her.

And Kyla awoke in that same position, too, her eyes open and focused on Cooper's chest.

"Morning. How you feeling?"

Kyla didn't move. She couldn't. "I hurt. Everything hurts. It all freaking hurts."

His hands roamed gently over her and kneaded the tense muscles at her shoulders, but he didn't say anything.

"Maybe I was a bit too open and honest there."

"No, you weren't. I want your honesty, Kyla, especially about how you're feeling and what's going on inside your head. I wanted to have my way with you this morning and had you not told me that, I could have hurt you. You didn't do anything wrong except make a play that will likely go down in July 4th football history. You might hurt like hell right now, but just know, you're already a legend around town."

She sighed, "Well, that makes it a little better at least." Her eyes flicked to the clock, "You have to go to work. I can get up. I don't need help."

Cooper sighed and lifted her chin. "Yeah, you do. And it doesn't make you weak to need it either. Not asking for it makes you stubborn though."

"You sound like my brother."

"He must be a pretty smart guy, too."

She scowled and swatted at his shoulder but didn't try to stop the smile on her face.

"We'll work together on making it easier for you to ask for help." He didn't wait for a response, instead kissing her nose and then her lips before pulling back. "I have to get home to change. You have the day off, boss's orders. You need to rest. Garage will be slow today anyway. I'll bring some lunch over."

"I have a ton of leftovers."

"All right, we'll have that then. You need me to stop and get something, you let me know."

His eyes heated with something she couldn't quite identify and she was too caught up in trying to figure out what that was to respond with anything other than a nod. He kissed her, his lips moving slowly over hers, drawing out her reaction until she was arching her sore back against him.

"Cooper. . ." She was panting when he finally pulled back.

"Not today, Kyla. I don't want to hurt you. Get some sleep."

Before he even shut the door Kyla fell back into a dreamless sleep.

• • •

Cooper had his hands inside the guts of a car. The garage was busy today. Phil and Jack were each working on vehicles in two of the other bays, and two of his other guys were busy with some detailing jobs. It was near lunch and he'd asked Kyla, who was feeling much better after taking a couple days to recoup from the football game, to run to the bank and then grab some pizza for everyone since none of them would likely get their normal lunch break.

"Yo, Cooper. We got company."

He looked up at Jack's voice and saw three cop cars pulling through the gate. Cooper wiped his hands on a rag. "Shut it down, guys. Close the bay doors. They aren't getting in without a warrant." He walked through the office and out into the lot, meeting Jackson, two other officers, and the chief of police, Martin Saybrook.

"What can I do for you, Jackson?"

Cooper intentionally directed his greeting to Jackson, blatantly ignoring the so-called head of the department. He ignored Jackson's glare and waited.

It was Saybrook who spoke though. He pushed forward, his arms crossed over his chest. He was dressed in his uniform, his black hair slicked back with too much product. "Mr. Moretto, we got word there's been some illegal chop shop activity going on. We need to look around, check out the books and the garage itself."

"You got a warrant?"

Saybrook grunted. "We don't need a piece of paper to let us in, Cooper. Now we can do this the easy way, or the hard way. You tell me how this is going to play out."

By now Phil and Jack were at his back. A glance behind him confirmed the bay doors had been closed and locked like he'd told the guys to do. His could see his other two employees were in the office.

"You aren't unlawfully entering my business, Saybrook. And save your tough guy act for someone else. I don't cave under your pressure like some of the others in this town. Now, get the fuck off my property and don't come back without that piece of paper."

Sayrook's meaty fist shot out and Cooper had just enough time to dodge it. Saybrook missed his intended target—his face—only grazing his jaw. No way was Cooper going to let this jackass hit him on his property. He lunged for the top cop.

One of the other cops took out his baton and lashed out at Cooper, slamming it into his ribs. He doubled over in pain and didn't see the officer's foot shoot out. Cooper stumbled, dropping to a knee while he tried to catch his breath, pain shooting down his thigh. He glanced up in time to see Jack holding Phil back from entering the scuffle.

"Stand down, Phil." Cooper ordered, before pushing to his feet. He directed his attention to Saybrook. "You might beat your way into getting your way with everything else, but I am not one of your cock-sucking whores. Beat the shit out of me, I don't care. But I will not give in to you."

"Coop, man, don't. We do not need you going to jail right now."

Saybrook leaned back. "Yeah, Moretto. Listen to your boy, Jack. Unless you want an extended stay in my jail, that is. I'd love to have you in a cage, where you couldn't get away from me."

"You're a sick bastard," Cooper hissed.

"I know," Saybrook crowed, his chest puffing out with what looked like pride.

Jackson cleared his throat. "Boss, I think we should go get that warrant. If a chop shop is what's happening here, they won't be able to hide the evidence." He leveled his gaze at Cooper. "We're coming back so don't do anything stupid. Or anything more stupid than usual."

Saybrook glared at the mechanics for another long moment before turning on his heel and heading back to his tricked out Escalade. How the town afforded to buy him that, no one knew. The cost alone was almost the entire department budget.

"Keep it calm, man." Phil mumbled as they watched the cops peel out of the lot.

"Shut the fucking gate and lock it. They want in, they're going to need to bust through it. Have one of the guys sit out front to let in customers."

"We're swamped," Jack said, but was cut off quickly by Cooper.

"I don't fucking care. Just do it."

Jack grumbled something before heading toward the gate, waving to the others to come out of the office. Just then, Kyla turned into the lot, smiling and carrying a bag and a couple boxes of pizza.

"What are you going tell her?" Phil asked.

Cooper sighed. "No idea, but I know I have to. She's going to freak out, but she needs to be ready in case they somehow get a warrant to come back here. And if Saybrook suddenly has a hard-on for me, I don't want her getting caught in the crossfire."

"Good luck with that." Phil muttered. "Hey Kyla. Perfect timing. My stomach was just telling me it was time to eat."

"Your stomach is always telling you that." Kyla teased as she handed him the food. She glanced back at Jack, locking the gate. "What's going on? Is the shop closing early?"

"Phil, take that out back, we can eat on the picnic table back there. There are beers in the fridge. Turn the stereo on, too. I think we all need a break."

Phil headed off to the back lot where they often partied or just hung out, and Cooper turned his attention to Kyla.

"Cooper, what's going on?" Her eyes were wide and he could tell she was nervous by the way she was fidgeting, shifting her feet and wringing her hands.

"We had a visitor and I want to tell you about it. Not to scare you, but just so you're aware of what's going on." He grabbed her hand and led her into the office, locking the doors. "Come here."

She went to him and immediately put her arms around his waist. God, this woman was amazing, he thought. Just that and he felt better. When she pressed tightly against him, he grimaced and sucked in a sharp breath.

Kyla glanced up and her face took on a concerned look. She lifted a hand to his jaw and he winced. "Cooper, you've got a bruise on your face. And your side. . ." She ran a hand along his abdomen. God, he wished these were different circumstances, her touching him like this, behind a locked door. "What happened?" He heard the trembling in her voice and it pissed him that she was scared.

He sat in the office chair and pulled her on his lap. Screw the pain, he had to reassure her right now that he was okay. She straddled his legs and waited.

"After you left, the cops came by. One of them was the chief, the guy I told you about. They made some allegations about us running a chop shop."

"But you don't. I mean, I've seen the books, and there isn't anything shady going on, like weird deliveries or unknown cars showing up and being ripped apart. You wouldn't exactly be able to hide that here."

"I know that, and you know that. Hell, everyone knows that, including probably Saybrook. But he wants to bust my balls for whatever reason and this is how he's choosing to do it."

"Did you let them in? And what does this have to do with your face being bruised?"

He buried his face in her neck and inhaled her sweet scent. His lips brushed the sensitive skin of her neck and he felt her shiver in his arms.

"Don't distract me," she whispered. "Tell me the rest."

Cooper lifted his head and sighed. "All right. We got into a tussle. The cops took a few shots when I told them to come back with a warrant. But it wasn't a big deal. Just a couple bruises, I'll be fine."

"Be fine. You'll be fine." She was looking at him strangely before she exploded from the chair and railed against Saybrook.

"That stupid jerkface! I cannot believe he came here, threatened you, and then hurt you. And I wasn't here. But let me tell you, if I were, I would have so given him a piece of my mind. I am so sick and tired of people taking the power they are given and abusing it. Why is he allowed to do that? Why doesn't anyone stop them?"

Cooper reached out and took her hands, yanking her toward him. "Kyla O'Grady, listen to me. You will not, under any circumstances give that man a piece of your mind. You see him, you walk the other way. No, you run the other way. I cannot have you anywhere near him. I've heard what he does to women, and I will not allow you to suffer that fate. And don't forget about what I told you we think he did to Cheryl. He will hurt you, Kyla, and make you wish you were dead. Maybe he'd even do worse. So please, steer clear of him. Promise me you will."

Kyla's eyes were round. "Fine, Cooper. I promise, I'll stay away from him. Pinkie swear."

"Isn't a pinkie swear some girl thing?" How she had him fearing for her safety in one moment and then had him amused in the next was beyond him. "I don't know if that works in this situation but, I believe you'll keep your promise."

"I always keep my promises. Especially to really hot, brave, kind mechanics who take care of Lola." Kyla wrapped her arms around his neck and she leaned in, gently pressing against him. "Now, about this bruise on your jaw: maybe a kiss will make it better?" Her lips brushed across his skin and his fingers pressed into her hips.

Cooper grinned. "I think that's a start." She was still kissing him, her lips moving down to his neck now. "Ya know, they got me in the stomach and thigh, too. I think those need a kiss."

He heard her soft laugh as her hands moved to the bottom of his shirt and slid underneath. "Well, let's see what we can do about that."

Cooper groaned as she dropped down and her lips touched his stomach, leaving kisses along his skin. He glanced at the door, thankful that he had the forethought to lock it.

• • •

"So, are you going to tell me what's happening with you and Cooper? We haven't had a lot of time to talk."

That was Sarah, who was sitting on the bed while Kyla was getting ready. It was a week following the disaster at the 4th of July picnic. They had finally rescheduled their date, but between work and his sleeping over every night, they were inseparable. Unfortunately all they did was sleep, which was more than a bit annoying. Something always happened to get in the way of their finishing. But tonight was the night. Kyla was determined.

"Things are good. We've been getting to know each other better. I didn't think he'd want to talk but he does, especially about his dad."

Sarah nodded. "Yeah, he and his dad were tight. Even though I was a couple years younger than him and the guys, I would go to the hockey games and his dad was always there, cheering Cooper on."

Cooper had talked a lot about his hockey playing days in both high school and college. Hockey was why he had a slightly crooked nose, the victim of a hockey fight after checking someone into the boards. She sighed. "I really like him, Sarah."

Sarah rolled her eyes. "Yeah, no shit. I mean, not to say I told you so, but well, I told you so."

Kyla shot her a mock glare and then went back to yanking the hem of the dress.

"All that is going to do is show more cleavage up top. Now stop it before you ruin the damn thing. You look hot," her friend scolded.

Kyla's stomach did another roll, definitely a good one. "So, am I all put together?"

Sarah grinned. "If I were into girls, I'd be doing you right now." The two burst out laughing and made their way into the small kitchen area. Kyla grabbed a bottle of wine and poured them each a glass.

"To liquid courage." she toasted, clinking Sarah's glass.

Her phone buzzed and Sarah grabbed it, "Oh I bet it's Cooper! Let's see what he says." She was squealing, but when she read the text her eyes narrowed, "Um, Kyla, what the hell is this?"

Kyla felt frozen in place. Something in her gut told her that it was another text, another threat, something else to add to her nightmares.

Sarah read the first text aloud. *"I'm coming for you, whore. You won't get away from me."*

Kyla grabbed the phone from a stunned Sarah just as another came in.

"You heard me, bitch. I will cut you up and leave you to bleed. See you soon."

She wasn't sure how long she stood there staring at the phone as if it was going to bite her. She fought the urge to throw up, steadying herself with a hand to the wall.

"Kyla, you okay?"

She jumped when Sarah placed a hand on her arm. "Yeah, I'm fine. Fine." Her movement was robotic. She could tell from Sarah's pursed lips that she wasn't buying it. She felt bad, guilty even, for lying and decided in that moment to not close herself off with her new friend. She wasn't going down that road again.

Just then a knock came at the door and they both jumped a mile. Sarah knocked into one of the wine glasses and it crashed to the floor, shattering everywhere.

Kyla ran to grab a towel and the broom while Sarah let out a curse and turned to greet Cooper. "Kyla and you need to talk. Now."

Cooper stood there, his hand still on the door-knob, taking in the scene. "What the fuck?"

Kyla stopped when she heard Cooper, fidgeting where she stood. Sarah grabbed the items out of her hand. "Go, Kyla. You need to tell Cooper what just happened. I'll clean this up and lock up when I go."

She was nervous, her voice barely above a whisper. "Are you mad?"

Sarah's head jerked up. "No! Kyla, why would I be pissed at you? I'm mad about that." Her eyes hit the phone Kyla gripped in her hand. . "But I'm not mad at you. I will be, however, if you don't give it up and let Cooper know what is going on."

Cooper came unstuck from the doorway. "Come on. We got time to talk." He tugged at her hand and she grabbed her wrap and purse. It was then that she got a good look at what Cooper was wearing. A pair of black dress pants, something she'd never seen him in, but holy heck, he looked good. This was paired with what looked like black cowboy boots and a dark gray, button-down shirt. Cooper escorted her to his truck and as rounded the hood she noticed his thick, dark hair lift in the breeze. Once glance at the sky confirmed dark clouds forming in the distance.

"What is going on?" Cooper said as he stuck his key in the ignition. The muscle in his jaw ticked and she could hear his voice vibrating.

She didn't back down though, or give in. Not until she said her piece first. "You look nice, Cooper." She reached over and interlaced her fingers in his.

His eyes shot to their hands and then back up to her. "You look better than good, baby. I wanted to say it when I first saw you. Hell, I wanted to cancel our date and take care of things right there, but we had an audience and clearly something is going on." He lifted their hands and kissed hers. "Talk to me."

"I will. Can we drive though? I can talk while you drive and then, once we get there, hopefully it will be all out and I can be done with it. I don't want to re-hash it a hundred times."

"The club is ten minutes from here, if that. This sounds like it might take longer than that."

She sighed. "It likely will, but we can sit in the lot until I'm done."

Cooper paused a beat but then started the truck and pulled out of the lot. She waited until they were on the street to begin.

"I got a text message. Actually two, tonight. And this isn't the first time I've gotten them. They're threatening and they scare the heck out of me. My brother has been trying to take care of it, filing violations of the order of protection and whatnot, but Frank's lawyers keep getting it adjourned. Anyway, just before you got there, Sarah saw them. Or one of them. It freaked her out. Well, and me too. And she told me to tell you."

"You weren't going to?"

Kyla hesitated and sneaked a look at Cooper; his jaw was hard as he concentrated on the road. "I was, but I wouldn't have done it tonight. I didn't want to ruin anything. Every time we try to go out, something interrupts and we don't get to have some peace. So I would have told you, but. . ."

"When, Kyla? When would you have told me your asshole ex is making threatening calls, or texts, whatever, to you? When he showed up and had a knife to your throat? 'Cause at that point, if there was a knife to you, I honestly wouldn't care less whether this night happened or not. I'd prefer you to be breathing."

"Cooper. I get it. You're pissed. I should have told you."

"Damn fucking right! I get you want to do shit on your own and not rely on me but *this* is something you tell the person you're with. How would you have liked it if I kept shit to myself about Saybrook? I did that with Jackson and were you not pissed at me for keeping it quiet until I saw you? For not calling you right away and letting you know I was okay?"

She stared out the window and swallowed the lump in her throat. Cooper was right. She tugged her hand from his but had no sooner set it in her lap than Cooper grabbed it again. "Don't retreat from me, Kyla." His voice was low, almost a growl. "Now talk. What else is there that I need to know?"

Kyla closed her eyes and made a spur-of-the-moment decision she knew in her gut was the right thing to do.

"I used to come home from college, during breaks and in the summer, and I'd sing wherever they let me. Whether it was the local clubs, karaoke, whatever it was, I was there, singing. Usually with my guitar or using the club's piano. I had been home or about six months, debating going back to get my master's degree or not when I met Frank. He was a cop, which in my town was a big deal, ya know? Everyone loved him, respected him, and everywhere he went, people listened. I don't understand why. He was just a cop, albeit it a charismatic one. But now, looking back, that was all he was. His eyes were empty. How did I miss that?" Cooper squeezed her hand in silent support and she continued.

"At first things were good, but then the red flags started flying and things I should have caught early on, I ignored. He made comments about my weight, about what I ate, and was always getting angry when I was nice to his friends. Frank's behavior got more and more controlling—everyone saw it. Everyone but me. Because when Frank apologized, he always made it up to me and made promises about our future. I thought if I just gave him one more chance it would stop." She paused. This next part was never easy to talk about.

"The first time he hit me was eye opening. He'd been angry I'd gone without him to a club. When I got home he pushed me against the door, screaming at me. He grabbed my arm and threw me toward the couch and I stumbled in my heels. I was straightening up when he smacked me across the face. He looked sorry right away and begged for forgiveness, blaming his job and the stress, and me being so pretty and his fear of losing me." She glanced over at Cooper. "I forgave him, even though I knew I shouldn't. And then it happened again and again and I lost myself, Cooper. I didn't know what I'd become or where the old me had gone. I stopped singing and playing music. After awhile I shut myself off from my family and friends and had nothing left except Frank."

"Baby," Cooper whispered. "You don't have to talk about this."

If only she could take that out. "No, you have to know who I am dealing with—who we're dealing with," she corrected. She was surprised she wasn't crying. Usually the tears came, but she felt stronger somehow, sharing her burden with someone—a man— who cared about her and wanted to protect her, not smother her.

"My brother, Mike, is the one who finally got through to me. He'd been trying to find a way to get Frank out of my life and bring me back home, and he hit the jackpot when he heard Frank had a piece on the side. A few actually. Mike had a PI follow him to get the goods and then cornered me, showing me that not only was Frank destroying my life, he was fucking around on me. Frank was having a grand old time while he kept me caged in like an animal." She laughed, a hollow sound. "I can't believe what finally did it was the fact that he had women on the side, not the beatings he'd give me every other day."

Cooper turned into a parking lot and parked the truck. He reached over and released her seatbelt, pulling her across the seat. She tucked her face into his neck. "My brother and I came up with a plan. I was going to wait a week, slowly get the few things I absolutely needed and give them to Mike or leave it at my mom's. I kept up appearances with Frank and I swear to god it was the worst week of my life, but I could finally see the light at the end of the tunnel.

"It was a Friday, and Frank was supposed to be out. Mike came over to get me out of there once and for all, but Frank decided to come home early. He was beyond furious, tackling Mike to the ground and pounding on him relentlessly. I was screaming, running for the phone and dialing 911. I slipped in the blood that was splattered across the floor, Mike's blood. He wasn't moving. I was so distracted and thought he was dead. I didn't see Frank coming, but I felt it when he got there. His fist cut across his body and landed on my cheek, but instead of cowering down like I'd done in the past, something inside me snapped. I fought back, kicking, biting, scratching, screaming, anything to hurt him. It didn't matter anymore if I lived or died. At some point I grabbed the gun out of his holster. I told him to stop. I warned him, but he kept coming, taunting me." She stared into Cooper's gorgeous blue eyes swimming with some emotion she couldn't identify. "I shot him, Cooper. When the cops showed up we were all bleeding out on the ground. I thought it would be over, that he was dead. But he survived and in many ways, my nightmare had really only just begun."

Shaking, she recounted her long recovery in the hospital, trying to get Frank fired and arrested, and not being able to find work. Her town had been divided, not sure whose story to believe.

"When I left town, it was because Frank had been reinstated pending the final investigation, which was bogus in and of itself. I mean, it had been nearly a year and they were still asking questions." She rolled her eyes in disbelief. "He pulled me over, fucked with my head, cuffed me to the car and then left me in the rain. I had to leave. I needed a new start. And now … well, I'm here and he's found me."

Cooper didn't say anything for a long time, he just held her against him, his hands sliding along her spine. Finally his voice rumbled through her. "That fuck shows up, Kyla, I will kill him. I swear to Christ he will not lay a hand on you ever again."

She closed her eyes and burrowed closer. "You aren't mad I didn't tell you before?"

His hands were at the side of her face as he stared down at her. "No. Fuck, Kyla, I'm upset you didn't tell me earlier, but I'm not mad at you." His lips crushed down onto hers and he took her mouth, possessing it, possessing her. She drank him in, moaning. Her hips undulated on his lap. Cooper dragged his mouth from hers. "We'll get through this. We're a team, you and me. Okay?"

She nodded. "Can we go eat now?"

Cooper grinned. "Yeah, let's get you fed."

Chapter 11

Cooper opened his door and slid out of the truck. He turned back and took her hand, helping her out of the truck. "Christ, I got a look at you in the room but fuck, you're gonna give me a heart attack." His mouth was crushing hers again before she could respond, his tongue pushing into her mouth without even waiting for her lips to part on their own. This wasn't one of his soft and sweet kisses, this was hard and deep and he was happy to feel her giving as good as he was.

It was Kyla who pulled back slightly from the kiss. "So, you like it then. . ."

He smiled. "Yeah, babe, I like it."

Kyla laughed as he grabbed her hand, following him.

As the two approached The Warehouse, Cooper marveled at the renovation Sam had done with the place. Every time he came here, seeing the building and knowing what it had looked like before, it floored him. The building was located in the industrial section of the town overlooking the water. The front and sides of the building were a mix of brick with alternating clear and opaque windows. It was well lit, unlike the rest of the area, which was dotted with similar buildings, although they looked to be abandoned. Off in the distance Cooper could make out the length of the pier extending far into the water, the pier where he and Kyla had first kissed. He smiled at the memory and pulled Kyla closer, settling her against his side. Cooper nodded to the bouncer and they were let in.

"Where are we?" Kyla asked.

"The Warehouse. Sam owns the place. He comes around the garage quite a bit so you'll meet him eventually, I'm sure." Cooper pulled her through the crowd effortlessly, his wide shoulders creating a path for them. She watched as he greeted just about everyone they passed, usually with a first name. A waitress materialized out of thin air as they hit the hostess station.

"Cooper, sweetie, haven't seen you in forever, table for one I assume? My section okay? Maybe we can make it like last time, I'll serve you dinner and then we can go have a bit of fun upstairs."

He tugged on Kyla's hand and brought her to his side, "How 'bout no. Table for two. In the back."

Cooper felt Kyla's arm slide around his waist and he tried to hide his smile. He looked down and saw Kyla glaring at the waitress. He had to admit, he liked her a little bit possessive. Unfortunately, it didn't seem to have any effect, because while the women eyed each other, she continued with her irritating voice. "Like I said, call me some other time. When you aren't so occupied."

Kyla leaned forward and hissed. "Trust me, he'll be too occupied to be calling you again, ever. So I wouldn't wait by the phone."

The waitress sneered. "Oh, he'll call. I know what he likes and how he likes it. And he always comes back. You're just his latest piece of ass to blow through town."

Cooper went still, scary still. He stepped between the two, pushing the waitress back with his presence alone. "Get out of my woman's face, and lose my fucking number. Don't think I won't be telling Sam about this little stunt you've pulled."

"Cooper," the waitress started, but stopped when he held up his hand.

Kyla dropped her hand from his waist, lacing her fingers into his. The hostess and a manager arrived at that point and led them to their table. Once settled, Kyla reached for a menu and finally peeked over the top. Cooper was smiling at her. "I'll be occupied, huh?"

"Oh shut up, she was ... I mean, she said it to you in front of me! How rude was that? You seriously had to get with her? Do you guys look past the bitch part just to get laid?"

"Sometimes, depends on how hot the woman is," he replied, laughing as Kyla rolled her eyes. He reached out and tugged at her waist, dragging her across the rounded booth seat so she was against him. "It's hard to find the total package sometimes, but when we do, all other bitches, as you say, go out the window. Then we got only one thing in mind, with one woman." He dropped a hand to her thigh, his fingers gliding over her skin to the hem of her skirt.

She watched his fingers go higher and she caught her breath. "That's good to know you're in the minority. Most guys are dogs, cheaters, getting all tripped up by the women around them, and unable to hold steady." Her tone was matter of fact.

Cooper reached for her hand and entwined his fingers with hers. He knew a lot of women had this issue, not feeling that they could trust the man they were with. Cooper knew that he would have an uphill battle, trying to convince her otherwise, but he would fight to prove her wrong. He regarded her with a thoughtful expression on his face. He reached out for her hand and squeezed, "I'm not, Kyla. I promise you. I'm sorry that's been your experience, but I will not do that."

"Can I get you something to drink to start with?"

Her head snapped up at the interruption and Cooper chuckled. "Kyla, what do you want to drink?"

"Beer is fine. And a glass of ice water, please, with lemon."

Cooper smiled at the waitress. "Two beers, ice water with lemon and how 'bout two of the burger specials with the waffle fries. Sound good, babe?"

"Sure, um, can I have my burger medium well, please? And no tomato? Thanks." Kyla glanced at Cooper, "I hate tomatoes. I like tomato sauce, but I hate actual tomatoes."

Cooper laughed as his hand moved over her knee, his fingers trailing lightly over her skin. "Important information to know. I'll remember that."

"So, your friend Sam, he owns the place? Does this give Felicia's place competition?"

"No, not really. It's only open Thursday through Saturday and for the occasional special event. Sam does security work that he doesn't talk much about. It takes him out of the country on occasion." Cooper's hand was all the way at the top of her thigh now, his fingers splayed across and dipping into her inner thigh. His fingers grazed the edge of her panties and she nearly came right there. His touch was a torture she never wanted to end.

"Cooper."

With his other hand Cooper grabbed hers and pressed it on his very hard erection. Hearing the hitch in her throat, he ducked his head and kissed her. The two were so engrossed with each other, they didn't notice the drinks arriving. Thankfully the wait staff was discreet, and the dark corner gave them much needed privacy.

"I need to breathe," Kyla murmured against his lips and pulled back. She squeezed the hand she held lightly over his jeans and smiled when he groaned. She picked up her beer and took a pull, watching as Cooper removed his hand from under her dress.

"Eat fast. I'm taking you home tonight."

When the food arrived she was happy they could talk casually and laugh at each other's jokes. She learned more about him as he told her stories of growing up in Ashten Falls with Tommy, Roger, Sam, Phil, Derek, and Sarah. She told him about her brother and what he did for a living. Kyla also told Cooper about her own college experience and her friends, and how she wanted to teach music, even just lessons someday, because that was her first love.

"So you're a musician and you're working in my garage? Seriously?"

"Well, I mentioned to Phil some things for the music store…" she trailed off, feeling suddenly shy.

Cooper nudged her thigh with his. "And I think they're great. Maybe this week you can see what kind of magic you can get going over there. The shop is pretty well organized and with the computer and phones networked, you can still do shop work from Music & Motors."

Her face lit up. "I take it you like that idea?"

"Hell yeah!" she enthused. She leaned in and kissed his cheek before taking a drink of water.

When they were finished Cooper got the check and paid, and finally stood. "All right, come on, we are going home." He was tugging her out of the booth when his phone rang.

"Shit," he muttered. "Hello? Fuck, are you kidding me? Well go check it out. I'm busy … fuck, damn. All right, I will stop by on my way home. Yeah. Later." He hung up and looked down at Kyla. "I gotta make a stop at the record store, the alarm is acting up again. Just be a minute. Then I want to get a look at what you got on underneath that dress for me."

The two climbed into Cooper's truck and motored over to the record store.

...

"I'll be right back," Cooper said as he headed through the hanging beads to reach his office at Music & Motors.

She nodded and moved restlessly toward the bins, giving them a cursory glance, before making her way to the piano. A quick check down the hall confirmed Cooper had disappeared and she was alone to enjoy the feel of her fingers running over the keys. It didn't take her long to get into *"The Heart Asks Pleasure First"* from *The Piano* soundtrack. Kyla was lost in the song. It wasn't until she played the last note that she looked up from the keys to see Cooper, leaning against the doorjamb. She squirmed under his gaze. "Sorry, I, uh, thought you were still in the office."

His eyes didn't leave her as he moved into her personal space. "That was freaking amazing."

She leaned her forehead against his, blushing. "Thanks."

He glanced around the space, still holding her. "Monday, I want you here."

At the confusion on her face, Cooper kept right on talking. "My dad loved this place. He and Steve, the terrible twosome people called them. Steve opened the bookstore and dad … well dad wanted to be all about the music. He wasn't the best businessman, but it stayed afloat, I sometimes think out of sheer willpower. When I came back from college after he died, everyone thought I'd sell it since I had bought the garage. But I couldn't."

When he closed his eyes, she kissed him softly. "You miss him. If you ever want to talk about him, I'm here."

"I might take you up on that sometime. Seeing as your car just kinda died right outside of town maybe, *maybe* it was my dad bringing me an angel. I've been struggling with whether to sell or just close it up. But seeing you at that piano, your fingers dancing over the keys and looking as relaxed and happy as I've ever seen you, I can't sell it now."

"Coop, this isn't a decision to make lightly. Just because I like it and want to help doesn't mean it will be a money-making success."

"Hey, I was ready to give up on this place. It wasn't making money, and I had no idea how to bring it to the 21st century and turn a profit. Now I can see just what it needs to be." His hand reached out and cupped her chin. "I still want to sell CDs and some vinyl, keep the video game area 'cause the guys and I like to chill there and so do some of the local kids, but the rest of it … Kyla, you could offer lessons, have a weekly open mic night for local talent, including you. With the school board cutting funding for most of the music programs at the school, we could fill that void and bring something good to town." His dark blue eyes were intent on her, "You think you can get on board with this?"

She bit her lip. This was a huge deal. Cooper was asking her to basically run the music store and come up with a concept to make a profit. She had ideas. A ton of ideas. But agreeing to this meant investing time and energy, and more importantly it meant staying. Instead of being terrified, Kyla was surprised at the excitement coursing inside of her. She'd found a place, finally. She had found a place where she could be herself and people loved her for it. Her past didn't brand her. She could do good here, even if it was just bringing music to those who wanted lessons or being a good friend.

She raised her eyes to his and smiled hugely. "Yes. Abso-freakin-lutely, Cooper."

Her eyes flicked over to the door, to the couch behind them, and then back to Cooper . "How well do the locks work in this place?"

Instead of answering, Cooper lifted Kyla in his arms, his mouth coming down on hers. She wrapped her legs around his waist, laughing against his lips as he growled, carrying her over to the couch. He bent slightly and dropped her onto the cushion, but their connection wasn't severed for long. He was on top of her in an instant and Kyla didn't hesitate before her hands were tugging his shirt out of his pants.

His hands roamed over her torso down to the hem of her dress. He pushed it up to her stomach, his eyes going wide as he caught a glimpse of her black lace panties. "Babe," he murmured, his fingers grazing over the thin fabric. "They look so much better on you than sticking out of your bag."

She shifted, lifting her hips to pull the dress up over her head, and dropped it on the floor next to her. Kyla wanted Cooper to see her, all of her, and for once she wasn't going to be shy about it.

All he could do was stare, his eyes covering every inch of her until she placed her hands at the waistband of his pants. He lifted off of her, grasping his shirt to pull it off and drop it on top of her dress. His hands slid over her breasts and around her back, unclasping her bra. His mouth covered a hardening nipple while his thumb stroked the other.

Her back arched, her head tilting back into the cushion. Her hands moved to his pants and she finished unbuttoning them, sliding her hand inside and along his dick. He was hard—she knew he was ready and she was getting close just from his mouth and tongue.

"Cooper, please," she begged.

At her plea Cooper's hand moved to her panties and snaked inside, cupping her mound. "You're already wet for me, baby. Love that." His fingers breezed over her wet folds and he slid one inside and then a second, her hips lifting up to meet his thrusts.

She felt the oncoming wave as it crashed into her and she held on to Cooper, her arms and legs wrapped tightly around him. She felt her bones melting into the couch when he whispered against her ear, "I need to be inside right now, Kyla."

"Yes, Cooper, now." Her legs dropped from his waist and she eagerly pushed his pants and boxers down. His fingers were peeling her panties down her legs when it happened.

There was a loud banging on the door and a muffled voice. "Cooper! Jesus, where you been, man?"

"You have got to be fucking kidding me," he groaned, his forehead leaning down against hers as the banging on the door increased. His fingers continued to press into her wet folds. "Whoever it is, I'm shooting them in the head. I don't care if it's Phil."

She could hear the door handle jiggling, "Cooper, get off!" and in a panicked whisper, she added, "I need my clothes unless you want whoever it is seeing me naked!" She was pulling at her underwear, and nabbed her bra.

He grabbed the blanket from the back of the couch and covered her up. "Relax, babe. Let me handle this." He was already off of her, tugging his pants up, but not before she got a good look at what he had been about to offer.

Dragging her eyes from his crotch to his face, her tone dead serious, she said, "Shoot them in the head. You have my permission."

"You got it." He kissed her forehead and pulled his shirt on, the top button of his pants left unbuttoned. Kyla was off the couch, holding the blanket to her front as she wiggled her dress over her head. She was pulling it over her hips when the door swung open.

A man walked inside and glanced between the two of them. "Oh fuck, Cooper. Sorry, but this is important." He looked sheepish as he caught Kyla's eyes. "You must be Kyla. Nice to finally meet you. I'm Sam."

"Hi, Sam." Kyla pulled her dress into place and tossed the blanket on the couch. "Nice to, uh, meet you too."

Cooper let out a growl. "Is this a social call? What do you need?"

"Word is that Jackson is looking for you. I figured if he needs to talk to you, no way am I letting you go alone, or have him find you alone." His eyes flicked to Kyla. "No offense, Kyla."

She shook her head, "None taken. I'm glad you guys have each other's back." She moved over to Cooper. "Go see what Jackson wants. I'll be in my room. Please call me, or have someone call me, if you don't come home tonight."

His body stiffened and Kyla started to shrink away, wondering what she said wrong. He pulled her back before she was out of arm's reach. "That motel is not your home. I'll be taking you home soon enough."

She blinked at him, not sure what to say. Thankfully she didn't have to think about it too much since Cooper was pulling her in for a heart-stopping kiss. "Let's get you next door so I can get back as soon as possible."

• • •

Kyla was in that place between asleep and awake when she heard a rustling and soft swoosh as something hit the floor. The covers moved back and when she felt the bed move, her eyes flew open, panicking as her legs kicked out. "No, no, no, no, NO!" she protested, her voice rising at each word. Her throat and chest constricted with fear. Frank had found her. He was going to kill her. She'd be gone forever and. . .

Her back slammed into a hard chest and a finger slid along her cheek. "Relax. It's me," he ordered, his voice a low rumble.

"Cooper," she breathed, unable to hide her relief before she remembered what happened just a few hours earlier. Her body tensed and she tried to move away.

He circled her waist and pulled her against him, leaning his head down, burying his face in her hair. "Just relax, take a deep breath." She felt his lips brush against her ear and neck.

"Is everything okay?" She didn't know why she was whispering, but it seemed Cooper was wired and she didn't want to increase the tension.

"Yeah. It's fine. Jackson had some information. He hinted that the coroner who fucked up Cheryl's autopsy is starting to drink. A lot. Jackson thinks the man might be close to cracking and wanted us to be aware." He kissed her forehead. "I was only gone a couple hours and I missed you like crazy."

"I missed you, too." She snuggled into him and wrapped her arm over his stomach as she pressed her cheek to his chest. "You help chase away the dark, Cooper. I hope this feeling never goes away."

His hand at her back stilled before lifting her up farther, his face mere centimeters from hers. "Forever. It's forever." He followed his own word with a toe-curling kiss.

Kyla released the tension in her body and relaxed against him. Soon the feelings she felt earlier in the music store, the tingling at her core, began to overtake her once again.

Cooper groaned, his hips lifting just a touch into her hand. "Fuck, Ky." Kyla took that as her cue and moved her fingers to the waistband of his boxers and pulled down, releasing his now hardened erection. She wrapped her fingers around its width while her thumb swiped the tip. She ducked her head down, intent on getting her mouth around his cock when suddenly her body was lifted in the air and she was turned around. Kyla had already gotten wet, just from touching Cooper, so when his tongue slid over her slick heat she nearly lost her mind.

Kyla was in mid-moan when her mouth covered him and worked him over. One of Cooper's arms was tight over her hips, holding her in place though her body was desperate to move against his mouth. He was teasing her with his tongue and mouth and she was doing the same. They were each driving the other to the edge only to back away slightly before starting again. Cooper's other hand slid up her tummy and to her sensitive nipples, pinching and rubbing it with his thumb and forefinger. His mouth moved away just a touch and Kyla moaned around his cock in protest.

"I'm gonna come baby and I know you're close. Let it go when you're ready." Kyla didn't know whether to laugh or cry in joy at his comment. How many men wanted to make sure their woman got off? How many put them first before their own pleasure? From Kyla's experiences, which were limited, and her friends talking, it wasn't many.

Suddenly Cooper's hand was gone from her breast and he pinched her clit just as he pushed two fingers deep inside her. Kyla came with a cry, though the sound was muffled. She felt Cooper's body tense but before he found his release, he was pulling her up his body and flipping her over on her back.

"Cooper." She moaned in protest.

She squirmed as Cooper's hands slid down her spine and inside her panties.

"I love it when you say my name." His hand moved and one finger slide inside her. He swiped his thumb across her sensitive spot before applying slight pressure.

Kyla ground out a moan as her hips lifted up towards his hand.

"Don't stop," she begged.

"One minute, Ky." He murmured and rolled away from her. He reached for his pants and grabbed a condom from the pocket. He tore it open, rolling it on before covering her body with his once more. He teased her entrance with his cock. Slowly he pushed inside, his eyes locked on hers until he was settled deep inside her. His thrusts began slow but soon they were at a fevered pitch. Kyla was keeping up with him, her nails sliding down the skin of his back. He arched his back when he felt her pussy clench around his cock as she came again. He buried his face in her neck as his own climax overtook him.

"Fuck, baby. Jesus H. Christ." Cooper's fingers grazed over Kyla's sensitive clit and she felt another spasm, though smaller, rock through her. Cooper chuckled and sat up enough to drag her against him. "My own personal firecracker."

Kyla sighed. "Mmhhmm. All for you Cooper. Just for you."

She could feel his heartbeat slowing as her head rested on his chest. Cooper tugged the blankets over them and tucked Kyla against his side. "Tomorrow night I want you in my house, in my bed, no more of this sleeping here then having to leave to go shower and change and come back. Yeah?"

Kyla moved her eyes to his, glazed over from the unbelievable orgasms he'd just given her and could only nod. She had tried to scowl at him when he flashed his knowing grin but it didn't last when he muttered "So fucking cute" and kissed her, again. "Pack your bags. We'll bring it over after work."

Kyla's mind whirled. Moving in with him? She hadn't known him that long, but it made sense. She more than liked him and wanted to be with him as much as possible. But what if they didn't mesh well? What if he was a slob and couldn't handle her need to organize things? What if he regretted asking her to move in? But the other voice inside Kyla was just as loud. What if he didn't regret asking her? What if it all worked out? She was quiet for a minute as she made her decision.

"I'll move in with you, Cooper. For now. But it's just temporary until we figure out this stuff with the text messages. And I find an apartment. We're still new and I don't want to wreck this."

Cooper shook his head. "We won't wreck anything as long as we communicate. And why waste your money on an apartment? I have a big house, we're together, and it's ridiculous to keep two places. And you're paying for this one with money you could use for your car. Or some more pretty underwear."

Kyla rolled her eyes. "Cooper, I won't make any promises other than tomorrow I will pack my bags and go to your house. For how long, I'm not sure. We'll just have to see how things go. All right?" She turned so Cooper's chest was pressed into her back. His arm wrapped around her front. She could definitely get used to feeling this warm and content.

"You got a deal," Cooper murmured into her hair.

Kyla smiled as she drifted off into sleep. She was in bed with her man who was holding her close after each of them having some pretty amazing orgasms. What more could she want?

Chapter 12

The store was buzzing with people perusing the music. A few others were on the couch watching some sports game on television. One of her new students was practicing the piano on the stage, which now had a curtain that she and Maggie had made. It was an awesome silvery gray with a sheer black panel over it. They had sewn long lines of shimmery, dark red and silver beading at random spots, which made it glitter when the light hit it.

Another group was just behind the big picture window in the parking lot at the dance block. It was really just a large, chalked-off square, full of design and colors. She let the kids who started hanging around do it and when it rained they got to do it again, which they loved. One of Cooper's friends had rewired the speakers so that whatever was playing inside, also played outside, though not too loudly since the town didn't want a party going on out there at all hours of the day and night.

Over the past week, Kyla had rearranged the flow in the music store, straightening the display cases and creating sections in the store. The television area remained relatively the same, it was just cleaner. But the CDs, records, tapes and other recordings were all arranged neatly, and in alphabetical order, in the front, just to the right of the door. She convinced Cooper to build a small stage along the left side of the store. That had been fun, watching Cooper and his friends arguing over how to get it done. Jack was all about precise measurements. Sam said he was just there for the beer. And Cooper wanted it done so he could get to more pressing matters, like finding out what she was wearing under the tight summer dress she was wearing. After hours of sawing and nailing and bickering among the boys, the stage was done. And, after everyone left and the door was locked, Cooper found out exactly what Kyla was, or wasn't, wearing.

Kyla was also busy arranging, advertising, and overseeing piano and voice lessons, among others, though those seemed to be the most popular. Cooper meanwhile, kept busy with the garage.

Cooper had asked her over breakfast this morning where the increase in profit was going to come from since it was becoming a hang-out, in his eyes, but the lessons were bringing in some money and a bunch of parents placed orders for equipment. Starting in September, Kyla planned a Friday night open mic night, which would bring business not only to Music & Motors but to the other stores nearby as well.

Kyla glanced up as Sarah walked in and heard her whistle. "Nice! I love what you've done with the place. I would have been here sooner but between the diner and Felicia giving me extra shifts, I've been dead tired."

Kyla tilted her head to the side, "Why are you working so much lately?"

"I've got something I'm saving up for and I'd like to get it sooner rather than later. I don't want to give too much away, but I'll fill you in when I can. How are things with you, here and at home?"

Kyla thought it was strange, how secretive Sarah was being, but she let it go. For now. She moved from behind the counter and the two settled in some comfortable chairs in a corner by the stage. "Things are good. It's an adjustment, living with Cooper and working with him, but he's so busy with the garage and with me working over here most of the day, we rarely run into each other until it's time to go home." She curled one of her legs underneath her. "He snores a little, but it's a cute kind of snoring. And he hasn't quite gotten the hang of putting the seat down when he's done, which has put him in the doghouse when, at two in the morning, I've almost fallen in to the toilet. But other than that, we seem to be making it work."

"Is this going to be long-term?"

Kyla chuckled. "You ask that question a lot."

"Well, I want to know if my new best friend is going to be sticking around town or if she is going to leave me high and dry."

"I thought Maggie was your best friend," Kyla teased.

"You're such a jerk. You *both* are my best friends, all right? Geesh! Now, would you please answer my question?"

Kyla sighed but was still smiling when she spoke, lowering her voice, "We haven't talked about long term really. Cooper wants me to stay, to move in for good, but I told him this was only until things with Frank and the text messages get sorted. I told him that then we'd talk. But to be honest, and I know I've only known him a short while, I can't imagine *not* being with him. So, I don't know for sure, but I do know that I like where I am and could see myself here, on a more permanent basis."

Sarah squealed and practically jumped out of the chair. "I knew it! And once again, I told you so. I have to go tell Maggie. And we need to go out and celebrate soon. Call you later!"

And like the tornado of energy Sarah could be, she blew out the door, likely off to fill in Maggie, and Justin, Rose, Steve and whoever else she ran into, what Kyla said. But since it was the truth, Kyla didn't mind.

...

Cooper was on his back and rolling out from underneath a truck when he heard someone come banging through the door between the office and garage.

"Phil, I thought you were leaving for the day or something? Forget something?"

The shadow he saw as he pulled out from underneath the car was definitely not Phil and as his eyes traveled up the body he had been getting used to looking at they stopped at the hem of her skirt, a smile spreading across his face. "I wasn't expecting you today. I figured you'd be tied up at Music & Motors most of the day." His gaze slid over her body, taking her in. "You're giving me a great view, babe."

Kyla placed a hand on her hip and hitched it out to the side slightly. She toed the under car roller he was laying on. "You got a minute?"

Cooper pushed himself up and stood. He was soon a breath away from her, wrapping her into a tight hug. "For you I always have a minute." Cooper pressed his mouth to hers his tongue pushing in to dance with hers. Kyla's arms wrapped around his back and she fisted his shirt in his hands, pressing her body tight to his.

Cooper leaned back, his eyes searching her face. "Everything okay?"

"Everything is great. I just wanted to come over and. . ." she trailed off, her hands drifting to the top of his jeans. She slipped her fingers insider and tugged his hips closer.

Cooper's eyes flared as Kyla licked her lips. Cooper tilted his head to the side as his fingers touched the skin of her thigh and skimmed higher.

Cooper's grip tightened and he bent down, his lips pressing into hers and kissing her sweet and soft. He smiled against her lips as they parted.

He heard her breath hitch as he kissed her. God she felt so damn good against him like that. "Aren't you worried about someone walking in us?"

Kyla's hand pushed up his shirt, and kissed the skin of his chest when he finally obliged and tossed it on the floor. She lifted her head, her eyes mischievous as she responded, "Nope."

Cooper's head fell back, a low growl in his throat as her tongue and lips were driving him wild. He moved his hands to her skirt as she worked, unsnapping the buckle and letting it fall to the floor. Cooper's thumbs hooked into her panties and they soon followed her skirt. His arms wrapped around her waist and he lifted her up. Kyla held on tight as he moved to the bench in the back. One hand moved to the wall, slamming into the button there.

Cooper's fingers feathered over her center even as the garage door banged shut. Kyla's hips surged forward.

"Fuck baby, you're already wet for me." As his mouth touched hers he worked his jeans down with one hand, the other teasing across her hardened nipples. Once his jeans were down he pressed forward, his erection teasing her entrance. "I need you Kyla. I didn't know it until I met you, but I have always needed just *you*." Kyla's heart melted at his words but before she could respond Cooper surged into her.

Kyla's fingernails dug into his shoulder as he thrust inside of her, one hand reaching to hang onto the edge of the table behind her. Cooper stayed inside of her for a beat, staring into her eyes as her body adjusted to the intrusion. He watched her closely. Cooper didn't want to miss any of her reactions.

"This is going to be fast and hard baby. We'll do slow and sweet later if that's okay with you."

Kyla's lips parted at his words. Cooper pulled out and Kyla moaned, but he wasn't gone for long. He surged back into her, his arm holding her around her waist, her legs wrapped around his waist. Over and over he took her to the brink, leading her there but pulling back just as she was about to crash over the edge.

"Cooper. Please."

Cooper groaned as Kyla ground her hips against him. "Come baby. Take me there with you."

Kyla let herself go, falling over the edge and crying out his name. Her pussy clenched and she felt Cooper thrust into her heat one more time before groaning out his release. They were both panting when Kyla's arms convulsed around him and she giggled.

Cooper kissed her shoulder and lifted his head. "Something funny?"

"Yeah." Kyla kissed him on the cheek. "I thought most businesses had a strict 'no banging the employees' rule." She was teasing. "Or at the very least, a 'no banging the employees' in the work area.

Cooper grinned. "I'm not most businesses." He burrowed his face into her neck before setting her down. "Though maybe next time, we do this in the office. I like a bit of variety." He set her down on the floor and they both began picking up their clothes.

Kyla kissed him on the cheek, her lips soft against his cheek. She had that just fucked look that made Cooper want to take her again and again. She was beautiful and she was his. He felt like the luckiest man on earth.

• • •

The frenzied sex in the garage was the best Cooper had ever experienced and that was saying something. But he lamented the lack of time afterward, which was strange since he was the one usually buckling up by now and trying to get the hell out. He was still hard inside her after they both came, and he wanted more. Cooper could tell by her glazed look she did, too. He groaned as she leaned into him and slid her hand down between them.

"That was sweet, so fucking sweet," he murmured into her ear as his fingers danced along her spine.

All he heard in response was a soft moan and her arms sliding back up and around his neck. Kyla was kissing along his neck and shoulders. He leaned back just a touch and lifted his eyes to hers.

Her arms tightened around him and she brushed her lips against his before burying her head in his neck. "So, lots of different ways, huh?"

His head bent and he whispered against her ear, "Yeah, lots and lots of different ways. We're going to be seriously exploring this. You going to be okay with that?"

"Yeah, I'm more than okay with that."

He kissed her neck and then lifted his head. "Probably should get you dressed, but I like having my hands on your skin."

"I like it, too." Kyla lifted her head, a mischievous smile on her face, then that smile suddenly died. "Fuck," she squealed and scrambled to get dressed.

Cooper's brows snapped together as he watched her turn frantic. "Kyla, what the hell?"

"Someone's here! Oh crap. Freakin-A. Hurry up!"

Kyla yanked up her panties and skirt, running her hands through her hair.

"You have *got* to be kidding me," he growled, snatching his shirt from the hood of the car and pulling it on. "Go out the back door." He nodded to it but stopped her before she could leave. "I'll make it up to you, tenfold. That I can promise you."

Winking, he slapped her ass. She shot him a mock glare and he chuckled, watching her hurry off. Cooper buckled his pants and ran a hand through his hair as Jackson banged on the door separating the garage and office.

"Customer service sucks when Kyla isn't around. Where is she?"

"Fuck you, Jackson!" he hollered back, but he couldn't hide the grin on his face as he went see what the cop wanted.

∙ ∙ ∙

Once Kyla cleared the back door she jogged back to the music store, straightening her clothes and fixing her hair as she went. She took some time in the office, trying to gain some semblance of composure, but she couldn't hide the grin on her face or the state of her hair.

Cooper walked in while she was at the counter ringing up a sale. One minute she was joking with customers, the next she saw his molten steel eyes on her as he leaned against the wall, and her body responded instantly. She locked the door behind the last customer a half hour later and stopped mid-turn when she felt two arms slide around her waist.

"I like watching you work. Didn't much like that old guy staring down your top, though." He slid one hand up and snagged the front of her tag at her cleavage, the other moved underneath her shirt.

"Cooper. . ." she started, not wanting to get into an argument when what she really wanted to get into was their bed and his pants, though not necessarily in that order.

"I'm just telling you how it is. If he wasn't a hundred and twenty five years old, I might have had to take him out, but I figured a guy at his age needs the excitement so I let him have it." Cooper chuckled as Kyla smacked him lightly in what he assumed was some sort of admonishment. "But in all seriousness, it doesn't bother me, not anymore because I've evolved, remember, and I also trust you completely. .

His hand moved higher, his thumb stroking over her bra-encased nipple. "Besides, after moving in together, I'm pretty sure the message has been received that you're taken and everyone knows I do not share. Ever."

She should yell at him, lose her temper, and give him a piece of her mind. But she couldn't with his thumb still working over her hardening nipple and his other hand sliding up the front of her skirt.

"Coop, I would never *let* another man touch me. But so we're clear, the same should go for you. Don't make me get into a catfight with some random bitch at a bar or, well, anywhere."

He bent down and kissed her smiling lips. "You got it. You're mine, baby, but I'm yours, too. Every inch of me." His lips moved to her jaw and kissed down her throat. "Now let me show you how a gentleman does things."

She snorted but tightened her hands around him. "Gentleman. Now *that's* funny seeing as you've got one hand down my skirt and the other up my shirt. In my workplace no less."

"I'm a different kind of gentleman." The words were murmured against her skin and she shivered from the vibration. His hand was over her panties, his fingers feather light as her hips pushed forward. She moaned, needing more. "He licked his tongue along her neck, sucking lightly at her skin. "Let's go home."

• • •

Kyla walked along the beach and sighed. She was relaxed, sated, after hours of being in Cooper's arms. When he'd had to go back to the garage, she'd decided to head down to the beach. Kyla strolled on the beach and let the cool water lap over her toes. She kept walking until she reached the pier, her mind busy with thoughts.

Looking back at the last six weeks, Kyla couldn't believe all she'd been through. Even with her Mustang Lola, breaking down, most of what happened to her had been good. She found a job she loved and in finding that job, she got to know great people. Heck, she even made friends. Her life was starting over and she was loving every minute of it. Especially those minutes that involved Cooper. He understood her and accepted her for who she was. He didn't judge her for her past, and he didn't treat her like she was a piece of a glass because of it. It was a normal relationship. Or at least what she thought a normal relationship was supposed to be.

She noted a few people at the far end of the structure, but otherwise the beach was quiet. Maybe she could find a perfect shell, a memento of this perfect evening in her life, among the items the ocean had churned up. She walked into the surf, shivering as the cool water hit her lower legs. Crouching down, she reached into the sand to pull a white object from it.

As cheesy as it was, she decided to give it to Cooper. Maybe he could find a place in his house for it. She spun around to head back up the beach but only found time enough to scream once and raise her arm to deflect the blow from the object coming toward her. She was only partially successful as she felt the object smack the side of her head. It was the last thing she knew as she lost consciousness, crumpling to the ground with the cold water folding over her.

Chapter 13

Cooper willed himself to stay awake despite the exhaustion he felt. It had been the longest day of his life. When he got to the hospital and saw her, Tommy had to hold him back from bursting into the emergency room. Tommy said they had to get her stabilized and cleaned up. Between the water, sand, and blood, she'd been a mess. When the doctor finally let Cooper in and he saw Kyla's bloody clothes on the floor, the bruises on her face, and the bandage on her forehead, he felt his heart skip a beat. He wanted to drag Kyla out of there and take her home, defend her to the death if he had to. Kyla had wormed her way into his heart and Cooper knew, that he would never let her go. But the possibility of her going, of her being taken from him, it hit home and scared the fuck out of him.

"Kyla. Kyla, you have to wake up. Come back to me, baby." Cooper heard his voice crack as he spoke. He'd been sitting there for hours, waiting impatiently for her to open her eyes. He wouldn't leave her side, he wouldn't let go of her hand. He needed to feel that connection, their connection.

He felt her fingers move, squeezing his gently. Her head moved to the side and she groaned. "Kyla, baby, that's it. Wake up and look at me. Let me see those beautiful eyes." Her eyes fluttered open and he smiled for the first time since he'd gotten the call about her accident.

"Cooper?" Her voice was raspy. "What happened?" Her legs moved under the blanket as she tried to lift herself up.

"No, Kyla. Just don't move, all right. You were on the beach, remember? You got hurt. We're at the hospital now. You've been out of it for awhile." Almost 24 hours. Cooper's jaw clenched. It had been the worst 24 hours of his life in fact, praying Kyla would wake up and come back to him.

"Oh yeah," she murmured. "Am I okay?" Cooper smoothed some hair from her forehead, careful of the bandage that now covered a large portion of it. "You're fine. Just a bump on the head. The doctors wanted to keep an eye on you. But we can talk about that later. Go back to sleep, doll. I'll be here when you wake up." He hesitated, as if he didn't want to give her any more news, then finally blurted out, "Ky, I called Mike. He's coming up here. He's worried about you."

Kyla tried to sit up again. "Mike's coming? When?" She trained her now wild eyes on Cooper. "Cooper, I don't think this is a good time for a family reunion. He's had to deal with enough of my crap and he got hurt by Frank already. He doesn't need this."

"I called him when I found out the ambulance brought you in. He's your brother and deserves to know what is going. You may think you need to protect him from Frank, but he sees it as his job to protect you, his little sister." Cooper took her hand in his and kissed her palm. "He's coming, Kyla. There isn't any stopping it. You're probably lucky he was able to convince your mom to stay home until he got here and assessed the situation."

"Mom knows?" she asked.

"Yeah. She's been calling me every three minutes to check on you. She seems really cool. I'm just sorry the first time I got to talk to her was to tell her that her daughter had been admitted to the hospital."

They tabled the discussion as a nurse and doctor walked into the room to check Kyla over. They wanted her to stay one more night, and then, they would need her to go to home with someone so they could keep an eye on her.

"That won't be a problem, doc." Cooper spoke up. "We live together and I'm not going to let her out of my sight."

"Cooper, I'm staying at your place, but you don't have to take care of me. I can go back to the motel or stay with Sarah. You have work and the thing with Jackson. I'm not your responsibility."

It took all of Cooper's will power to not respond to Kyla. Instead, he waited until the doctor and nurse left. He carefully laid down on the bed next to her.

"Cooper, what are you doing? I don't think the hospital allows visitors to sleep with patients."

"I don't care what the hospital policy is, Kyla. I need you to listen to me." Kyla's mouth closed and she waited for Cooper to continue. "I get that you don't want to be a burden. I get that you want to be independent and be your own person. And I'd never try to change you, or force you to do something you don't want to do. But you have to understand, Kyla, it is my responsibility to take care of you. It always will be. And I wouldn't have it any other way. Wanting to protect you, to make sure you're safe and loved, that isn't a bad thing and it doesn't mean you're giving anything up by letting me do that."

"But Cooper, we just started this and it's all so much. I don't want you to regret this or think I'm a pain in the ass with a bunch of drama following her."

He shook his head. "Enough, Kyla. I don't think that, and I won't ever. You're right, we haven't known each other long, but I can tell you that I've wanted you since the moment I saw you and that hasn't changed. In fact, that feeling has just grown. Now, you're not going back to the motel or staying with Sarah. You're staying at home, with me." He kissed her lightly and then smiled. "And of course, if you want to take care of me, in whatever way you can, I'm all for that."

Kyla laughed softly. "All right, Cooper. If we can take care of each other, be each other's responsibilities, and protect each other, well then, I'm on board with that."

At that point the nurse came in but didn't say a word about Kyla being snuggled up with her man in the hospital bed. Instead she headed for the IV stand and injected something into her IV. In matter of minutes Kyla drifted off to sleep. Cooper remained at her side, dozing off with his woman in his arms.

•••

Sometime in the night Kyla woke up again, her eyes adjusting to the dark. She pulled herself up a bit on the bed, pressing her hand against the large bandage on her forehead. She turned in Cooper's arms and snuggled against him.

"Cooper." She kissed his jaw, a light touch but one that had him stirring.

"Right here, babe. You need something?"

"Yeah, you. And I want you to tell me what happened."

Cooper lay facing her, stroking her cheek with his finger. "Scared the hell out of me when Tommy called. A few fishermen were walking down the pier, saw someone go after you, and heard you scream. Whoever did it pushed you into the water and you weren't' moving. One of the guys called 911, another dropped his gear and jumped off the pier to get to you. If they'd backtracked on the pier and then took the hill down to the beach, you'd have drowned before they could pull you out." His voice was rough, his emotions laid bare. "Tommy and his partner were first on the scene. He called me while he was working on you and told me to get to the hospital and to call your family. Jesus, Kyla, I thought you would be gone when I got here."

She tried to blink back the tears but failed as they began spilling over. "I'm sorry." She knew it was an odd thing to say, but she felt badly for making him worry.

"Don't be sorry. You didn't do anything. Just the thought of losing you … it was not a good thought." Cooper kissed her nose and settled back. "Whoever did this, they hit you with a piece of driftwood. It was found down the beach, your blood all over it. They didn't find who it was; they did trail some tracks in the sand and the cops are still looking. Jackson is heading the investigation." He started to shake his head as Kyla narrowed his eyes. "No, it's okay. He seems to like you and wants to nail the fucker who did this to the wall. And more power to him, I say."

"But he hit you." Maybe he could forgive, but she couldn't forget the bruises he came back with the day at the diner.

"Jackson has to do his job, and that day he had to send a message for someone. He did, we tussled, and I gave as good, if not better, than I got. But all that shit is being put on hold until we find this asshole."

Kyla burrowed into the length of Cooper's body. She traced her fingers along his shoulder and down to his waist, resting it there. "And you called Mike." It wasn't a question. She remembered him saying that when she first woke up. Her feelings about Mike knowing what was going on, and getting involved again after the last disaster with Frank where he got hurt, were mixed.

"Yeah. I found his number in your phone, which you left in our bedroom. We'll talk about that later. You need to take it with you everywhere." When she nodded, he continued. "Mike was planning on coming down anyway, wanting to straighten things out with you. He loves you, though I did tell him that if he upsets you, I'll kick his ass." Her eyes grew wide. Mike was nearly as big as Cooper. Maybe two inches shorter but just as broad. Cooper continued, "He then told me if I broke your heart he'd tear me to pieces and throw whatever was left into the ocean. I think we bonded over all that actually."

She couldn't help but grin. "Mike has never liked anyone I've dated. You should have seen the way he hated Frank. Open hostility like I've never seen. That was one of the reasons I backed away from everyone when I was with him. I hated being around that." She sighed, her eyes meeting Cooper's. "Is that who they think did it? Frank? Did he find me?"

Cooper kissed her, his lips soft against hers. He was careful with her, no doubt knowing she was still sore, but he tugged her tightly. "Don't know. Cops in your hometown are searching for him. Cops here are keeping an eye out, too. They found a bunch of searches on his computer, one for this place, some for places out west. He had you flagged at work, probably got your information when you opened your bank account and transferred funds from the old account. But you don't have to worry about this anymore. Until we catch the fuck who did this, me, the guys at the shop, your brother, even Jackson, we all have your back."

Kyla yawned, already tired again.

"I love you." The words floated softly, sweetly in the air between them.

All thoughts of sleep flew out the window. "You love me?" Her tone was one of incredulity, "How can you ... I mean, we just. . ." She was trying not to panic, and she was losing the battle. "How can you love me?"

"'Cause you're funny, cute, gorgeous, have a body that makes me hard every time I look at you, a contagious laugh and a smile that lights up whatever room you're in. You sing and I swear to god I'm in the presence of an angel, but it's matched by that sweet devil of an attitude you got no fear throwing around." Cooper ducked his head, his nose touching the side of hers. "I knew I wanted you the second I heard your voice, and I knew I loved you not long after that."

She was trying to hold back the tears, but a few leaked out of her eyes, trickling down her cheeks. He swiped them away with his thumbs. She was thrilled that he loved her, but those words, words she desperately wanted to say, stuck as a lump in her throat.

"Don't cry, baby. It's okay, you don't have to say it back," he assured her. "Just say it when you're ready."

"I ... Cooper..."

His expression was soft, the blue in his eyes getting deeper, more intense. "Shh, I know. Go to sleep. You need to rest up and get your strength back." His lips were at her ear as he whispered, "And just know that I am going to keep you naked in our bedroom—hell, the entire house—for awhile once the docs clear you to go home."

His eyes held a promise in them and that promise made Kyla squirm in the best way possible. "'Night, Cooper."

"'Night, Kyla."

• • •

"Cooper, I've been resting. I'm fine," she protested the next day when he insisted she spend the afternoon in their bed. "I need to get back to work. I have a ton of things to do at Music & Motors. And if I stay away from the shop too long it will be like a hurricane went through again."

Cooper set her bag down on a chair in the corner of the room and turned to her. "Lift your arms." It was an order more than a request, but she did it anyway. He tossed the shirt on the floor and she saw the heat flare in his deep blue eyes. He paused a beat before he spoke. "You heard the doctor. He wants you to take some time off, and since I'm your boss, you're off for a week, which is good, because I still plan on getting you naked a lot over this week."

Kyla rolled her eyes. "God, you're bossy. You're lucky I find that incredibly attractive in you." She wrapped her arms around his neck. "Come to bed with me?"

He grinned. "Hell, yeah. I planned on it. But, all we're going to do is sleep."

Kyla snapped. "Oh for god's sake, Cooper, I got bumped in the head not hit by a car. I'm fine."

His arms tightened and he became scarily still. He was silent for a long time, spinning it out and making Kyla shift in his arms. Finally he said quietly, "You have no idea what I felt, what went through my head when I got that fuckin' call. So if I want to take care of you and not overdo things, even though it kills me 'cause all I can think about is stripping you out of all your clothes and fucking you for hours, then I am going to take it slow. You understand that?"

"I didn't think about that. I should have. And so I do understand, as long as you understand I'm going to be fine. I'm not going anywhere, honey. Not ever."

Cooper relaxed, his hand on her back rubbing small circles over her skin. "Let's get to bed."

She grabbed a t-shirt he tossed at her and pulled it on. She wiggled out of her skirt and threw that on the floor before crawling under the covers. Once Cooper was undressed, he slid underneath and she snuggled up against his chest. Cooper looked down and saw Kyla's eyes fluttering closed and not long after her breathing evened out. Having Kyla in his bed was bittersweet. He'd wanted to bring her here, cook dinner and then sit on the beach after. He knew he didn't have to seduce Kyla, but he wanted to show the romantic side of himself and give her something that she clearly hadn't had when she was with Frank.

Instead Cooper brought here to recuperate after getting clubbed over the head and pushed into the bay. He could only imagine what she had experienced. He sighed, staring at the ceiling as his thoughts raced. He wanted to find the bastard responsible and beat him into oblivion. All of the emotions Kyla had brought up inside him—the undeniable constriction on the left side of his chest, the overwhelming need to claim her as his and protect her until his last dying day—all of it scared the fuck out of him but he wouldn't trade it for the world.

• • •

She awakened abruptly when Cooper jerked, then jumped out of bed, grabbing for a gun he stored in the bedside table.

She hadn't seen a gun since the night she shot Frank and it threw her off balance. She needed to push back against the building fear.

" I heard a noise. Just going to check things out. Go back to sleep," Cooper said.

"No, I will wait until you get back." She reached for her phone. "I know I can't fight these battles alone now, Cooper, but that doesn't mean I can't call 911 if I have to."

He grinned at her. "Going to start calling you my wingman." He winked and then disappeared through the bedroom doorway.

He returned in less than five minutes. "Just Tommy and Phil checking on things," he reported as he sat on the edge of the bed, his hand skimming along the hem of his shirt and then under it. "I'm sorry if I scared you. Sarah is coming over with your stuff later." He tucked some stray locks of hair behind her ear. "But you need to get a bit more sleep first, or try at least. You need all your strength if you're going to be having my back."

She nodded, shooting him her best mischievous smile. "Oh, I have your back. And your front, and your sides." She lifted up on her knees and kissed him hard. "So don't doubt my strength. I'm feeling better already, so hurry up with the guys so we can get started. You are going to be the one who needs lots of energy."

He took her hand in his and moved it down his body to the front of his cargo pants, pressing it into his hard length, groaning as she flexed his fingers around him. His other hand reached lower, grinning as he felt her already damp panties. "I highly doubt that will be a problem." His free hand was under her shirt, his thumb sliding over her hardened nipple. Kyla arched her back, was pressing her chest into his hands when suddenly he stood. He kissed her one last time and strode from the room, laughing softly as he did.

She glared at his back. "Tease!" she hollered after him, huffing before settling back down and going to sleep.

Chapter 14

For the next couple of days Kyla was happy to follow Cooper's direction and take it easy. This meant lounging around his house, reading, watching television, and listening to music. And baking. The first day, when Cooper came home from work, she had made chocolate chip and peanut butter cookies with the ingredients Sarah had brought over since Kyla wasn't allowed to drive anywhere. More of Cooper's rules. Kyla didn't mind her imprisonment though, because she knew she needed to stay close, recover from the concussion, and hopefully in a few days the cops would catch Frank.

Today she was sitting on the stool at the breakfast counter, flipping through a magazine as she waited for dinner to finish. She'd called Cooper earlier and asked if she could use the grill, to which his answer was no.

This conversation did not go well. At all.

"But, Cooper, I can handle the grill, I won't get hurt," she said, her tone annoyed. "It's not like the grill can reach out and beat the crap out of me and drag me under water."

He was silent. Perhaps it was too soon to joke about such things, at least with Cooper. "Babe," he finally spoke, "I'm not worried about you getting hurt from the grill, though knowing you as I do, I am sure you could find a way to hurt yourself. The grill is just … well, it's a guy thing. I man the grill. Take out the steaks, do whatever you were gonna do to them marinade wise, and I'll throw 'em on when I get home."

"But I wanted to. . ."

"Kyla, seriously, I'm lying under a car right now and I don't have time to argue about this. I know you are totally capable of using the thing, but I just want to be the one who does. I'll be home at six."

Now it was her turn to be silent. She was trying to do something nice. "Fine," she huffed out. "But just so you know, you've gone backwards on the evolutionary scale and I'm highly pissed off about it. And to think you were making progress. Shows how much I was paying attention. I'll talk to you later. Maybe." She didn't give him time to respond, instead tossing her phone over into the couch and stomping to the freezer. She grabbed the steaks and put them in the marinade, finishing the mashed potatoes, which would just need to be reheated later. Glowering at the bags of cookies on the counter and the dishes she washed, she marched out onto the back porch that was elevated on stilts, overlooking the water.

The sun was in a prime spot right now and so she tossed out her towel on a chair and settled in on her stomach, unclasping her bikini top to avoid tan lines. She turned up the music pumping out of her mp3 player, something to match her mood, which meant the broody music of Pearl Jam.

Cooper had said when she came to stay with him he wanted this to be permanent, not just her staying here until Frank was caught. But sometimes his over the top manly ways and beliefs annoyed the crap out her. He wanted to be the one who used it? Well, whatever. It was his grill, it was his house and his things so if he wanted to do it, she'd not make an issue out of it. "Who knows how long I'll be staying here anyways," she muttered to herself. .

She must have fallen asleep because she awoke with a start to footsteps coming toward her on the wraparound porch. She turned her head expecting it to be Cooper or Jack, who had spent the day hanging around the house to keep an eye on her. But then the sound stopped and she heard a thud, prompting her to lift her head more.

Concerned, she reached around her back and put her top back on, then rolled off the chair and was taken off guard when something slammed into her. She hit the floor hard but pushed back against her attacker. Kyla screamed and the attacker's hand struck out to cover her mouth. The grip around her neck tightened and she could feel the air being squeezed out of her as the person tried to drag her around the other side of the porch. Kyla tucked her head down slightly and bit at the forearm around her neck and chin. The attacker howled and dropped the offending arm, giving Kyla a chance to move out of reach.

"Kyla?"

It was Cooper. She hadn't heard his car pull in, but she could tell he was close. She struggled to her feet but only got two steps away when a hand reached out and yanked her down by her hair. Kyla shrieked from the surprise and went down hard on her knees, not sure whether she was going to pass out or vomit. Whoever was behind her must have heard Cooper too, because they ran in the other direction and into the trees at the side of the house.

"Kyla! Jesus Christ, Kyla!" She could hear the panic in Cooper's voice and that hurt her heart almost as much as the new injuries she'd sustained.

"I'm fine," she croaked out. And she was for the most part. Compared to the knock to the head and the near drowning, this was nothing. She moved each limb carefully, finding nothing broken. She lifted a hand to rub her throat where she'd been choked. "Where's Jack?"

"He got hit on the head, but he's fine. Tommy is on his way. Don't move, we gotta get you checked out, and then the EMTs will take you to the hospital."

"No! I'm fine. I'm not going there again."

"Kyla."

"Cooper, don't argue with me about this. Please." The last word cracked. She was so tired. Her body was tired of getting her ass kicked, and her brain was fried from the chaos around her.

He didn't say anything but slid his arms around her waist to help her up. Kyla leaned into him, choking back a whimper. "I got you, Kyla. You're going to be okay."

"No, I'm not." She was trembling, but this time it was more from anger than pain. "Jack got hit in the head, I've been attacked twice. It's not going to be fine. It's not going to end until one of us is dead." Frank was such an asshole, she thought to herself. Why couldn't he just let her be?

He picked her up and carried her inside, settling into the couch with her on his lap and rubbing his hands over her shoulders. He didn't say anything, but she watched the muscle in his jaw jump as he tried to control his fury.

After Tommy looked her over, Kyla took a deep breath and leaned into Cooper, burying her face in his neck. "All I've been is a huge pain in the ass. I should have taken care of this on my own, and not gotten you and your friends involved."

He moved her so he could look her in the eye. "Kyla, whether you and I were together or not, you still work for me. And the guys like you, thinking of you as a little sister. At least they better be. Anyway, they'd be volunteering to keep you safe, which is what they're doing now." He kissed her mouth, a sweet and sexy kiss, his tongue taking a lazy journey as it explored her mouth. Finally he leaned back. "Besides, it's not just the guys. You have your brother, Sarah, Maggie, Rose and Steve. Babe, everyone is in your corner. As for me, I'm not going anywhere, not now, probably not until you're sick of me."

She smiled at the teasing in his voice. "What if I don't ever get sick of you?"

Cooper's arms tightened around her and she melted into him further. He dropped his forehead to hers. "Then I'd be the luckiest fuckin' man alive."

She bit her bottom lip and closed her eyes as she let the love and warmth he was exuding flow over and into her skin. "So, does this mean you'll continue to evolve and I can make steaks on the grill? Because seriously, a grill is not guy territory. Or it shouldn't be."

He tilted his head to the side and grinned. "Hmm, we'll see. I think maybe with some up close and personal training, hands on, of course, I might find myself able to be okay with that." He leaned forward and brushed his lips over her cheek, then over her lips. "You ready to talk to the cops now?"

She hadn't acknowledged anyone else was in the house, other than Tommy for those brief few minutes. Jack was at a barstool in the kitchen, holding an ice pack to the side of his head and speaking to the cops, one of whom was Jackson. Tommy was still lingering on the porch.

"Have they been watching us?"

"I don't know. Don't care either." He kissed her again, his thumbs tracing over the welts on her neck. "Come on, let's get this over with."

She nodded and stood, linking hands with Cooper and heading outside. After answering a million questions from Jackson, she went about mothering Jack and his injury, which he was not happy about.

A car pulled into the drive and everyone froze. Jackson's hand went to his gun. Kyla squinted at the car, and then her eyes widened. She bolted out of Cooper's arms and down the steps.

"Kyla!" Cooper yelled, but she was already gone and at the driver's side door just as the man inside swung his leg out and stood up.

She threw her arms over the tall, blonde and blue-eyed man and burst into tears, sobs she knew could be heard from the porch.

"I'm Mike O'Grady," he said while still holding her in a bear hug. "You must be Cooper? Nice to finally meet you."

Kyla winced inwardly. She hadn't been the one to tell him about Cooper. And now, seeing him here, ready to help, to drop his commitments at home for her, she felt bad for the rift she'd left between them for so long.

Cooper lifted his chin in greeting. "Jackson, this is Mike, Kyla's brother. He's an assistant DA in Pennsylvania. Mike, this is Jackson, detective with the local PD."

She finally stepped back but kept a grip on Mike's arm, wiping at her tears with the other. "I'm sorry, Mike. I should have called you. But I am so glad you're here…"

Mike hugged her again. "The past is past, Kyla. I messed up. I let you down and I'm not going to let that happen again." He lifted her chin, eyes narrowing on the swelling and bruising around her neck that was starting to show. "What's wrong with your neck? I thought you were hit on the head?"

"Some psycho attacked Jack and then me, just a little while ago. I didn't ask because I was too busy biting the fucker. He pulled my hair, Mike. Can you believe that? What a sissy move! I mean. . ." she trailed off, something nagging at the back of her mind.

"Yeah well you always pulled hair growing up when you fought, too. Never heard you call yourself a sissy."

"That's because I'm a girl and you were a boy who deserved it for those freaking charley horses you'd give me." She turned to Cooper "Mike and I used to have some knock-down, drag-out fights growing up."

Mike snorted a laugh. "Mainly because Kyla was always stealing my GI Joes to have weddings with Barbie and all her friends." He added to Cooper, "Kyla always thought Ken was too much of a preppy snob to be with Barbie. Said Barbie needed a real man."

She glared as the guys cracked up. "Shut up! Barbie may have liked her heels and fancy clothes, but she needed a guy who could kick ass, not some tennis playing pansy." She followed up with a gesture they'd couldn't mistake.

Cooper grinned, grabbing her hand and nipping at her extended finger. "You guys want to stay for steaks? Kyla took about twelve out earlier because apparently she thinks I can eat them all."

"Sure," Mike and Jackson said, heading inside first.

"Well, you look like a guy who needs his protein and meat has protein."

"I am, babe, I just don't usually eat all that at once. Otherwise I'll get a gut. Now come on. Let's get this impromptu dinner started."

...

Cooper insisted that Mike stay in the guest bedroom, the one on the other side of the house, farther away from their bedroom.

"You like Mike?" she asked as they climbed into bed, whispering as she laced her fingers through Cooper's.

"Yeah, he seems like a good guy, a good brother. He did everything he could to protect you. He was willing to give his life for you, Kyla. That makes him a pretty amazing guy right there."

She sighed, turning into him. "Yeah, he is pretty awesome. Just don't tell him I said that." She kissed his shoulder, then his jaw and chin. "I needed to hit rock bottom, but if he'd taken me outta there before I could make that decision myself, I'd have gone right back to Frank. I needed to be strong enough to be ready to leave. By then Mike was still there, ready to lose his own life to protect mine. I wasn't alone."

Cooper was silent, his fingers gliding along her hip. "You weren't alone then and you aren't now." He looked into her eyes. "I never thought I'd feel like this, Kyla. Thank you for giving me the best gift I could have ever wanted."

Shyly pleased, she leaned her forehead on his chest. "Whatever."

He smacked her ass, grinning at her surprised yelp. "Don't 'whatever' me. For the last five years I refused to believe I would ever find the one woman I needed to make me whole. Figured I was just meant to be alone. But you changed that the minute your car broke down and you called for a tow." Cooper kept his fingers dancing across her skin in random patterns. "I was engaged to this girl I dated all through college. She left me when she realized my one goal in life was to stay here, open a car shop, and raise a family. She wanted more—bright lights, big city, money. I wasn't good enough for her and she let me know it by stepping out on me. Repeatedly."

Kyla was tense as she listened to Cooper's story. "Does she live around here? Because I don't know whether I should kick her ass for breaking your heart or thank her for giving me a chance to be with you."

"My baby has claws. Feisty," he said in that sexy voice she loved. Kyla snuggled against him. "But no, she doesn't live around here. She left town with a friend of mine from college. The guy I caught her cheating on me with. But that's over. My point in saying all this is that I was so focused on work and avoiding exploring my personal life, I didn't have any expectations of ever finding someone, of having a future. Now it's all I can think about."

She felt the weight of what he was saying on her settling around her. But it wasn't a heavy constriction in her chest. It was light and comfortable, like a blanket being pulled around her, warming her insides.

"How much of your stopping had to do with my Mustang? Come on, tell me truth."

He laughed full out. "Gotta admit, I heard the make and model and it got my attention. It's not often a mechanic gets his hands on a beauty like that. But the beauty I got in my bed is a hundred times better."

"That's a good thing, 'cause where the car goes, I go. So you're stuck with us both."

Cooper lifted her up over his chest as his hands slid down into her panties. "Wouldn't have it any other way."

She rested her cheek on his chest, listening to his heartbeat. "How is Lola anyway?"

"Things are looking up. She's still on life support, but a few parts have come in."

"You're keeping a tab still, right? So I can match the hours of work?"

"Kyla." There was a warning tone in her voice.

"No, you have to, Cooper. That was our deal. The fact that I'm naked in your bed doesn't change that."

He sighed, she hoped because he respected her narrowed eyes and stern look. "Fine. We'll talk about it later. Are you planning on staying in the city, even after she's fixed?"

She looked into his face, biting her lower lip. "Yeah, I mean, I want to. I just have to find an apartment someplace."

"No reason to do that since you'll be sleeping with me at night and waking up with me in the morning. Why waste your money? And why schlep our stuff back and forth? Your stuff is already here."

"Yeah, but isn't this kind of soon, to move in together? I don't want to ruin this by being an idiot and going fast."

Cooper gave her an amused look. "Babe, you've been in town almost three months. In that time we've seen each other almost every day. You've been living here for over a week and before that I was at your place. If we were going to kill each other, I think we would have already." He squeezed her bottom. "And we won't ruin it so long as talk to each other and we listen. That means when one of us says or does something stupid, or that we don't understand, we talk it over. And there will be no stewing over shit, either."

"Well, Mr. Bossy, seems like you have it all figured out."

Cooper smiled and nipped at her lower lip. "Nah, just know what I want. So no more freaking out in your head about shit. Like the grilling thing. You hung up on me."

"I did not. I said my piece and then hit the end button."

"Before I could respond or say goodbye," he retorted.

She felt her cheeks flush. "Whatever."

"Not whatever. I'm only letting it go because we kind of talked about it afterward. But seriously, babe, it's not a big deal. You cook dinner all the time for us. I can't bake to save my life, or do anything else with a stove really, but I can grill. So let me help you out in areas I can. And grilling is one of them. And it has nothing to do with me not wanting you touching my stuff. In fact I want your stuff everywhere and your hands all over my stuff. But the grill … let me do it. Or we'll do it together."

Kyla sighed, "Deal. But that means that we'll cook together too, so you can learn how. How have you survived not knowing how to cook, anyway."

"The diner. Or pizza. Or anything that comes in a box-I can cook if it comes in a package."

She laughed, "We have a lot of work to do, then." She leaned over and kissed him. "'Night, Coop."

"'Night, Ky." His hands continued their lazy movement over her body until she was asleep.

Chapter 15

Cooper watched Kyla walk into the music store on her first day back, then parked his bike out front as a decoy before he headed over to the garage. He couldn't help but grin—other than the psycho after the love of his life, he was living a dream.

As he rounded the corner he stopped and then ran a hand through his hair. Jackson was outside his car in the lot talking to Kyla's brother.

"Hey guys. What's going on?"

"Just wanted to meet up, trade any info. Kyla go back to work today?" Jackson asked.

"Yeah, she insisted on handling the lessons she has planned for today through Saturday. Sarah has been manning the register when she can between jobs, and even some of the guys have pitched in, but only she can give the lessons. Kyla doesn't want to let the kids down."

Mike sighed. "That's my sister—always concerned about everyone else when she should be focusing on herself."

Jackson cleared his throat. "Look, sorry to interrupt this, but I got a shitload of cases I need to get working on. Cooper, I stopped by to say that forensics came back and we got nothing so far. The locals in Pennsylvania say Frank is still in the wind but seem to think he was in town when the attacks on Kyla took place but they want to find him so they can have a chat and confirm that. They are also trying to get a warrant for his phone and computer. Hopefully that will be enough to show he is breaking the Order of Protection and put his ass in jail. Has Kyla gotten any other calls?"

"Nope. Things have been pretty quiet, though we're both on edge, waiting for the next shoe to drop." And that was the truth.

He didn't even want to fall asleep lately, worried that someone would break in and he wouldn't be ready.

"Well maybe he's given up. Or drove off a cliff. That would make closing this case a hell of a lot easier," Mike muttered.

Cooper snorted. "Yeah well, hopefully you and the cops in Kyla's hometown can step this up since someone is trying to fucking kill her. I would think this is a priority, unless your douchebag boss has you busy busting the balls of innocent people again."

"If the cops in Pennsylvania are right about Frank and his alibis, then we have to start looking somewhere else. All indications are that this Frank guy is not the one going after Kyla. Whoever this psycho is, he's latched onto your girl. That isn't a good sign. So fuck you, Cooper."

Mike held up his hands, standing between the two. "Enough. This is about my sister, not about whatever is going on in this twisted town. We can deal with that later. Right now, let's all stay smart and alert about this fucker who wants my sister dead."

Cooper lifted his chin. "Kyla is my only priority. Everything else is on the back burner until I make sure she's safe and this asshole is caught. Now I gotta get to work. Call if you hear something."

With that he headed into the shop and opened for the day, but before he slid under the car he dropped in at the music store, just to make sure Kyla was all right.

• • •

On the first open mic night at Music & Motors, Kyla couldn't stop smiling. The turnout was awesome. She wandered around the floor, greeting other members of the community who had come, including Steve, Rose, Sarah, Justin, and Maggie. Her eyes swept over the many familiar faces and fell on Cooper, who stood along the wall near the television. Kyla had spent the last several days moving furniture around to maximize the space.

Sarah moved closer as the last participant left the stage. Well, next to last. "You're up, Ky. Get those fingers on the ivories." Kyla grinned, that familiar thrill of performing flowing through her body. She had never dreamed of being a rock star or song writer. She was content playing, performing, and teaching others.

The only hitch in her usually steel nerves was the fact that it had been a while since she'd done this. Kyla had been practicing all week—it was time to see if she was ready. She made her way to the stage and settled on the bench in front of the piano, adjusting the microphone before taking a breath. She started the introduction and one of her students joined in soon after on guitar. As she sang the lyrics to Rascal Flatts' *Bless the Broken Road,* Kyla looked over the crowd again and found Cooper watching her. She held his gaze the entire time, knowing in her heart and deep in her soul that she was in love with him.

...

When the song ended, the place erupted with claps and cheers. Kyla was beaming as she stood up and spoke briefly to her students. The kids looked thrilled and in awe of Kyla, and Cooper didn't blame them. The woman had talent, that was for sure.

He met Kyla at the edge of the stage, pulling her into his arms and twirling her around. Music was already flowing through the speaker system as people mingled. Out of the corner of his eye, he saw some of the kids dancing in the parking lot. A few couples even started dancing in the store itself while others were checking out with their purchases. Hell, maybe this place would make a real profit by the end of the year. He also couldn't help but notice a few of their guests made their way toward Steve's bookstore while others left Music & Motors to stroll into a small art gallery that had opened across the street. Maybe Kyla was right. This sort of thing might just liven up Main Street and bring the community together more.

"How'd I do?" She was grinning from ear to ear.

"Perfect. Most beautiful and talented woman I know." He buried his face in her neck. "You're amazing."

Kyla sighed and melted into him. "I love you, Cooper."

Cooper's heart beat hard in his chest as her words caressed every inch of him. "Love you, too." And then she was gone again, floating off to help out at the register with Sarah and Maggie, leaving him to absorb what she'd just said. His heart felt light and it was like a weight had been lifted from his shoulders. Before finding Kyla, he'd come to believe that he'd never find the one for him. Especially after his last relationship which ended in betrayal, and having to put up with Marla and her clinginess. Funny how the universe worked, bringing him the love of his life when he'd finally given up on love. He grinned as he watched her with her friends and customers, her smile lighting up the room. She was happy and he loved seeing her like that. He made a vow to himself to keep her that way, always. She deserved that and more.

From nowhere, Sam slapped his hand on Cooper's shoulder. "This is why I don't get involved with women, man. She's got you looking like a puppy dog, ready to follow her around wherever she leads you."

Cooper grunted but he didn't bother to hide the hint of a smile on his face. "Fuck you, Sam. She's not leading me around by my dick. She's not that kind of girl. And honestly, I can't wait until this happens to you. Do you think I expected to find my better half on the side of the road? Not in a million years, man. But I'm damn glad her car broke down where it did and I was there to help out. So you just wait. It'll happen and I'll be there to say 'I told you so.'"

Sam crossed his arms over his chest. "Yeah, you would do some shit like that, but it's not going to happen, so save your breath.

I'm not letting a woman get me tied up in knots. But listen, in all seriousness, no matter how much I bust 'em on you, I am happy for you guys. I think she's way too good for you, but. . ."

Cooper pushed Sam toward the door and grumbled, "Get the hell outta here unless you're buying something." Sam's laughter could be heard as he left, and despite the ribbing Cooper took over Kyla, he didn't give a fuck.

Cooper talked to some more folks who had stopped by the store but soon his thoughts turned to Kyla. Finally, as the last person left, he looked around to join her and his heart stopped when he saw Maggie and Sarah getting their coats—alone. "Where's Kyla?" he asked as he stalked toward them.

Sarah's head snapped up and she furrowed her brow. "In the office. We put the couches back and she wanted to put the cash in the safe."

Cooper let out a breath of relief. "Thank god. All right. Thanks, guys, for everything." He locked the door behind them and went in search of the love of his life.

...

Kyla had her back to the door. She was bending over the desk to grab her jacket when large hands grabbed her by the hips.

"Not leaving without me, I hope."

Kyla stilled at his words, her body tingling where his fingers touched the exposed skin of her stomach. She tried to turn her body, but he held her there, pressing himself against her.

Cooper pushed her shirt up higher, leaning his chest over her back. He sucked in a breath as his fingers drifted over her breasts.

"Now why would I do that? You're my bodyguard tonight, aren't you?"

"I'm always your bodyguard, doll." His voice had a teasing tone to it, making her shiver and melt against his hard body.

She groaned as he nipped at her earlobe, her jaw, and then down her neck. Just his touch was bringing her dangerously close to losing control. As it was, she couldn't think straight, her eyes closed. Cooper's fingers grazed over her panties, already wet with anticipation for what was to come.

Kyla twisted in his hands, this time successful in turning toward him. She watched him for a beat before moving her mouth over his, the heat between them unmistakable. She scooched up on the desk and yanked him toward her, pushing his own shirt up over his abdomen. Her fingers trailed over his skin, sending shivers throughout his body. His hands shook as he pushed her skirt up higher and then he lifted her slightly before reaching for her panties and ripping them away from her body. She glanced down as he stuffed the shredded fabric into his pocket but was soon distracted by his tongue licking down her neck and to the swell of her breasts.

Cooper rubbed her nipple between his fingers, his mouth taking the other, until he elicited a moan.

He glanced up as she unbuttoned his jeans and pushed them down. She was ready for him, had been since they'd left their bed this morning.

"I can't get enough of you," Cooper murmured against her mouth.

Her eyes were heavy-lidded and she reached her hands around his neck and pulled his head down to her mouth. When her teeth grazed his ear he slammed into her and she responded with a cry as he thrust into her over and over, one hand on her back pressing her against him and the other tangled in her hair.

"God, you're beautiful."

Cooper's whispered compliments pushed her closer and closer to letting go of that control she was holding so tightly.. She whimpered. She'd never felt this cared for, this special.

"Cooper..."

"That's it, love. I'm going to bring you over. You want that, baby?"

"Yes!" she cried, her head dropping back. He moved his mouth to her neck, licking and sucking every bit of her skin.

"Good, now open your eyes. Look at me, Kyla." Cooper's hand fisted in her hair, and she focused on his dark blue gaze. He stroked one more time, grinding his hips as he did and her body shuddered with her release. She buried her face in his neck as they both tried to catch their breaths, sweat coating their skin.

After several minutes he pulled out, grinning at her mewled protest of their lost connection. "What do you say we go home for round two?"

"Best idea you've had all day. Well, second best." She laughed softly and straightened her clothes before putting on her jacket.

Cooper's rumbled laugh wrapped around her, and for the first time in a long time she didn't feel broken. She was home, in the place she was supposed to be.

...

Her cell phone was ringing off the hook, but she was laying on her back on the couch, with Cooper in front of her, kissing the hell out of her.

"Cooper, I need to get that. It's the third call. . ."

"Nuu uhh. You stay right here." He reached behind him and swiped the phone off the table before putting it to his ear. "Hello?"

"Cooper!" she hissed. Now the man was answering her cell phone? She was going to kill him. But hopefully that wouldn't happen until after he took her against the wall.

"Who the hell is this?" Cooper growled as he hit the speaker button. .

"It's Mike. Listen, I know you probably don't want to deal with this, but they found Frank in Ohio. Apparently he was going to head out after you when he got wind of the investigation. He realized shit was about to hit the fan and he hit rock bottom. When the cops nabbed him, they checked his phone—he made the first few calls, but then stopped when his captain came down on him about flagging you. He was never in Maine though and has an airtight alibi for the attacks. He was being interviewed by Internal Affairs."

Kyla could only sit staring at the phone as if it had eight legs and sharp, poisonous fangs. "What did you just say?" But she didn't give him time to repeat it. "He has an alibi, but are they sure?" She glanced over at Cooper to gauge his reaction. His body was solid as a rock and he looked beyond pissed off.

"I know, Kyla. If Frank has been locked down, he couldn't have been the one who got to you on the beach." Silence reigned. Finally Cooper took the phone, leaving it on speaker.

"Mike, it's Cooper. You said he only made the first few? What about the others?"

"They found nothing and he is adamant he wants nothing to do with Kyla. But even if it was him, the cops have him now. He's been in custody since the day before yesterday and will be until he is sent to face charges here in the next month. The court denied him bail."

"Fuck, if it's not Frank, then...," Cooper trailed off and sighed. "Thanks, Mike."

"I know this sucks, not knowing who is coming after me, but I have to admit I'm just glad Frank's ass is in jail. Hopefully he gets a hairy cellmate named Bubba who likes pretty boys," Kyla couldn't resist saying.

Cooper shook his head. "Remind me never to get on your bad side, doll."

He disconnected the call without out so much as a goodbye, and Kyla saw that as her signal to tug Cooper back to her, her fingers sliding inside his still unbuttoned jeans. "So where were we? Cause the news we just got, well that's worth celebrating."

Cooper groaned "Sorry, babe, but we're going to have to hold off on that party for a bit. It's great that fucker is locked up, but that doesn't solve the mystery of who did this to you." His finger traced her pouting lower lip "But I'm still up for a wild night in bed."

Chapter 16

Kyla rummaged through her beach bag. "Anyone have any sunscreen I can borrow? I can't find mine."

"I have some you can use," Sarah spoke from the porch railing she was leaning against. "Are we heading to the beach, or what?"

"Yeah, I'm ready now. Let's go." Kyla grabbed her bag and slung it over her shoulder. "All I want to do is fall asleep in the sun and forget about the drama for a few hours. Do you think we can manage that?"

Sarah laughed. "I hope so. We all need a break. Or a vacation. Maybe one to an island somewhere in the tropics."

"I'm all for taking Cooper to a tropical island, but I don't know if he'd go if he didn't have a car to fix."

"You make Coop happy, Kyla. I am really glad your car broke down three months ago."

"Me too, Sarah."

Sarah threw an arm over each of Kyla's shoulder in a hug. "I'm going to mix some more margaritas to take to the beach. Be right back."

No sooner had her friend disappeared than Kyla's phone rang and she answered on the second ring.

"This Kyla?"

"Yeah. Can I help you?"

"Watch your back. Someone's coming for you. Soon."

"What? Who is this?"

The phone disconnected and Kyla looked down at her cell phone. Her body felt numb and she knew just what an antelope felt like when hunted by a lion. "What the fuck was that about?" she muttered.

"Kyla?" Sarah was at her side in two steps.

"Whoever that was just told me to watch my back. I didn't recognize the voice. And they didn't tell me who was coming or who they were. Great. I had a few days of peace and now Cooper can go back to freaking out. Fuck."

"So much for a relaxing day at the beach. Come on, let's go find the guys." She was already picking up towels and bags.

"Sorry, Sarah."

Sarah stilled and reached over to pat Kyla's hand. "Hey, don't apologize. This is not you. It's the fucker who is doing this. We will nail his ass. But let's go tell Cooper so he can have his shit fit and the guys can get a plan. Then we can eat some cookies. I need food at times like these."

"Me, too." Kyla agreed.

The women linked their arms and headed for the stone steps leading up to Cooper's porch, ready to take on whatever the world would throw at them.

• • •

"Cooper, whoever made the call clearly wanted me to know whatever was happening so now we know to expect something. I even texted Jackson already. So relax."

He ran his hands over his face and looked up as Sam walked through the front door and into the kitchen.

"Hey, Sam. Can you tell Cooper to stop freaking out please? Everyone is on this. We've just received a warning that something is about to go down. It's all good," said Kyla.

Maybe she was trying to convince herself. Maybe she was trying to convince Sam and Cooper and everyone else who was on edge. Maybe it was both. She just knew for sure that she wanted to avoid another sleepless night for Cooper.

"Call was traced to the motel," Sam said. "Jackson went over there and is interrogating Morris now. I don't know what the fuck he has to do with this. Kyla, are you friends with him or something?"

"That's just ew." She scrunched up her nose for emphasis. "We talked maybe four times. He was always staring at me in that creepy way. I don't know why Rose ever hired him. He is just … creepy."

"Rose has a big heart," Cooper explained. "And Morris might seem like a creep and be an asshole whenever he opens his mouth, but he's never done anything that crossed the line. He's all talk. And I saw the way he'd watch you, but he knew, from the time I walked you home from the pier, that you were off limits. If he called you to warn you about something going down, maybe he isn't as creepy as we thought."

But if he was trying to help her, why hadn't he just said who he was? It didn't make any sense to her. But then, what part of having an insane psycho stalker made any sense at all?

...

The weekend was quiet. Nothing much had come out of what Morris had to say. Mainly because before Jackson could get much information, Chief Saybrook had ordered he be cut loose. This had not made Jackson or Cooper happy, and for the first time Kyla could see the two men had a similar distaste for the top cop. What made it worse was that Morris had gone to ground and no one could find him. Not even Sam. This was alarming in itself, but Kyla could see Cooper was trying to keep his worry hidden. At least from her.

On Sunday, the guys were sprawled out on the furniture in the living area watching a football game. The weather was cooling off as September approached, but the leaves were gorgeous and the frothy waves on the bay, the smell of sea salt in the air was, to Kyla, perfect. She had made a bunch of finger foods for them to munch on and had a pot of chili simmering in the Crockpot for dinner. She was leaning against the kitchen counter, her head bent as she looked through a cookbook when she felt Cooper at her back, his arms circling her waist.

"Food smells amazing."

She nestled into Cooper's hold. "Thanks. It's my mom's recipe. She'd make it for us for our Sunday football feasts. Course, we always watched the Steelers. Not those guys."

He grinned and nipped at her jaw. "Babe, this is a Patriots' house. Gonna have to get used to that."

"This is something we're going to have to disagree about. My mom is sending my jersey and I sleep in it. So. . ."

"I don't think so. You sleep in that, it'll be off before the covers even get over your body. You'll be sleeping naked."

"That isn't much of a deterrent, Coop."

His head tipped back and he laughed. "I'll remember that, babe. You need any help with this?"

"Nope. Thanks for asking though. We just need to grill the meat when it's close to dinner time. That's your deal."

"I ever tell you you're amazing?"

She felt her insides melt and she sighed. "Yeah. But not today."

"Well, you are. You don't always have to do this though. I like you for more than just your cooking and hosting skills. Those are just a bonus."

She laughed at his teasing. "Yeah, two more checks off your list, huh? Tall, I can cook, and host a helluva party."

"You're also sweet, gorgeous, strong, you press tight against me when you sleep, and give me a reason to breathe."

"Cooper . . ." His head dipped to her mouth as she breathed his name.

"God damn it! I fuckin' hate the Broncos! Cooper, man, stop making out with my sister and get over here. You're missing the game."

Cooper shook with laughter as she felt her face blaze.

"Shut up, Mike! I swear I will tell Mom you're being a pain in the ass."

"Whatever." Mike muttered and turned back to the TV. Yeah, pulling the mom card always worked.

Her phone vibrated on the counter and she grabbed it.

"Come to the bar while I stock before it opens? I need to talk to you about Tommy."

Kyla lifted a brow at Sarah's text message and showed it to Cooper.

"You mind if I go hang with Sarah at the bar? She has to go in early and since you're watching the game, I'll be safe there. Doors will be locked and the bouncers get there early, too. I will leave by three-thirty to be home for dinner."

He hesitated.

"I'll take her over there," Jack said as he strolled over to the breakfast bar that separated the kitchen and living room. "I gotta get going anyway."

Cooper glanced between her and Jack, clearly not convinced it was a good idea, or that he could win this battle.

"Have fun, baby. Call me and I'll come by to get you."

She wrapped her arms around his neck, kissed him, and whispered into his ear, "Thank you."

He twisted his head, his eyes melted and he leaned into her body. "You owe me later. And I promise to collect."

His mouth touched hers lightly and then he turned to Jack. "Don't motor off until she's inside. Thanks, man."

• • •

"Thanks, Jack!" Kyla hollered from the doorway and made her way inside the bar, closing and locking the door behind her. She headed for the counter, glancing around at the empty stage and dim lights leaving shadows in the corners and recesses of the booths. Kyla crossed her arms over her chest and shivered.

"Sarah? You in the back?"

A bang from the stage made her head twist in that direction. She squinted at the shadow she saw behind the curtain and walked forward.

"Sarah? What are you doing? I thought you were restocking."

Another loud thud and grunt, all the more closer as she reached the edge of the stage.

"Sarah?" Her voice was barely a whisper as she spoke. She felt her stomach twist as her eyes adjusted to the lighting. Something wasn't right. She knew that with every fiber of her being. She wanted to be sick. She wanted to run. But her feet were frozen to the floor.

The shadow grew bigger and she finally managed to step back. A body, larger than Sarah, much larger, fell through the curtain.

Kyla felt her breath hitch in her throat and as her eyes adjusted to the light her hand flew to her mouth. "Morris?" She whispered his name, the sound coming out like a hiss.

The man's head turned and she saw the wicked slice along his length, the copious amount of blood pouring from it. His lips formed a word, but the only sound that emerged was a gurgle. She didn't need sound though. She could read his lips.

"Run."

And she did. Kyla turned and bumped into a table, her foot catching on a nearby chair. But she kept moving toward the door.

"I don't think so."

Marla stood against the exit. Her eyes were wild, her bleached hair was wild, and although she had on jeans and a black t-shirt, she looked anything but normal. She was crazy. And not because of the large hunting knife she had at her side. It was her posture, the way she flipped the knife around in her fingers, and the deadened tone of her voice when she spoke again.

"Run, Kyla. Please fuckin' run because I want to be the one who guts you. I want to watch you bleed just like Morris, but I want you able to talk, to scream while you do. I've dreamed about it since that day I saw Cooper watching you. I knew you had to die."

"Marla. I don't know why you're doing this. I didn't do anything. . ."

As Marla stalked forward, Kyla walked backwards toward the bar. The door to the back rooms was at the end of it. If she could get there, she might be able to get to a room and lock herself in.

"You did everything!" The scream ricocheted off the walls of the bar.

"But what did Morris do? I barely know him." She didn't dare take her eyes off of Marla, but the lack of any sound from the stage did not bode well for his survival.

"Cooper was *mine!* You took him from me, you took away the life I was supposed to have. I gave myself to him when we were kids. We were meant to *be!* And you stole that. I could have had him if I just had a little more time. But you came to town, all damsel-in-distress and with a psycho for an ex. Cooper had to save you, he had to claim you. And you didn't tell him no. I warned you, but you wouldn't give up and go home!"

Kyla swallowed. This woman was not stable and her shrill screams were getting more erratic. She gripped the edge of the bar with her right hand and her left dipped around the corner, searching for anything under the counter she might be able to use as a weapon.

"But Morris?" she asked again. She had to keep the woman talking, had to keep her distracted.

"Morris was watching you, too. He liked you, but he backed off when Cooper stepped in. He came into the bar here. I gave him a few freebies, made him want me like all the men want me." Marla sneered before continuing. "Morris was my partner until he got a fuckin' conscience and decided you and Cooper fit together. He didn't want to hurt you. He liked you too much. Said you were nice, even though you barely gave him the time of day. He was *weak* to your charms, just like Cooper! But I will cure them of that."

Kyla's fingers wrapped around the neck of a bottle in the nick of time and she pulled it out just as Marla lunged. Kyla moved fast and jumped back while swinging the bottle toward Marla's head. One shot. Kyla was sure she could knock her out and run.

But it didn't happen. Marla dodged and instead of her head, the bottle shattered against her shoulder. Marla's animal scream tore through the bar and she came harder at Kyla. Both women stabbed out with their weapons. Kyla felt the moment the jagged edge of the broken bottle sunk into Marla's flesh thigh and the blood began pooling out to drip on the floor. She dropped the bottle and moved three steps backward toward the door before turning to run. She made it only two steps before she felt the searing heat in her shoulder as the knife sunk into her flesh. Her scream was cut off as Marla grabbed her hair and yanked her back into the bar.

Kyla fell to the ground, but used her arms, biting through the pain as she scrambled through both of their blood wetting the floor.

"You're mine, bitch. Don't worry, you won't go fast. I want to play."

Kyla kicked out but missed her target. Instead the world went dark as the knife handle knocked her into unconsciousness.

• • •

"What the fuck? Why are you here?" Cooper exploded as Sarah walked through the door into the house. The action in the room was as electrified as a live wire as all of the guys jumped up, grabbing jackets and phones.

Sarah's eyes were round, puzzled as she watched the flurry of activity around her. "What the hell did I do?"

"Kyla got a text from you, asking to meet her at Felicia's 'cause you had some restocking to do before opening."

"Uh, no. Wasn't me. My phone was stolen last night from the bar. Are you. . ." Her face was pale. "Oh my god. Cooper, it's a Sunday. No events were scheduled for tonight so we don't open until six. I'm not even working today."

Cooper had already grabbed his gun from the desk drawer and was at the door. Phil, Tommy, and Mike were behind him.

"Sam, see if you can find Marla. Mike, call Jackson. Let them know what is going on. Sarah call Felicia, give her a heads up. Jesus motherfucker god damnit!" he roared.

"Man, calm down."

"Phil, get in the car and drive. We have to get to her. I swear to god. . ."

Cooper didn't have to finish that statement. He was already yanking the door open, then hauled ass to the car, not saying a word as he jumped into the passenger seat.

Phil stomped on the gas, gravel flying as they roared off.

Cooper had a tight grip on the gun in his lap, his other fist clenched. He had to stay in control. He had to get to her. If anything happened, his world would be over.

Phil spoke up first. "We'll get to her, Coop. She's strong. She'll fight back. She didn't find you to lose you. She's stubborn, she's got a temper, and you only gotta know her for about two minutes to know she won't be beat down."

He only nodded. He believed Phil's words in theory. He knew Kyla was strong and could fight. She'd had to deal with that asshole ex of hers to survive. But against a physical weapon, those were just words. And no amount of pep talks could soothe the ache in his heart or the fear in his mind.

Chapter 17

Kyla lay on the ground, wincing with each racking cough through her body. She had only been out for a couple of minutes. But in that time Marla had dragged her to the stage, somehow hefting her onto it.

She blinked several times, trying to clear the fog. Her fingers worked into the back of her jeans, trying to grab her phone. A rustling somewhere above her caught her attention and she jerked her head to the side. Marla crouched and spoke, her tone dead and distant but her eyes filled with intent.

"Kyla, Kyla, Kyla … this is what happens when you don't do what you're told. This is going to be quite the mess to clean up. Blood leaves such a horrible stain." Marla straightened and after some rustling Kyla heard her captor move behind the curtain at the back of the stage. She used that time, unsure of just how much she'd have, to pull her phone out and dial 911.

She tried to lift herself up but the pain in her shoulder wound made her fall back. She choked out a sob and dropped to her side as the phone rang.

"911, what is your emergency?"

"This is Kyla O'Grady. I'm at Felicia's. I've been attacked. It's Marla, she's crazy. I'm bleeding bad. Please hurry."

The sound of a door opening made her freeze, but instead of turning the phone off, Kyla scooted her body to the edge of the stage and dropped the phone over the side, wincing at the clattering noise it made. She silently prayed it stayed on, but she couldn't tell from her vantage point.

She heard the curtain rustle and lifted her head. Her eyes followed Marla's movements as she came closer, but her eyes stopped on the knife in her hand. Kyla knew that, despite the overwhelming desire she had to sleep, she had to force herself to stay awake. If she lost consciousness, it would be over. Kyla would not let this woman win. She would not lose the life she had been rebuilding here in Ashten Falls. And she definitely would not lose Cooper.

Marla grinned down at her from a few feet away. "Ready to play?"

"Fuck you," Kyla spit through clenched teeth.

"Not nice!" Marla screamed and raised her arm.

• • •

"Jesus," Saybrook muttered as he entered the strip joint. "Could you be any louder, Marla? Shut your fuckin' mouth." He headed for the stage where Marla stood over Kyla, ready to strike. He took out his gun and trained it on Cooper's woman, smiling as she stilled.

He glanced around and saw blood on the stage, along with Morris's big, greasy body. "Damnit all to hell."

Marla moved toward him. "Martin, I did what you said. You told me to get rid of my problem, so, I am." She waved her hand at the scene in front of her.

"You made a mess is what you did. How do you expect to clean this up? There's blood everywhere and that bitch isn't even dead yet."

"I want to play with her first," Marla begged. "She needs to suffer for taking Cooper, for distracting him."

Saybrook took two steps and grabbed hold of her arm hard. "Are you kidding me? You really are crazy. Only psychopaths play with their kill. You need to kill her and move on. Have you not paid attention to what I've been telling you?"

"But Cheryl was beat up, before she was drowned. So you had to have played with her first . . ."

"This isn't about what I did to Cheryl!" he roared, his words echoing off the walls. Marla's body shook in his arms as he yelled. He didn't want Cheryl's name mentioned again, especially by the likes of Marla. Marla couldn't compare to Cheryl. If only she hadn't betrayed him. If only she'd wanted him the way she wanted Roger. Then none of this would have happened.

He shook Marla, hard. "Don't mention her name again. Ever. Now finish the job so I can clean up your mess. I'm going to the truck to get some plastic. She better be dead when I get back."

...

"Fuck!" Cooper growled out. "Drive faster, Phil!" They were only two blocks away, but that felt like a fucking lifetime. He tried to call up her smile in his mind, the way she looked when he made her come, the soft look she got when he told her he loved her, but they were gone. All he could see were images of Kyla, beaten, battered and bloody. He physically hurt from it and wanted to hit something, anything, to make it stop.

"We go in half-cocked, we could get her killed," Tommy broke into his nightmare as Phil squealed the tires wheeling into the parking lot. "Just keep your motherfuckin' head, Cooper."

"Yeah, I got you." He was already out of the car before Phil came to a full stop, then racing across the parking lot, Tommy and Phil on his heels. He could hear the sirens getting closer and out of the corner of his eye he saw Sam's Charger pulling into the lot.

Cooper glared at Tommy, who was punching something in his smartphone. "What the fuck are you doing?"

"I'm calling Jackson to let him know we're here so AFPD doesn't shoot us," he muttered and was already running for the back of the building with Sam.

• • •

Kyla turned her head as the chief of police walked out the door. He was going to help Marla cover this crime. He was going to help this woman kill her. She had to get out of here.

"Now, let's finish what I started, shall we?" Marla moved fast, stabbing downward with the knife.

Kyla jerked her head to the side and rolled just out of reach. She heard it slam into the floor of the stage but she didn't look back. She was in full-on scramble mode to get some distance between her and the maniac. She pushed up with a grunt, the pain in her shoulder worse than before, but she ignored it. When she heard Marla's breathing get closer, she swung around and kicked out hard at the woman's knee. Marla grunted and her forward progress was stalled as she wobbled and stumbled.

A quick glance revealed Marla no longer had the knife in her hand. This was at least progress. Kyla took a step back, about to turn tail and run like hell when Marla lunged. She felt the fist connect with her cheek, her head snapping to the side.

That was enough. With pain radiating in her face, she ran at Marla and tackled her around the waist. Marla hit the hard floor of the stage with a thump and cushioned some of the impact for Kyla. Kyla raised up and brought her hand back before landing a blow to Marla's jaw. Somewhere in the background she heard yelling and a ruckus at the door, but it didn't register. She reared up and hit Marla again, ignoring the pain of the woman's kicks and scratching.

"Kyla!"

Kyla recognized Cooper's voice, but it was muffled. And she couldn't afford to back down. She had to keep fighting. If she gave Marla even a second, her life could be over. And that was *not* going to happen.

Landing another punch, Kyla didn't see Marla's fingers reach up and grab the shoulder with the knife wound and press her fingers into it. The pain radiated through Kyla's body and it took a second for her to realize the cry she was hearing was her own. It threw her off balance and that gave Marla an in.

"They won't be in time," Marla cackled—actually cackled—and struck out with her fist, snapping Kyla's head back and rolling Kyla onto her back.

Marla grabbed Kyla's hair, then scrambled to a half-standing stance as she tried to drag her. Seeing Marla bent over with her legs and vulnerable, Kyla pushed up with her hips and kicked out and up with her feet.

Marla howled as Kyla's foot connected with her pelvis and she crumpled to the floor, writhing in pain. Apparently getting kicked in the vag hurt like hell, something Kyla hoped she would never have to remember for the future.

"I'm in here!" Marla was struggling to get up and even as Kyla limped backward, unable to run as the pain and exhaustion started to overwhelm her, Marla's unabashed hatred and rage radiated throughout the room.

"Stay down, bitch!" Kyla screamed. Marla's mouth twisted into a murderous grin and she continued her advance, trapping Kyla at the edge of the stage. If Marla rushed her, she'd topple over. It was only a few feet, but in her condition it was not something she wanted to endure. Kyla's eyes flicked around the room; she saw light entering the bar from the doorway and could just make out the shadows running toward them.

Using the adrenaline pumping through her system Kyla took a breath and rushed Marla, spinning her around in the process.

She heard Cooper's voice scream her name, but Kyla was hell bent on finishing this.

She grunted as her shoulder connected with Marla's chest but ignored the pain and pushed through. Marla's arms wheeled back as the woman crashed over the side of the stage. Kyla heard a sickening crack, her eyes registering that Marla was on the ground, her head at a strange angle and blood pooling underneath her.

Kyla didn't have time to celebrate as the pain she'd tried to ignore shot through her. She groaned and crumpled to the stage.

• • •

Cooper ran toward Kyla and didn't stop, not even when Marla's head hit the floor, the audible crack hard to miss. His sole attention was on Kyla. He jumped on the stage and his arms caught her just as she lost consciousness.

"Holy fuck," Tommy breathed, rushing to Kyla.

Sam headed over to Marla to check her pulse. "Marla's dead. Guys, give me your guns," he commanded. "Whether Jackson is on our side or not, I still don't trust AFPD. And if Saybrook is here and sees 'em, we're fucked. I'm going to run them to the truck before the cops get here."

The guys handed over their firearms and Sam was gone in a flash.

Cooper held Kyla in his lap, the palm of his hand resting gently on her cheek. His thumb caressed the bruise already starting to form where Marla had hit her. "Come on, baby, you can't leave me. You can't shake up my world and then leave. You hear me? Please."

Kyla groaned in response. "All right, already. Why is everyone being so loud?" Her voice was barely a whisper, but it was something. He couldn't help but laugh, relief flowing through him. It only increased when Kyla squeezed his hand.

"Keep her talking, Cooper," Tommy instructed. Cooper nodded but never took his eyes off the woman he didn't ever want to go a day without seeing. "You have to stay awake, Ky. Let Tommy do his thing, but keep those gorgeous eyes open for me."

"I got it. Stay awake, I think I can do that," she murmured. He felt her body shudder against him.

"You're just going to do what I asked? Without argument? Must have been quite the blow to head for you not to argue."

"You know you love it when I argue with you. It keeps you on your toes." Kyla gave in to a little laugh but her body tightened in response.

Mike crouched nearby. "Kyla, seriously, don't ever fuckin' do that again. Ever."

She struggled to open her eyes and turned her head toward her brother, who looked as white as a ghost. "Hey, you know me. I got a hard head. It's going to be fine."

Phil stood at the edge of the bar. He shook his head slowly and muttered, "Fuck me. The woman is bleeding on the floor of a titty bar, and she is the one reassuring you guys everything is fine."

"What can I say, Phil, a woman's work is never done." Kyla coughed and closed her eyes. "I'm cold." She shivered in Cooper's arms as Tommy barked for a blanket. When it settled over her, she snuggled against Cooper and her eyes closed again.

"Don't you fall asleep, Kyla. You and I gotta have words about this mess. So don't be doing anything stupid like checking out on us. You understand me?" Jackson said from nearby.

Her eyes fluttered again and she held his gaze a long moment before speaking softly, "On one condition. You be nice from now on. Be the guy who has been helping to keep me safe these last few months." It was dirty, and a possible deathbed promise, so how could Cooper feel like laughing at her gall?

Jackson nodded but muttered to Cooper, "Your woman's fuckin' crazy."

Cooper grinned and Jackson stalked away.

"We have to get her to the hospital" Tommy said softly to Cooper. "She's losing blood fast."

Cooper nodded and lifted Kyla in his arms. He set her down on the stretcher, leaning down to brush his lips against her forehead. She grabbed his arm and he could tell her grip was weak. "We're going to get you fixed up, Kyla. And then this nightmare will be over. It'll finally be over."

Chapter 18

"Are you done yet?" Seriously, Kyla had never fussed so long on a pedicure in her life.

"Stop your whining."

She shot Sarah a glare, but the woman just grinned and went back to painting Kyla's toes.

"I'm not whining. But dinner is going to be done soon and I'm starved."

Since the attack a week ago, Sarah, Mike, Rose, Maggie and Cooper—especially Cooper—had made sure she rested. They accomplished this by hovering and not letting her do anything for herself. Kyla wanted to work and she needed to get out of this house. She wanted her normal.

When she'd arrived at the hospital, the doctors had blood at the ready, thanks to Tommy. Her shoulder wound required 37 stitches, but other than that, there was no lasting physical damage. Her body still ached, but the bruises were fading.

Cooper was wired the first couple days, not wanting to let Kyla out of his sight. She'd wake up in the middle of the night and he'd be sitting up in bed, eyes wide open and watching her.

"Cooper, it's okay. Go to sleep." She'd said this on the second night and Cooper had settled next to her, his arms curled tight around her.

"It's like if I blink, you're going to be gone. I can't get rid of that feeling, Ky. I can't get the images of you, of your blood, out of my head. I won't ever forget that or the fear that came along with it." He had whispered in her ear and Kyla knew it was her turn to comfort him. She had rested her cheek on his chest.

"Cooper, I don't know how to get rid of those images. Sometimes I see scary things too, and I can't get those pictures out of my brain. But thinking about you, here, wrapped up with me, that helps. We're okay, Cooper. I'm okay. And I promise, I'm not going anywhere."

"Damn right you're not." His words had been muffled as he kissed her neck. "Let's get some sleep. I think we both need it."

Kyla had stayed awake until she felt Cooper's breathing ease and felt his body relax. Only then did she close her own eyes.

Their talk seemed to settle Cooper's mind a bit, but not by much. He was still overprotective and bossy. But she was happy to deal with that part of him if it meant he would get some sleep at night. She had to remember he had gone through an ordeal, too. Not only had he seen her almost die at the hands of a psychopath, but he also had to deal with the fact he hadn't been there to protect her from it. For a guy like Cooper, this was a blow. So she was going to give him time. And besides, sometimes being taken care of was nice. How many times would she get the chance to have someone waiting on her hand and foot?

Still, Kyla had convinced him to let her go to work starting Monday. She had lessons to make up for, and according to Steve, the kids had been hanging around the bookstore, constantly asking about how she was doing and giving him cards and flowers to pass on to her. She had quite the collection she planned to take to the music store and display on the counter.

"All done." Sarah capped the polish and both women turned as Maggie came through the door.

"So, you're staying then." Maggie declared. "I mean, if you're running the store now and staying with Cooper, you aren't going home with Mike, right?"

She nodded. "Nope. I'm here to stay. This is my home now." They turned their heads toward the men in the next room: Cooper, Justin, Phil, Tommy, Sam, Derek, and another friend Kyla had only recently met, Roger, sitting on the couch watching a game. Edith and Sheena were fighting in the kitchen over whether the salad dressing had enough spice to it. "Besides, even with Frank in jail, what do I have to go back to? Mike likes it here, and my mom is going to come stay for the holidays. And anyway, my heart, are here. I couldn't even consider leaving."

Sarah threw herself at Kyla, hugging her tightly and Maggie joined in. Sarah spoke first, sniffling as she did, "Good, because if you were leaving I might have had to follow you."

The women were still crying when Coop was suddenly filling the doorframe.

"Is this a hug anyone can join?"

Kyla smiled at her man. "Jealous?"

"Am I jealous of hot women hugging on each other? Hell no. Just wondering if I can be part of the action." He grinned as Kyla shot him one of her patented glares—she had a feeling she was going to need a lifetime supply of them. "That isn't too effective when it's cute as hell, doll." He winked and then headed out to the grill.

"Whatever," Kyla muttered, smiling as Sarah cracked up.

Maggie left their huddle and came out from the house a few minutes later, pitcher in hand. "Who needs a refill?" Both Sarah and Kyla offered their near empty glasses before leaning back on their lounge chairs.

Sarah broke the comfortable silence a few minutes later. "I am so happy this whole mess is finally over. Now things can get back to normal."

Maggie lifted her glass "To normal." The three clinked their drinks together.

Kyla nodded. "Frank is in jail, likely forever. Marla is dead. Saybrook is in jail. Cooper and I are good. Felicia's is re-opening and the music store is doing well. The only downside is a man who everyone thought was creepy had to die to show the world that, in the end, he did the right thing."

"As cliché has it sounds, you really can't judge a book by its cover." Sarah's words were quiet but the contemplative mood was interrupted by the guys' laughter.

Kyla looked over and flashed a bright smile to Cooper, who had his ever watchful eyes on her. He winked. She pushed herself off the chair and started to stand.

"This is what I wanted. Happiness, family, laughter, friends, love. Never would have thought I'd find it on the coast of Maine. But I am certainly glad I did."

• • •

"I can't believe Kyla's phone caught all that went down during the attack. Who knew we'd get a confession about Cheryl over all this. Maybe Roger can finally move on now."

Cooper glanced up from the grill at Sam's comment. "Feds say it's not a complete confession but they have enough to hold him while they search his place and look into the rest of the claims we were making."

Mike snorted. "I wonder how he likes his new digs in the federal penitentiary. Hopefully he gets a big, burly cellmate to keep him company."

Cooped flipped the burgers. His gaze moved to Kyla, sitting with her friends on their porch, finally safe, before he addressed Sam and Mike. "I imagine he's in solitary. Or at least I hope he is. I think him being left alone to have to think about everything he did, the fear he caused a lot of innocent people, the crimes he committed over the years, especially what he did to Cheryl, is a much better punishment."

"Yeah." Mike took a drink of his beer. "There was another good thing that came out of all this." At Cooper's raised brow, Mike grinned. "You and Kyla. You guys are playing house and I imagine there will be more plans for the future soon, am I right?"

Cooper plated the food and the men headed inside. "If you're asking if I'm spending the rest of my life with her, you can bet your life on it. I almost lost her. I don't ever want to feel like that again."

Sam leveled his gaze at Cooper. "Good to hear, Cooper, 'Cause I'd have to kick your ass if you didn't. Or take her for myself."

Cooper punched him in the arm as he laughed. "You can try, buddy. But she's had the best, no way she's settle for anything less."

"What are you guys laughing about?"

Kyla settled against his side and he wrapped his arm around her waist. He kissed her on the lips. "Nothing babe, just Sam and your brother being hilarious."

"God, can you two stop making out in front of me? I don't know whether to punch something or throw up," Mike complained.

Kyla stuck her tongue out at Sam and her brother. "One day you two will find this and wonder why you waited so long. And Cooper and I will be here to say that we told you so."

Sam shook his head. "Nah, not me Kyla. Besides, the best girl I know has been taken. But if you decide to dump this guy's sorry ass, you know where to find me."

Kyla chuckled. "That's not going to happen. I kinda like his ass."

Cooper rolled his eyes. "All right, let's get this conversation off my ass. Go get your girls, time to eat."

Kyla headed for the porch to get her friends and for the first time since he saw her and her Mustang on the side of the road, Cooper didn't feel on edge. He wasn't worried about her safety. He wasn't preoccupied with what he had to do to take down the crooked top cop. His town was safe and hopefully, on its way to being cleaned up for good. Everything was falling into place and Cooper was content.

It was about damn time.

Slow Ride

• • •

"See you soon, little sister."

It was Cooper who gently pulled her back from their hug and he offered Mike his hand.

"See you for Christmas, Mike. I'm looking forward to meeting the rest of the family."

Mike slapped him on the shoulder. "Mom is ecstatic. She's already started making Christmas cookies. She's sending them to Kyla to freeze for Christmas. Hope you got a big freezer."

Kyla groaned, her eyes round. "Oh dear lord. Be prepared."

"Hey, I like cookies. Just might have to get some more running in if they're as good as those ones your mom sent last week."

"My ass is going to be huge," she complained.

Cooper's body shook. "Good thing I like your ass then. A lot." He winked and she couldn't help but smile.

"Enough of the googly-eyes. God, you two. . . ." Mike shook his head and shot a glare at Cooper. "She's my sister, man."

"Sorry, I can't help it. I have a hard time keeping my hands to myself when she's around."

"All right, enough!" Her eyes danced between the two. "Mike, you need to get on the road. Be careful and call me as soon as you get home. I'll worry."

Cooper lifted his chin, his face serious. "Seriously, Mike, call. She'll drive me nuts if you don't."

Her brother grinned. "Will do, man. Later."

They watched as Mike got into his car and backed out. She settled against Cooper and sighed, her voice soft when she finally spoke. "I lost a lot of time with him."

Cooper brushed the hair from her shoulder and kissed her neck. "That's all behind you now. Nothing but good in front of you. In front of us."

Kyla twisted her head and caught his eyes. "Do you still want me hanging around without the chaos swirling around me?"

He arched a brow. "I've wanted you since before the chaos and stayed because I wanted to be here beyond it. Yes, I still want you." He bent his head and touched his mouth to hers. "Don't ever doubt that, Kyla."

She finally let out a breath and relaxed. "Okay. Let's go inside now. I'm cold."

"Got just the thing to warm you up." He smacked her ass and pushed her inside the door. "Don't make me chase you, baby. You know I always win."

Kyla squealed and ran from him, "Cooper!"

"Only because I let you," she teased and he flashed her that wicked grin that started her engine every time. "Oh really? We'll see about that. . . ." he challenged.

Cooper came at her and she squeaked, turning and running for the hallway. She was laughing; any fear she had to this kind of playfulness was completely gone. She felt his arm wrap around her middle as she turned the corner into the bathroom. "Not very effective when you're giggling like that, babe." His head dipped down and his lips brushed against the skin at her ear. "Hmm, the bathroom. Good choice, Kyla. I've been wanting to take you in here for awhile now."

Cooper's hand moved to her pants and in half a second he had them undone and sliding down her legs. His hand moved between her legs and she arched back against him. "Want to give that to me, baby?"

His finger pressed in and she groaned out, "Yes."

Cooper turned her in his arm and grinned against her mouth. "Told you. I win."

Her mock glare made him laugh, and even more so when she had the audacity to pout. "I wasn't prepared. You cheated." No one had said hands in her panties were part of the game. Not that she was complaining.

Cooper just shook his head. "You keep believing that. But just remember this for future reference: if this is breaking the rules, I will be doing it a lot."

Kyla breath caught as she looked into his eyes. And then he went about breaking the rules. Repeatedly.

More from Crimson Romance
(From *Wildflower Redemption* by Leslie P. García)

Aaron Estes stood at the window, one hand pulling back the drapes to clear his view. Outside, clouds hovered along the horizon, but he doubted it would rain.

Someone from town— Ross something? —had stopped by earlier and offered to do work. The handyman had scoffed at the chance of rain. "Always cloudy," he'd grumbled. "Never rains."

Aaron had shrugged and told the man politely that he didn't need help. And he didn't—at least, not physical help. Spiritual help, maybe, mental health—the kind of health that comes with peace and contentment. The kind of health he'd probably never find again. He closed his eyes and listened for any sound of six-year-old Chloe waking, but heard only silence. Unwelcome memories tried to push in, and he pressed his lids tighter against his face, unwilling to give in again to the pain.

The memories came anyway: the loud, angry words of a marriage shattering. The cheery morning greeting from the one thing he and Stella still shared—a tiny, precious miracle of motion and light.

Chloe's loud kiss and plaintive complaint when her mother tried to leave without kissing Aaron goodbye hovered near the surface. He could still feel Chloe's huge kiss on his cheeks, hear the petulance in her voice when her mother tried to step around them.

"Mommy, you forgot Daddy's kiss." Stella pecked him on the cheek, and Chloe tugged on her mom's blouse.

"Mommy, don't be silly. Mommies kiss daddies on the mouth."

With lips so tight he could feel her anger, Stella stood on tiptoe and touched her mouth to his. Then he watched as Chloe grabbed her mother's hand, delighted that she was playing mom today, not cop. To Chloe, the world was a game, and everyone in it, players.

He closed his eyes, but the burning didn't go away, so he went back to staring blindly outside. There were no daffodils here, as there were in Alabama, but he heard that just miles north spring came in on carpets of bluebonnets and waves of flaming Indian paintbrush. All the locals raved about the Texas wildflowers. They said he should go see them, but he knew he couldn't.

The scene he'd rushed to just over a year ago crowded in: the hysteria, the cop cars with their flashing red and blue lights; the crumpled body of a child, an injured teacher being wheeled toward an ambulance; and an officer who knew Stella pulling him aside. She'd taken a bullet for a kid, the officer told him. Unfaithful, maybe, arrogant often—but nobody doubted Stella Estes's courage.

The tears rolled down his cheeks and he wiped them away with the back of his hand, trying not to remember that there'd been blood on the daffodils the day the world ended.

• • •

Luz Wilkinson tugged on the girth again and nudged Pompom's belly with a knee. "Let it out, girl," she urged. The little pinto sighed heavily and turned around to nose Luz just as the cell phone in her pocket went off. Her horses would have shied at the sudden blast of sound, and the other ponies would have lifted their heads and pricked their ears. Pompom stood there with that complete lack of interest that indicated absolute lack of intelligence.

Frowning over the pony's deficiencies, Luz fished the phone out and hit the button to silence it. She didn't recognize the number. She hoped it wasn't a bill collector, but knew that it probably was.

"Hello?"

"Uh...hi. Is this Eden Acres?"

"Yes." Luz scratched Pompom's ear while she tried to connect a physical image with the deep, masculine voice. She often toyed with visualizing strangers from their phone calls, and almost always was wrong. Silence pricked her into awareness. Perhaps the caller expected someone more enthusiastic, more helpful. Someone who could offer more than one word answers...

"May I help you?" she prodded when he didn't go on.

Another long pause, then came the abrupt questions: "I heard you have therapy horses? And ponies?"

Luz hesitated. Sometimes children from a group foster home came out to ride, and occasionally a counselor who worked with troubled children recommended exposing them to riding. But therapy? She wouldn't go that far.

"We have horses and ponies," she said carefully. "But who told you we have therapy horses?"

"Esmeralda Salinas," the voice said, no longer hesitant.

Luz wrinkled her nose, picturing the elegant redheaded school guidance counselor with her neat suits and perpetual pep. Living in this tiny community, they'd crossed paths several times. They didn't much like each other, but Esmeralda loved horses. That was usually a sterling quality, but this time, Luz's main yardstick for measuring "good folks" didn't hold water, because the counselor struck her as conceited, plastic, and sneaky. Although they avoided each other as much as possible, she boarded the woman's pricey Appaloosa. Undoubtedly Esmeralda would have liked finer stomping grounds for the horse and herself, but no one else boarded horses in this arid, dying community. Very few still owned livestock.

Nevertheless, Luz was surprised that the counselor had referred any male new to town. The director of the children's group home was an elderly woman, and the other referrals were long-time residents, parents in established relationships, but Esmeralda sending a guy her way? He was not single, then, apparently.

"You're Ms. Wilkinson?" Doubt tinged the deep voice. She'd confused the caller. Didn't matter. Confusion was a constant companion these days.

"Yes," she replied. One word again. He could state his business or not. She didn't care.

"Ms. Wilkinson, I need to talk to you about riding lessons for my little girl, Chloe. Or maybe—" Another brief pause, as if he wasn't sure what he wanted. "Maybe even buying a pony. I need advice on what would be best."

He was a client then. She should be happier than she was. She pasted a smile on her face, hoping it would make her voice warmer, more caring. "Great. Advice is what we do best." Quick questions confirmed he knew how to find Eden Acres, and she clicked the phone off and returned it to her pocket. She realized, a little late, that asking the man's name might have been both friendlier and more professional.

"Screw it," she muttered with unusual ire. "Professional never worked for me, anyway. Come on, old lady. Some kid might actually get a pony ride today."

Half an hour later Luz was feeding the menagerie when she heard tires on the gravel drive. She called the motley collection of rescued animals her menagerie, because it took too long to go into the species, circumstances, and problems she dealt with trying to feed and shelter them day to day. Candy, the burro, butted her as she turned away, and the kitten with no name left its feeding dish to run away from some unseen menace, almost tripping her. She wiped her hands on the sides of her jeans and shut the door separating the odd animals from the handful of horses that were both her treasures and bread-earners.

By the time she made it outside, a dark-haired, broad-shouldered man was leaning against an SUV, frowning. He wore long sleeves and a tie, hardly south Texas pony-buying attire. But she wasn't expecting anyone else.

She walked over and held out her hand. "I'm Luz Wilkinson. Welcome to Eden Acres. Are you—?"

"Aaron Estes." He shook her hand briefly, and then cast another look around the premises. Not disapproving, exactly, she thought. It was more a look of disappointment.

"Why don't we go into the office?" she suggested. "It's cooler." And it was well decorated with new paint and shelves of her mother's trophies, recently polished.

They walked into the barn. The half-open stall doors caught his attention. He pointed at one of the horses. "Pretty. Yours?"

"No." She shook her head, and paused to pet the broad blaze of white running down the mare's face. "This is Domatrix. One of my boarders."

"Doma—isn't this Esmeralda's horse?"

"Yes, as a matter of fact." She leaned against the stall door, slanting a glance at him, surprised that Esmeralda had apparently described Domatrix in detail to a man new in town. No wonder Aaron Estes hadn't flinched at the name, even shortened as it seemed to be. Then again…she thought of the tall, regal redhead and the dearth of men in Rose Creek. A man with a daughter likely meant a married man. That would lessen Esmeralda's interest. Wouldn't it? She pushed away from the mare's stall, and he followed the remaining few feet to the office. She waved a hand at the chairs and took her own place behind the small, bare desk.

"So tell me how I can help," she invited.

He looked down for a minute at his hands before looking at her. When he did finally lift his eyes, she could see why Esmeralda had pounced. The man's perfect features and startling green eyes would stop traffic in lots of places, let alone this one-horse, one-eligible-man town.

"My little girl—Chloe—needs a hobby. Something she'll like that's safe."

Luz studied him, perplexed. Somehow the pieces of the big, attractive man across the desk didn't add up. She supposed she was using stereotypes, but he seemed too hesitant and unsure for his own body. Not as if he was uncomfortable in his own skin, maybe, but almost as if he were fearful of something.

She puzzled over the discomfort he seemed to feel, trying to figure out his connection to Esme. He wasn't family; the Rose Creek gossips knew everyone and every relative, no matter how far flung. The counselor had aging parents and a half-brother down in Laredo. A friend? She discarded that. Esmeralda didn't work weekends, and if he were a friend, she would be here. So the relationship had to be professional. Maybe the daughter he'd mentioned was Esmeralda's client?

"'Safe as opposed to bike riding or playing with dolls? Or safe, fun, and a perfect springtime activity—I'm not sure I know what you mean by safe," Luz admitted. "Riding has risks—the same as pretty much everything."

Aaron Estes growled something that sounded profane and hunched forward over the desk, his face tight. "Don't you think I know that?" After a moment, his face muscles eased into smoother lines. His lips twitched, as if they'd known how to smile, but forgotten. "I'm not as weird as I seem. Just a tad nervous and overprotective."

"But you're not in denial," she observed. "That's got to be good." She smiled. "So, tell me about your Chloe."

Pure, absolute love washed across his face. His lips remembered how to smile and he straightened in his chair. "Chloe's my life," he said simply.

Luz returned the smile, but prodded gently for more insight. "How old is she? Does she like horses? Has she ridden before?"

"Six, yes, and no."

Luz blinked, trying to understand the simple, one-word answers. Saw the dimples appear, and then deepen in Aaron Estes' cheeks. She'd always had a weakness for dimples, dammit! Was he one-upping her? "So, is this payback, or do you always keep things so short and simple?"

He actually chuckled. It was a short little rumble of laughter, but a chuckle.

"Payback, definitely. I was nervous enough about calling and you were anything but friendly."

She thought back on her hesitation to answer the phone, how she'd focused on the pinto rather than concentrating on encouraging conversation. He had her pegged, but she didn't care. Wouldn't. She needed customers, but wasn't in the market for relationships of any kind. And professional? She allowed herself a quick mental shrug. She no longer had a profession. She'd been a teacher, and a good one. She'd surrounded herself with kids and poured energy and love into their lives. Then she'd lost it all, including her daughter Lily. Not her daughter, she reminded herself: Brian's daughter, given to her as one more false promise. Now she rescued discarded animals when she could, and was going broke doing it.

So she pounced on something he said. "You were nervous? About asking if we had ponies?" Slight derision might have crept into her words, because he flinched and drew away again.

"Not about ponies." He paused, looking for the right words. "We don't know each other. Esmeralda recommended riding as a form of therapy." He shrugged. "Telling a stranger your kid has problems is hard."

Her cheeks burned with embarrassment. "I owe you an apology—of course it is." She stood up abruptly, annoyed with herself. "Guess it's attack a stranger day—I'm just not sure why. Would you like to look at Rumbles? She would be the pony Chloe would work with first."

"Sure." He got up too, ignoring her apology, and stretched. Outside the office, one of the horses whinnied, and another kicked at the stall. The pungent scents of the stable reminded her it was time to muck stalls—again. Already. Out of the corner of her eyes, she saw his nose wrinkle.

"Do you even like horses?" she asked, curious.

He slanted a glance down at her and shrugged. "Don't know. Haven't been around them. Not really an animal person."

Before Luz could murmur a response, he stopped, turning towards her and holding his hands out in apology. "Not that I don't like them, exactly. I used to travel, and before that—well, I just wasn't raised around them."

"Okay." Luz gave him her own shrug. "So I guess Chloe's mom will be the main go-between here?"

A muscle in his jaw twitched, and the nervous tension he'd shown in the beginning visibly tightened his body. "Chloe's mom," he said through clenched teeth, "is dead."

In the mood for more Crimson Romance?
Check out *The Rebel's Own* by M.O. Kenyan at
CrimsonRomance.com.

Made in the USA
Lexington, KY
01 December 2014